The Cankerworm

Suzanne Swift

Jane May Publishing

All enquiries should be made to the author
suzanne@suzanneswift.com.au

Cover photo by Ana Gizdovska on Unsplash

First published in 2022 by Jane May Publishing (Australia)

ISBN: 978-0-6454330-0-5 (paperback)
ISBN: 978-0-6454330-1-2 (ebook)

 A catalogue record for this book is available from the National Library of Australia

For Michelle and Jessica

Acknowledgements

I would like to thank Ursula Benstead, Lyndell Browne, Amanda Holder, Oly Koziaris, Eileen Mundy, Georgia Taylor and Sara Vidal for your feedback and encouragement and for your willingness to tell me when something wasn't working even when I thought it was.

I'm also grateful to the Yarraville writer's group for providing a sense of accountability and for the lively and inspiring discussions and feedback which helped us all grow as writers.

Thank you to my former counselling clients and to other victim survivors I've known. Although the characters in "The Cankerworm" are entirely fictional and not based on any of you - it was your courage to seek healing and tell your stories that played a significant role in my desire to write this book.

Finally, my thanks to Keld, for the many hours spent discussing minor nuances and major changes, for your help in overcoming the practical and psychological obstacles that got in the way and for the support and encouragement you have lavished upon me throughout the process.

O Rose thou art sick.
The invisible worm,
That flies in the night
In the howling storm:

Has found out thy bed
Of crimson joy:
And his dark secret love
Does thy life destroy.

WILLIAM BLAKE

The canker galls the infants of the spring
Too oft before their buttons be disclosed.

WILLIAM SHAKESPEARE

...the cankerworm spoileth and fleeth away.

NAHUM 3:16 KJV

Chapter 1

Tracy and a tall stranger named Sam sat opposite Annette. Well, maybe *sat* was the wrong word. Intertwined on one stool, they were making out in front of her as if she wasn't there. Sam's tongue circled around Tracy's lips, periodically darting in and out of her mouth like a frightened goldfish. *Gross!*

Tracy slid off Sam's knee, stood to face him and leaned in close to his ear. Sam attempted to slip his hand into the back of Tracy's waist high Levis. Annette smiled. *Ha ha, too tight!*

Annette shifted on the hard, wooden stool and adjusted the waistband of her own jeans which dug hard into her belly. Both she and Tracy had to lie flat on the bed to zip their jeans up. Annette bought hers even tighter than Tracy did though, because she just didn't fill them out as well. She was slimmer—too boyish, perhaps? Let's not sugar coat it, she was just plain *skinny*, like her mum said. Eighteen and still waiting for proper boobs to appear. Probably too late now, she would be stuck with these AA cup bumps forever.

Sam gave up his quest for skin and pulled Tracy in closer, hands lingering on her hips instead. Soon those jeans would be coming off the same way they went on.

Enough with the staring, besides being uncool, it was not helping Annette's mood. She swivelled around on the barstool. A well-dressed man in a corner booth was watching her. Turning away quickly she gazed down at her half empty glass of bourbon and coke. She swished it around a little and nodded her head half-heartedly in time with the music. The band had packed up and gone home an hour ago. Now a DJ presided over the entertainment. The Bee Gee's, 'Stayin' Alive', blared out through the sound system. He didn't seem to realise it wasn't that kind of pub. A few stragglers on the dance floor attempted to dance to the disco beat like they had to the heavy metal band, not appearing to care what anyone thought of them. Drunken smiles on their faces, some with their eyes closed, headbanging away when they should have been doing John Travolta moves. A sting of envy jabbed at her. At least they were enjoying themselves.

Sharing the Carlton flat with Tracy had been fun at first. So much better than the long nights alone in her bedsit. They didn't bear thinking about. Going out on the town, listening to music, drinking. Especially the night she met Alex —here—right here at this table. She allowed herself a moment of nostalgia. Imagined him smiling across at her, and then, just as quickly, shut it down.

Not much had changed on the other side of the table when she looked up again. Sam and Tracy were still completely oblivious to her—fondling, kissing, exploring. Annette let out a loud sigh, which was pointless, because she couldn't be heard over the music anyway. She drained her glass. The alcohol had stopped giving her that pleasant buzz a while ago and this was getting tedious.

"I'm off," she yelled. Tracy and Sam kept at it. She waved her hand in front of Tracy's face. "I'm leaving now."

"Oh umm... do you want me... ahh... us, to walk home with you?"

Tracy's question seemed to be directed towards Sam, as much as to Annette. He nodded his agreement. Tracy flashed him a warm smile.

"No, it's okay," Annette said. "I'll be fine."

Definitely a case of three's a crowd.

As she made her way towards the door, she glanced at the guy in the booth. Dressed in a black suit and loosened tie, he wasn't her usual type, but he looked okay—older—but okay. He grabbed his half-full glass and walked towards her.

"Can I buy you a drink before you go?" he asked.

What was the alternative? Go home alone? Avoid Alex and the wounded puppy way he looked at her now that he was sleeping on the couch? Listen to Tracy and Sam having it off in the next room all night?

"Why not," she answered.

Nestled in the dimly lit booth with him, she sipped on a Fluffy Duck. He drank a more sophisticated, Whisky Sour. Tracy caught her eye from across the room.

Oh, so she hasn't completely forgotten I exist.

Annette shrugged, then smiled at her friend. Tracy gave her a wink and turned back to Sam.

Annette and the stranger exchanged names, but soon gave up trying to talk over the ever-increasing volume of the music. The cocktail tasted lovely. So sweet and creamy, like drinking dessert. She really should pace herself, but it was a little too late for that. Besides, wouldn't it make things easier later, easier to let go, to relax? A shiver went through her and she gulped down the rest of her drink.

The man gestured at her glass and mouthed, "Another?"

Annette nodded. He gave her leg a squeeze just above the knee and her breath caught in her throat. Fair enough though, he was buying her expensive drinks. She managed a hesitant smile. The man made his way through the three-deep crowd at the bar and was soon out of sight.

The first time she'd tried a Fluffy Duck was the night she'd met Alex. It was New Year's Eve and the Union Hotel was abuzz with excitement. The last night of the 70's and the pub had a late licence, so drinks were available until midnight. At about ten to twelve Alex had bought her and Tracy two cocktails each, and himself two pots—just in case. He had laughed at her whipped cream moustache and seemed to think everything she had to say was important. At midnight the band played 'Auld Lang Syne' and he asked permission to kiss her. A long, slightly drunken kiss that she still hadn't forgotten.

When the lights were turned up—that awkward time when the negotiating about the rest of the night usually started—Alex asked her on a real date, to the movies. Wrote her number on the back of his hand and said he'd call the next day. And he did call.

Their relationship moved forward quickly. When Alex's lease on his flat was about to expire and he suggested moving in, Annette didn't give it a lot of thought. Logically, it followed that if it felt bad being alone, then having someone around who liked her would take away the bad feeling. Tracy was okay with Alex moving into the flat. Another person sharing the rent suited both of them.

It was great for a while. Alex went to work early in the morning. When he got home in the late afternoon they would cook together before Annette left for her shift at the restaurant. They laughed and had fun as they experimented in the kitchen.

Later, if Alex was still awake, they would have a few drinks together, go to bed, make love and talk into the night. Either way, he always woke up when she got into bed and held her for a while—even if they didn't talk or have sex.

That's how it was in the beginning anyway.

The man slid into the booth and cupped his hand around her ear.

"Sorry, they've finished serving drinks, but don't worry, I know where we can get one," he said with a wink.

Annette looked across at Tracy's table. It was empty.

"Let's go," he said and grabbed her hand.

Although it was still Autumn, a chilly breeze struck her as they stepped out of the warm, noisy pub into the laneway. At the corner, he let go of her hand and fished in his pocket for his car keys while she waited to see which way they were headed. Why didn't she bring a coat? The biting Melbourne wind set her shivering. Goosebumps appeared on her bare arms. She rubbed them and wished he would hurry up. The footpath was almost empty.

Was it really true that drinks had finished? People usually flooded out pretty quickly after the flow of alcohol stopped.

The drone of a lone car passed by and faded into the distance. What *was* that sound? Straining to hear, she caught fragments of a lilting voice accompanied by the gentle strums of a guitar. The music was coming from the other side of the street. About half a block away a bus was parked. Not a public transport bus because it was painted so brightly. She'd seen that same bus parked there before. A streetlamp softly shone, illuminating the inside of the bus and the face of the man in the front seat who was playing the guitar. She peered at him, curious, and he looked directly at her.

Now, the man from the bar hurried along in the opposite direction, looking straight ahead until he stopped in front of a white Mercedes. Annette paused, she felt drawn to stay and listen to the music. The man opened the passenger side door and shot her a puzzled look. After lingering for a moment longer, she rushed to catch up, tottering a bit on her heels. Just before stepping into the car, she looked back, the young man in the bus was still watching her.

The man's South Yarra apartment was very posh. Polished white marble bench tops in the kitchen and plush, black leather couches in the lounge room.

"Welcome to my humble crib," he said, with a flourish of his arm.

"Very cool," she responded.

Flicking through a large selection of records, he chose one and held it up to show her. "Hope you like jazz," he said.

She didn't, but she smiled and nodded anyway. The strange, too-slow-for-the-beat music thumped softly out of the sound system. The speakers were built into either side of the stone fireplace. The whole setup must have cost a fortune. All very fancy—too fancy. She tightened her grip on the armrest.

After another drink on the couch, he kissed her. His lips a little too wet, the pressure a little too hard. Inexplicably, she thought of Alex again, and how his kisses felt just right.

When the man leaned in again, she stiffened and moved away a little. Should she leave? He would be disappointed though—perhaps even annoyed.

He leaned against the back of the couch.

"You're very beautiful you know," he said, running his hand along her thigh.

She sat perfectly still. As his hand crept higher, she closed her eyes.

***

Daylight was peeking around the edges of the heavy, velvet curtains when Annette slipped out of bed and dressed. She sat on the bed and watched the man sleeping. A small, round puddle of drool had seeped onto the pillow from his slackened mouth. The wrinkles around his mouth and eyes were way more obvious this morning.

So nice though, not to feel alone for a while and so easy to get his undivided attention. At least—that was—until he'd finished with her, at which time he'd abruptly rolled away and fallen asleep, snoring softly. Was it worth it?

He shifted on the bed, stretched, opened his eyes.

"Good morning." His voice was groggy with sleep. "Come back to bed for a while."

He stretched out a hand towards her. It was clear to her what this invitation would involve, and she couldn't think of anything she wanted less right now.

"No, got to go sorry."

"Do you need a lift somewhere?"

"No thanks. Is there a tram stop near here?"

He gave her directions, then asked, "Can I get your number?"

Why did he bother with the charade? So that she wouldn't feel hurt? Someone this rich and successful would have no interest in her. And besides, this was probably yet another stupid, alcohol-fuelled mistake.

"What for? I don't think you'll call me."

She felt like shit this morning—used. Why the bad feeling, when she was willing enough last night?

He smiled. "Don't be silly."

In the lounge room, she found a scrap of paper and a pen on the kitchen bench and scribbled down her number. Back in the bedroom, she pressed it into his palm. He squeezed her hand and said he'd call soon. Annette nodded. *Yeah sure.*

She snatched her hand away and walked out into the chilly morning.

Now that she was alone again, she felt relieved—relieved

to be away from him—from all of them. When Alex came into her life, she was sure she'd broken this pattern—she was *in a relationship*. But no, nothing had changed. Here she was again. The same slutty behaviour. Why did she do it? This wasn't what she wanted.

***

Annette and Tracy were clearing tables at Le Plat Brasserie. What a busy night! Finally, all the patrons had left, and Annette was carrying her last pile of dirty dishes out to the kitchen. She came backwards through the swinging doors and the head chef walked past the doorway at the same moment. Crashing straight into him, she dropped the top few plates which shattered loudly onto the tiled floor. He backed away from her, throwing up his hands.

"You have all the grace of a baby elephant Annette!"

Annette froze. Tracy came in with another load of dishes and skirted around her.

"Are you okay?" Tracy asked, as she headed for the sink.

Annette nodded. She walked over and put the rest of the dishes on the bench, then returned and knelt to pick up the pieces.

"I do not know why the manager gave you this job. You are an imbécile. Stupid, clumsy…", the chef continued.

Annette didn't look up until she saw his shiny black shoes move away from her and heard them clattering across the kitchen floor. Soon after, the back door slammed. *Thank God!*

Avoiding eye contact with the kitchenhand, she dropped the broken pieces in the bin and then wiped up the mess.

The chef's abuse was a nightly occurrence, but it still frightened her when it happened. She wished she could quit but was trapped in this dead-end job. How else could she pay her share of the rent and food? He yelled at Tracy too, but she didn't seem so upset by it. Not much seemed to faze her. Annette admired that; she wished she could brush things off so easily.

When she went back out into the dining area, Tracy beckoned her over to the bar. The barman had gone home. They were the only ones left in that part of the restaurant.

"What'll you have?" Tracy asked.

Annette smiled and pointed to a bottle of Cointreau on the top shelf. Tracy poured them both a shot. They squatted down behind the bar. Tracy gulped hers straight down. Annette—not used to the strength of undiluted alcohol—sipped at hers.

"He's just a mean little man, don't worry about him," Tracy said, then pointed at Annette's nearly full glass. "Drink up."

Annette drank it all down, squeezing her eyes shut and shaking her head.

Tracy laughed. "That's better. Stuck up bastard he is, I'd like to stick his petits pains up his skinny, little arse!"

Annette giggled. The alcohol was soothing. Tracy poured them both another shot. This time, Annette drank it straight down.

They punched their timecards, changed out of their uniforms and headed down the street towards their favourite pub. As they walked out into the crisp night air, Annette left the worries of the restaurant behind her. The shots had really kicked in now. She was excited about what the rest of the night would bring.

"We need to talk about Alex." The seriousness of Tracy's tone pierced through Annette's high spirits like a pin piercing a balloon.

She didn't want to think about Alex right now.

"Can't we talk about it later?"

Alex had said he would move out the week after the relationship ended. Three weeks later and he had only moved as far as the lounge room. Tracy had already asked her once to get him to leave. He was still paying his share of the rent, but there was tension in the air. Annette knew that Tracy felt it too.

"No, we cannot talk about it later. He needs to go. I can't cope with him moping around the place."

Annette felt guilty, she couldn't even look him in the eye, let alone tell him to leave the flat.

"Perhaps you could tell him?"

Tracy took Annette's arm and stopped her abruptly in the middle of the street. She turned to face Annette.

"What? No, I'm not the one who broke up with him. He's a hunk who adores you. And, he seems like a decent guy. I still don't understand what he did that was so bad you had to end it." Tracy raised her eyebrows, as though waiting for an answer.

Annette struggled to think of a response. Deep down she knew the breakup wasn't his fault. They were so good together until the arguments started.

Looking back, she couldn't really make sense of what went wrong. It must have been frustrating for him. Even at the time she knew she wasn't being fair.

When he was there, she wanted him gone. When he was gone, she wanted him there. If he was asleep when she arrived home from work, she would huff with disapproval as she climbed into bed. He would wake up and reach for her, but she would roll away. Why had things changed so dramatically? And so fast? She felt lonely even when he was right next to her.

After the initial excitement had waned, there was this sense of unreality during sex, a weird disconnect. Like she was playing a part, her body responded, but as though it was somehow separate from her. And, instead of the warm afterglow of the first weeks, a cold emptiness descended in the quiet that followed.

Of course, Alex didn't have any idea what had changed either. He clearly didn't know how to fix it. How could he possibly understand what she needed when she had no idea herself? And as her discontent increased, so did her drinking. She guzzled bourbon and coke when she could afford it. If she was skint, there was usually a leftover cask of Fruity Lexia from which she could squeeze the last drops.

The loneliness that was staved off temporarily, was back with a vengeance. Finally, she broke up with him. What else could she do?

Tracy was still standing there with that expectant look on her face. Annette could tell that she was getting pissed off. This was concerning. Maybe Tracy would make her leave instead. Tracy was her only friend; she couldn't really afford to upset her.

"I'll tell him tomorrow," she said.

They walked on in silence until they arrived at the Union. Annette noticed the strange, brightly painted bus sitting across the road. Why was it there again? The thought crossed her mind only for an instant, and then they were inside.

The pub was dimly lit and felt warm and welcoming. It was busy though, and there were no free tables.

Tracy pointed out two older businessmen who had eaten at the restaurant earlier. One of them had flirted with Tracy as she waited on their table. When the men spotted the girls, they invited them over.

Over the course of the next hour, the four of them had drinks. A lot of drinks. Annette tried a Tequila Sunrise, then a Gin Sling, and then decided on yet another Tequila Sunrise. Tracy was mixing her drinks too.

The blonde man with a tight perm was focused on Tracy, but the one with greased short back and sides zeroed in on Annette. He leaned in towards her. Close enough for her to smell his wine-soaked breath. He snaked his hand around her waist. She didn't like it, or him either really, but she didn't move away. His hand moved lower to squeeze the cheek of her bum.

"What a bad girl you are," he said, leering at her.

Suddenly, she couldn't breathe and began to feel sick. Her feet felt like they were stuck to the floor. He continued to rub her bottom through the fabric of her thin skirt. Then he kissed her—a slobbery, unpleasant kiss—she still didn't move. She couldn't.

Finally, after what seemed like hours—but was probably only seconds—she stumbled back away from him.

"I need to... need to go to the bathroom," she said.

Tracy broke off her conversation with the blonde man and turned to her. "You look awful, what happened?"

Annette didn't respond but picked up her bag and made her way towards the toilets.

"Wait up!" Tracy called out from behind her.

Annette didn't turn around though; didn't stop moving until she was safely inside the powder room of the ladies' toilets. She flopped onto a low bench and leaned her spinning head back against the wall. Tracy came in and sat beside her.

"I feel sick. That man... he was disgusting," she said.

Tracy nodded her agreement

"The blonde guy is kind of cute, but yeah, the other one looks like a real sleazebucket."

"I need to get out of here," Annette said.

Tracy shrugged. "Yeah, well I'm supposed to be with Sam anyway, so that's cool."

Tracy grabbed her hand as they came out of the toilets

and dragged her around the other side of the bar from where the two businessmen were sitting. Annette was relieved that she couldn't see them through the crowd.

When the girls emerged into the night air, Annette's head started to spin again. She stopped, closed her eyes and tried taking deep breaths. It didn't help. She let go of Tracy's hand and slumped down in the darkened doorway of a department store.

Everything seemed surreal. As if through a fog, Annette saw a middle-aged couple walking past, shaking their heads.

Tracy's voice sounded far away when she told the couple, "This is none of your business, move on!"

And, then, to Annette, "What are you doing? Are you okay?"

After that, it all faded away into blackness.

Chapter 2

"Hey Annette, how are you feeling this morning? My name's Mark, by the way." Morning, what happened to the rest of last night? Immediately upon lifting her throbbing head she felt sick. And, each breath was a harsh reminder of her parched throat. She opened her eyes and looked in the direction of the voice. A young man—maybe early to mid-twenties—was standing next to her. An extremely good-looking young man. He seemed vaguely familiar. How did he know her name?

Annette looked around. What was this place? A bus. Was it *that* bus?

She was laying across two seats. Legs draped over the armrest of the aisle seat. Tucked in around her was a multi-coloured, crocheted blanket. Relieved, she noticed her handbag poking out between the folds of the blanket.

Her heavy head ached even more when she lifted it to see above the seats. A guitar on a stand was up at the front of the bus. Stacks of pamphlets in crates sat beside the driver's seat. Down at the back of the bus, were two young girls around her age. They chatted in low voices, glancing in her direction now and then. She lowered herself back down, out of their view.

"You don't look so good. Big night last night?"

She sighed. "Yeah, I guess it must have been," she said.

"When you passed out your girlfriend tried to wake you but couldn't. So, we offered to bring you in here, to sleep it off."

Mark walked towards the front of the bus. Though he wasn't particularly tall; he still had to bend forward a little, so as not to hit his head. He returned with a carton of juice and a paper cup.

"Here... you're probably a bit dry."

She nodded. That was an understatement, she could probably drink the whole carton. Their hands touched briefly as he handed her the cup. She sculled the cool orange juice straight down. Much better.

"Another... please?" she asked.

"We park in different areas of the city. This is one of our regular spots," he said, pouring more juice into the cup she was holding out towards him. "Usually, we drop the volunteers off at home and take the bus back to the church, but because you were still here, I called a parent to pick up the kids and I stayed back there." He gestured towards the back of the bus.

So, she was alone and passed out on these seats. And, a total stranger was sleeping a few feet away. Why did Tracy leave her here? The nausea returned. She thought she might throw up.

"You look quite pale."

For a few moments she didn't speak or move and eventually, the urge passed.

"I think I'll be okay."

She sipped the juice, more slowly this time. He seemed like a nice person, not particularly dangerous. She started to feel a little better. This was the strange bus she'd seen parked near the bar. That's why he looked familiar.

Mark squatted down beside her; and her breath caught in her throat with the closeness of him. What would it be like to run her fingers through his thick, black hair or touch his smooth-shaven face? With an involuntary shake of the head, she shook the thoughts away. Her head started hammering again and she cupped a hand over her forehead.

"Headache as well?" he asked.

"Hmm," she said.

"Alcohol will do that to you."

A little annoyed—but also embarrassed—by his stating of the obvious, she shifted the conversation away from her out of control behaviour.

"Why do you park here in the middle of the night? It seems like an odd thing to do."

"I'm a youth pastor. We do outreach to..."—he hesitated—"...troubled kids."

A pastor, Annette didn't think he looked like a pastor. He was young and seemed friendly enough. He didn't quite fit her impression of a clergyman. Weren't they usually stuck up and unapproachable? She was curious, she didn't know much about religion.

"I don't know what that means. What do you do to them?"

He smiled. "Well, we don't *do* anything to them. We just chat with them about what's missing in their lives."

Tears pricked at her eyes. The words cut deep, straight to that empty void deep inside. She tried to push it away, like she usually did, but couldn't. Was she really going to cry —right here on this bus—in front of this man she didn't know? She managed to blink the tears away.

"How about you? How are you doing?"

Had Mark noticed her shift in mood? Perhaps it was

only a coincidence that he seemed to take the opportunity to dig around a little? Maybe she should tell him about her shitty life. He seemed genuinely interested. But where to start? Early, when her father abandoned her? Or, maybe with her stepfather's appearance shortly afterwards? What about when her mother wanted her out of the house and she subsequently dropped out of school?

Or, maybe best to start later, with the drunken one-night stands and her miserable, going nowhere job. Or even, that she had co-habited with twenty-year-old Alex at the tender age of eighteen.

"I guess that should be pretty obvious to you after what happened last night."

He nodded. "Hmm... there is a better way to live you know."

Was he judging her? No, he was just concerned.

"I'm sure there is."

"God will accept you, you know, no matter what you've done."

This was starting to sound like a spiel he probably gave to everyone who wasn't a Christian. And what did he mean? *No matter what you've done.* Her life wasn't ideal, but he didn't know that. Lucky, she hadn't confided in him. He didn't want to help her, he just wanted to criticise her.

She grabbed her bag and shuffled herself up and around to a seated position. The blanket fell to the floor. Mark stayed squatting beside her.

"How about you just fuck off out of my way! I don't know you and what I do with my life really is none of your business."

His eyebrows flew up and his mouth dropped open. Only for a moment though, then his smile was back in place. Immediately she wished she hadn't been so harsh.

Still not moving, he said, "I'm not saying you're a bad person, we've all sinned and fallen short of the glory of God. I just want to show you how you can be happy. Are you happy?"

That awful empty feeling swept over her again. Threatening to overwhelm her. No, she was not happy, not happy at all. She didn't move. The concern in his blue eyes and the promise of his words, held her there, giving her a tiny seed of hope.

"We're having free food and a singalong tomorrow evening. I'd love to see you there."

He walked to the front of the bus and grabbed a leaflet from a pile. The girls down the back of the bus giggled. They were watching him too, but they turned back to each other, when she caught them looking at him. He held out the leaflet towards her.

Shaking her head slightly, she said, "I don't think I'd fit in. And I really don't have any interest in religion."

The invitation and warmth in his expression didn't waver.

"That's okay, it's those who don't feel they fit in who are the most welcome." He continued to hold out the printed piece of paper.

These last few words brought on a sudden yielding towards him. A softening, like butter melting in a pan, that took her by surprise. Despite this, she did her best to maintain a tough exterior.

Without another word, she took the leaflet from his outstretched hand, shoved it roughly in her bag and left.

***

Annette walked home, conscious of still being dressed for the night before. She hadn't been able to check a mirror.

Mascara was probably smeared halfway down her face by now. She turned into the doorway of an apartment block and got out her compact. Yes, hair wild and unbrushed, but mascara not too bad. She ran her brush through her hair and wondered what Mark thought of her. Didn't matter though, he was a pastor. And besides, she had enough problems. Still, she couldn't stop picturing Mark with his wavy hair, concerned, gentle eyes and warm smile. She wanted to see him again.

When she was nearly at the flat, hazy memories of the night before began to intrude. Tracy had abandoned her. What a callous thing to do, to leave her there overnight with a stranger and not even try to get her home. And before that, something had happened, yes, that man had touched her and after that everything had unravelled. No, she wouldn't think about that now, it made her feel bad. She would rather concentrate on Mark and how he'd told her she could be happy. She so wanted that to be true.

Alex was on the couch asleep when she opened the front door. A few empty beer cans were on the coffee table. Even though she shut the door ever so gently, he woke up and blinked, revealing only the slits of his sleepy eyes. Then he stretched out and yawned.

"Hi," he said. Eyes fully open now, his smile faded. "Didn't make it home last night?"

Annette sighed; she really was over this too. Him, being here—still in her life—when there was nothing left between them. She walked straight past him into the kitchen without responding. Then stopped in the kitchen doorway and surveyed the scene.

"I planned to clean those up this morning," Alex called out from behind her.

Dishes were stacked up haphazardly on the sink. Food scraps—gnawed bones still sitting on the plates—a few blowflies buzzing around them. Fat spattered over the tiles above the stove. It looked as though Alex and his mates had eaten here last night. Somebody had cooked chops.

Abandoning her plan of finding a drink in the fridge, she marched into the bedroom and slammed the door. This was her life. She sat down heavily on the unmade bed. Living in this shithole with people who didn't care.

Turns out Tracy wasn't a friend after all. She had thought that Tracy would look out for her. It was obvious now though, that she was just as alone as ever. The tears and sadness that she'd held back on the bus, threatened to overwhelm her again. She gulped them down and was left with only anger.

Tears had never helped her when she was still at home. Tears didn't bring her any comfort from her mother. Rose had to manage her own misery, so there was nothing leftover for Annette. And, tears brought her even more trouble from her father. Was it normal to make a child *stop* crying by threatening them with a leather belt? Effective though, she stopped her grizzling quick smart.

The bedroom door pushed open and Annette gasped.

"Sorry, didn't mean to scare you."

Alex was standing there with a large bottle of coke in his hand.

"Want some?" he asked, offering her the bottle.

Although he smirked a little at his double entendre, she could see that he was nervous. Why was he doing this? He was just making life difficult for them both. Couldn't he just accept that it was over?

"Fucking knock, you fucking prick!" she shouted. "You don't sleep here anymore remember."

Alex walked towards the bed, an anxious smile stuck on his face.

"I told you a month ago that it was over, that you're a

hopeless case, going nowhere."

She sighed, shaking her head. Maybe she was talking about herself. Maybe, she was truly hopeless at life. At least come Monday, Alex would go to his job as a plasterer. He might even run his own business one day. He'd often talked about it. Her job was going nowhere, her life was going nowhere. Yes, Alex swilled a few beers, but she had never seen him pass out drunk like she had last night. She smiled a grim smile. Alex moved towards the bed again.

Pointing a finger at him, she said, "Get your stuff out today, Tracy wants you out."

Where would he go? Would she miss him at all? He sat down on the bed.

For the second time that day, she said, "Fuck off." This time though, it came out as a whisper.

"You don't mean that," he said.

No... she didn't.

He gently slipped his hand around her waist and his touch felt so good. For the last month he'd left her alone and that was how she'd wanted it. But now, she felt that familiar stirring.

"I miss being with you babe. You know I still... care about you," he said. "I don't really get what happened."

He placed the coke bottle down on the fabric-covered wooden box that doubled as a bedside table. Then, he leaned across and nuzzled her neck. Annette closed her eyes. Alex leaned back, slid his hand under her T-shirt and undid her bra. Then he cupped her breast in his hand and gently rolled her nipple between his fingers.

From a faraway place, sensible, rational thoughts were trying to gain traction. It's not fair to string things out. To let him believe she still cared. Having sex would complicate the situation even more. This felt good though—really good. After laying her down on the bed, he lifted her skirt and slid his hand inside her knickers and began to move his fingers. She moaned softly. At the start, before things went bad, it had felt like this.

When he brought his mouth to hers to kiss her, she smelt the stale beer on his breath. In an instant, the exquisite pleasure which had been building to orgasm, vanished. Now, disoriented, disconnected, she began to sob—great heaving sobs.

"Shit! What's wrong?" he asked.

He took his hand out of her pants and smoothed down her skirt.

"I didn't hurt you, did I?"

Unable to answer, she shook her head. He put a hand on her shoulder.

"Please tell me what's wrong," he said, as he tried to pull her towards him.

She shrugged his hand away from her shoulder.

"Are you going to tell me?"

Annette shook her head again. This time he tried to put his arm around her waist. How easy would it be to let go and melt into him? To let him comfort her. To comfort each other. In some deep, hidden away part of herself, she knew this weird behaviour had nothing to do with him. The urge to reassure him, to say out loud that it wasn't his fault, that she didn't understand what had happened either, almost won out. But no, she had to shut him out. Send a clear message. They weren't together, it hadn't worked. Letting him back in would be a big mistake.

"Okay, I guess I'll just... leave you alone then."

He got up and left the room, closing the door softly behind him.

Annette continued to cry, and it felt like a dam breaking, rising up and overflowing. Over the sound of her own sobs, she could hear Alex run the tap and clatter around in the kitchen. She was glad he couldn't hear her anymore.

When she was all cried out, she considered getting up and facing the day. Alex was still at home though. She took a large swig from the bottle of flat coke that Alex had left on the bedside table.

Oh God, now he'll be thinking we're back together.

What was wrong with her? Why didn't she stop him? Why couldn't she ever just say no?

A need for the bathroom soon drove Annette from the sanctuary of her room. When she walked past the kitchen Alex came to the doorway. She could see the concern in his eyes. She didn't linger though—didn't give him time to speak. Finished with her quick visit to the toilet, she hurried back to the bedroom, shut the door and crawled in under the doona.

The muffled sounds of sport on the TV came from the lounge room. Knowing Alex was out there was strangely comforting. Although she didn't want to be close to him, she didn't want to be alone either. Clearly, he was upset by her outburst. She knew he wouldn't intentionally do anything to hurt her, and he hadn't. Her reaction had come as a shock to her as well. Why had she suddenly felt so bad? Maybe, because of her conversation with Mark. He was so clean cut. And the girls on the bus, they looked about her age, but she was sure they didn't act like filthy, low-life sluts the way that she did. What had just happened with Alex was a perfect example.

The sounds of the TV, a distant lawn mower and kids playing football in the street, drifted into—then out of —Annette's awareness. Half awake, then half asleep, worn out by the events of last night and the morning, she soon slipped into a fitful doze.

Annette dreamt of a garden. Not a beautiful exotic garden, but a few straggly plants and weeds in the backyard of an ugly fibro house. A single pretty, purple pansy flowered among the sparse weeds and half dead bushes. Freshly planted in the middle of a small trough dug out of the soil.

A beautiful woman came out of the house, her hair in a French twist—perfectly coiffed—makeup immaculate. Her floral dress floated gracefully around her legs as she walked. With a glass of wine in her hand, she took a seat on the verandah. A man came out of the house carrying a bucket. He filled the bucket from a tap on the back wall of the house and walked over to pour water carelessly onto the pansy. The pansy drooped under the weight. The woman sipped her wine and watched expressionless. Again, and again he filled the bucket and doused the pansy—ruthless with the water. The trough deepened and widened, filled and over-flowed. The pansy bowed and then flattened into the dirt. The man seemed to glide through the water without effort. Single-minded in his mission until the whole back yard was under water, the level almost, but not quite, reaching the height of the verandah. The man then placed the bucket down on the verandah and walked inside. The woman still didn't move.

Annette woke with a start, feeling even more disturbed than before. She pulled the doona off the bed and walked out into the lounge room. Curling up on the old armchair across from Alex, she covered herself with the doona. He offered to make her a cup of tea and with gratitude, she nodded.

Chapter 3

Annette stood across the road from the church hall. Hovering at what she estimated was a safe enough distance—partially hidden by a tree. From here, she could watch people going into the church without them seeing her. They were all like the girls on the bus—happy, chatty, giggly. Another wave of self-doubt swept over her, but the hope of seeing Mark again kept her from leaving.

How many times this week had she stared at the crumpled leaflet Mark had given her?

DAWN OF HOPE CHRISTIAN FELLOWSHIP
Join us at 5pm, Sunday 9th March 1980 for an evening of
fun, food and song.

The Clifton Hill address was written underneath. The church hall wasn't far away—a short bus ride. She had looked up the word fellowship in the small dictionary that Tracy kept in the scrabble box. *Fellowship; Friendly association, especially with those who share one's interests.*

Well, she was quite certain the people there wouldn't share her interests and that she knew nothing about theirs.

She was nothing like them. And Mark would be the only person she had even met before. Hanging around alone, like a desperate idiot, while the Christians all chatted with each other, was the nightmare scenario she couldn't stop picturing.

On the other hand, though, she hadn't been able to get Mark out of her head since they'd met. That tiny seed of hope was still germinating. Based on what, she wasn't sure. Just a growing certainty that she couldn't continue like this, not if there was even the slimmest possibility of a better life. In the end, she'd rushed her makeup and nearly missed the bus.

God, imagine walking in late!

Completely behind the tree now, she took out her compact to do a final check. After touching up her lipstick, she smacked her lips together to spread the glossy crimson evenly. Happy that her wavy, blonde hair was behaving today, she swished it back behind her and smoothed a few wispy strands down. Dark brown mascara highlighted her large brown eyes. Good choice not to add the blue eyeshadow today. Most of the girls going in didn't even look like they were wearing makeup. She grabbed a tissue from her bag and squeezed it between her lips, patting off some colour. Hmm... better, she didn't want to look like a tart. She put away her compact and turned her attention back to the hall. Still no sign of Mark.

What did Mark think of her? Did he think she was pretty? The evidence was that boys, in general, found her attractive.

They told her; *bodaciously beautiful; I get lost in those awesome brown eyes; I want to pash those perfect lips.*

Tracy told her; *I would kill to have your figure, and, that gorgeous mane of golden hair you have, oh my God.*

Alex told her too; *You are a total fox, babe.*

And she trusted Alex.

Still she couldn't see it herself. Eyes too big, face too thin, hair too frizzy. Were they lying to her? Or, did she see something different? Was that because of what went on inside her head? That wasn't pretty at all. Look what a bitch she'd been to Alex. Poor Alex. She'd ignored his advances since yesterday. Now, he was more miserable than ever.

Mark had stepped outside and was talking to a teenage boy. Angel like, in flared white pants and a white T-shirt. Now that she had laid eyes on him, there was no turning back. She took a few tentative steps out into the open and stood there shuffling her feet. Would he notice her? A few moments went by until Mark looked up. After speaking to the boy again briefly, he gestured towards Annette then walked across the street to where she stood. Her heart started to hammer. He was even more attractive than she remembered.

"Hi." His voice was cheerful. "Aren't you coming in?"

"Well, I'm not sure. I don't know anyone..."

"You know me," he said.

Then he smiled and placed his hand on the small of her back. Was she imagining that look in his eye? Maybe she just wanted it to be there. Yet, there was a part of her that didn't want that. Didn't want him to look at her that way. She was confused. What did she want? For him to save her from her miserable life. And the happiness he promised. That's what she wanted. Any other kind of interest in him was a waste of time. Surely a pastor wouldn't allow himself to lust after someone like her.

He took his hand away as they approached the hall. She could still feel the heat from his touch.

"Don't worry, I'll take care of you," he reassured her, as they walked inside together.

But he didn't take care of her. People wanted to talk to

him constantly. He had been so focused on her and her wellbeing on the bus, yet as soon as they were inside, his focus was on everyone else. She was left leaning against a wall alone, like a leftover plank of wood.

Older women ran the kitchen. They brought out hot sausage rolls, party pies and egg and lettuce sandwiches. On her way back to the kitchen, one of the women handed Annette a plate from the stack on the table.

"Help yourself love. There's punch over there as well." The woman indicated towards the other end of the table.

Annette was pleased. "Punch?"

The woman frowned as though she could read Annette's thoughts. "Hmm, non-alcoholic, of course. It's made with dry ginger, pineapple juice and lemonade," she said. The woman walked away, shaking her head a little.

Not used to such an abundance of free food, Annette filled her small paper plate with two of everything. The food tasted good. More importantly, eating gave her something to do. The punch was sweet, and she liked it. A real drink would have been better though.

A girl in a preppy pant suit separated herself from a large group close by and approached Annette.

"Hi, I'm Julie."

"I'm Annette."

"Great that you could come today and learn more about us. So... do you live around here?"

"No, I live in Carlton."

"Oh, there's a girl at our church who goes to University High. That's near Carlton isn't it? Is that where you go?"

"Ah no... I don't—"

An amplified voice cut through the hubbub asking people to come in and be seated.

"Sorry, will have to catch you later. Duty calls," Julie said with a smile, and hurried off towards the main part of the hall.

Mark was nowhere to be seen so Annette headed to the back and sat down on the floor—cross-legged like everyone else.

Printed songbooks were handed out. On stage now, Julie announced the song number and led the singing in a sweet, clear voice. She was backed by a hip young band—a guitarist, keyboard player and a drummer. Annette joined in —this was kind of fun. The music was upbeat and the tunes easy to follow.

After about ten songs Julie closed her songbook, left the stage and re-joined her friends on the floor in the front. Mark walked onto the stage from off to the side and approached the microphone. An expectant hush came over the group. He waited a few moments and then began to sing.

"We try to do it on our own. We stumble and we fall."

Annette sat mesmerised by his soft, husky voice and his rock star look. White clothes set off by a white electric guitar slung across his chest. The band stayed silent, eyes on Mark. He pushed his foot pedal and strummed his guitar gently before singing the next lines.

"You watch us struggle, and with a gentle voice you call."

Mark nodded to the drummer and the rest of the band joined in, still soft, subdued but with the beat becoming ever louder.

Mark's voice, stronger now, "Only when the hurting is too great, do we offer up the broken pieces. We find You in our darkest night, and sing praise to You, sweet Jesus."

The music swelled even louder as Mark continued, his eyes closed. Voice more insistent, passion evident on his face. Annette glanced around and noticed plenty of other girls also had their eyes glued to Mark. Perhaps they were wishing he was something more than their spiritual leader.

After the crescendo, the song didn't finish. Mark continued to repeat the last line.

"We find You in our darkest night, and sing praise to You, sweet Jesus."

Most of the group joined him in singing the same line over and over. He closed his eyes and swayed with the music, raising both arms in the air as he sang. Then the crowd stood, almost in unison. Annette jumped up when she realised that she was the last one still sitting on the floor. Mark's audience swayed with him.

Almost everyone had one arm or both arms lifted in the air now. They were waving their raised hands from side to side slowly in time with the music. Everyone was singing. The same few words kept repeating. Annette sang along. She had never experienced anything like this before. Everyone looked so happy with their closed eyes and smiling faces. Transported to some other wonderful place. She wondered whether that place was somewhere worth going.

Now people around her started muttering.

The girl to the right of Annette was repeating, "Thank you, thank you Jesus."

Annette couldn't decipher what the boy on the other side of her was saying. Was he speaking in another language? Voices raised even louder after the song finally came to an end. Now it was getting a bit weird.

Mark's voice quieted the cacophony.

"Praise God, Praise God, Praise the Lord Jesus Christ."

He placed his guitar on a stand and the rest of the band took seats on the side of the stage. Mark lowered his head and the whole room followed suit. Annette lowered her head but kept her eyes on Mark.

"Lord, we come to you in prayer. We commit this time to You. May those who already know You be strengthened. May those who don't know You hear you calling them home. Speak through me Lord."

Mark went on to talk about a different life. A life in which whatever you'd done in the past, didn't matter. Where all that went before, was forgiven. A life in which you could be loved unconditionally and accepted, no matter who you were, or where you came from. He leapt about on the stage as he spoke, almost bursting with heartfelt fervour. The excitement about all this was contagious.

At the end he asked, "Who among you wants this better life for yourself. I plead with those of you who are still unsaved. Jesus pleads with you. Come forward so that we can pray together."

For a moment, Annette considered walking to the front. No, it was all too unfamiliar and strange. Besides, she was still a long way from believing her past didn't matter.

One at a time, they straggled forward. A pimply-faced teenage boy in clothes that didn't fit properly, a thin girl in a long green and red tie-dyed skirt and a conservative looking young man in a shirt and tie. The three stood at the front facing Mark.

"Lord accept these three lost lambs into your fold. Forgive them their sins. Elevate them, lift them up to be with You." His voice boomed louder and louder into the microphone. "They are renouncing the old ways, the old habits. They are renewed in You. Lord bring down your Holy Spirit upon these three..." Mark opened his eyes for a moment and looked directly at Annette. "...and upon anyone else here who is still caught up in the grip of Satan. In the name of Jesus, I ask you to set them free."

Shocked, Annette dropped her gaze. Could he be right? Perhaps she was being controlled by the Devil. As bizarre as it sounded, maybe it was true. She certainly didn't feel like she was in control of her bad choices.

Mark closed his eyes again and concluded his prayer

with a loud "Amen" that was echoed by the whole group.

After that, he formed a huddle with the three and they placed their hands on each other's shoulders. They stayed in the circle with Mark, for what seemed like a very long time. She wondered what he was saying to them.

The larger group started to break up and people were leaving. Should she wait for Mark? She sat down on the floor again. A few adults appeared at the front entrance jangling their car keys.

When the room was nearly empty, except for the small group near the stage, she finally gave up on him and walked towards the door.

"Hey, are you leaving?" Mark called out, rushing up to her. "Can I have your phone number? I'd like to call you to organise a time to meet up with you."

Out of his pocket he pulled a pen and a photocopied scrap of paper.

Dotted lines followed the headings; *name, address, phone number.*

Annette filled in only her name and phone number —she didn't want him showing up at the messy flat—and handed it back to him. Then, she walked quickly from the hall, head down, to hide the grin that had spread across her face.

***

"Do you know if anyone's called for me?"

Two whole days and Mark *still* hadn't called. Maybe he already phoned, and Alex hadn't passed on the message. She didn't want to ask Alex though. Better to continue to steer clear of him.

Since being left stranded last Saturday night, Annette hadn't spoken to Tracy much either. Tracy had abandoned her. Really, she should have it out with Tracy. That would be the mature way to deal with it. At least now though, she had broken the ice.

Tracy looked surprised. Maybe by the question, or maybe, that Annette was talking to her again.

"No, no-one's called, I would have told you," she said.

Okay, judging by Tracy's tone, they couldn't just pick up where they left off. She would have to address what had happened.

Annette sucked in a breath. Trying her best to keep her voice casual and light, she began, "You remember last week when you left me in the city—"

"What do you mean *left you*? What was I supposed to do? You couldn't walk, you wouldn't have even been able to get to the tram stop."

Tracy was one of the few people to show an interest in Annette since she'd left home. More than that, meeting Tracy had been a turning point in her life.

She reflected on the chain of events last year that had led to her leaving home and ultimately to finding the job at the restaurant.

Tension between Annette and her stepfather, Bob, had been building for a long time. Simple things like a TV program would cause her to blow up at him. Bob wanted to watch the news, while she wanted to watch the latest bands on Countdown. Sometimes, she even shocked herself with the words that spat out of her mouth. Never, had she talked back to her father—she was too scared of him—but with Bob, she didn't hold back. When she started in on him, he would stay silent at first, which infuriated her even more. Then, she would ramp up the abuse until, finally, he would make some remark about her needing to cool off, pick up his newspaper and go and sit out on the porch. Knowing that she had rattled him though, gave her some satisfaction.

Rose hated it when Annette acted this way, but she couldn't help it. Bob was an easy target for the rage that bubbled up inside.

A few months after Annette's seventeenth birthday, Rose had shown her the classified ads for bedsits.

"Now wouldn't you like to have a nice little place to yourself?" Rose asked. "Look, you could afford this and still go to school if you wanted," she said, pointing to an ad for a self-contained bungalow.

So, her mother wanted her out of the house. Annette couldn't believe it. First her father had abandoned her, and now Rose wanted to get rid of her.

"You don't want me here anymore?" Annette's voice cracked.

Rose began to cry.

"Of course, I do. I just can't stand the fighting anymore."

"Well, why don't you throw him out? I'm your daughter!"

Rose didn't answer and left the room still crying.

Annette pulled the newspaper towards her. The bungalow was thirty dollars a week. Annette was working after school as a cashier at a supermarket. If she took a packed lunch to school and asked for some extra shifts at work, maybe she could manage. It wasn't such a bad idea; it would be great to have her own space. And, if they didn't want her there, why stay?

She packed one afternoon and—while Bob was still at work—Rose drove her to her new place.

"I do love you, you know," Rose said, when they arrived at the bungalow.

Annette was still pissed off. On the other hand, she was also excited about the prospect of having her own place. She didn't tell her mother this though; she wanted Rose to feel bad.

"Yeah, well it's impossible to tell."

Annette managed to finish two terms of Form 6. One more term and she would have matriculated, but it was a struggle to pay the rent and buy food with only the after-school supermarket shifts. Leaving school was an easy choice. She'd always felt different to the other kids at school. Not that she was actively disliked—if she was, it wasn't obvious to her—but she'd never developed really close friends. School was a lonely place and she wouldn't miss it. And, besides, what was the point? No-one cared whether she succeeded at life or not.

Rose visited her regularly at the bedsit, bringing a few groceries and toiletries. Annette didn't tell Rose that she'd left school—it was none of her business. She was cool towards Rose, pretending that she was about to go out, so the visit would have to be cut short. Eventually, Rose just stopped coming.

After that, being alone in the bedsit every evening and weekend with only a portable black and white TV for company brought on a new level of crushing loneliness. This went on for a few weeks during which every negative thought about herself was magnified. And, the fear that came with living alone was unbearable. The long nights were the worst. Scared to go to sleep because she'd heard a noise outside. Staying awake for hours and finally falling asleep with the TV on. Then later, waking in a cold sweat, believing someone was right there beside her bed. In the end, she started to believe she might turn into a crazy person if this went on too long. So, when she saw the job at Le Plat advertised, she applied straight away.

The new job gave her respite in some unexpected ways. Apart from having something to do at night, she found a new friend in Tracy. Tracy introduced her to alcohol and showed her how easy it was to meet boys. Alcohol helped with the bad feelings. Boys helped her avoid being alone. And, living with Tracy helped with the middle-of-the-night terror.

Right now though, she was putting all that at risk.

"I mean... I just want to know what happened," Annette backpedalled.

"That guy from the bus offered to help. He and one of the boys who was with him carried you into the bus. They told me you'd be safe, that they were Christians. He said he was a minister so I assumed they would look after you." Tracy looked positively wounded now. "I've been wanting to ask you about the whole thing, but you seem to have been avoiding me."

Annette suddenly felt guilty for being so angry with her, "I thought you just left me."

"Well, I didn't... just *leave you*." She paused for a moment and then smiled, a nervous, little smile. "And, even if I did, you can't make me responsible for you. You really shouldn't get so pissed that you pass out, it's just not safe to do that."

It hadn't occurred to Annette until that moment that Tracy was right, she wasn't responsible for her. Tracy wasn't her mother. It wasn't Tracy's job to take care of her. She really shouldn't have got that drunk that she couldn't get herself home. More evidence of her rotten life. Passed out in the street like a homeless person.

A wave of self-disgust swept over her. Mark was right, she really was in the grip of Satan. No matter now though, Mark would help her, he would save her. She sighed as she remembered the touch of his hand on her back.

"You're right, I do need to change," Annette admitted.

"I'm not saying that, I'm just saying, you know... I was worried about you."

Annette gave Tracy a sheepish smile. "Well, maybe I

should be thanking you because I am glad I met him."

Tracy's eyes popped wide open. "Met who? The minister?"

"Yes, the minister. His name's Mark, and I like him," she stated simply.

"But he's a minister and he's older, isn't he?"

"Maybe a bit older, I'm not sure. And, what's the problem with him being a minister? Annette asked.

Tracy didn't answer, but that dubious look was still on her face—eyebrows knitted, tight-lipped unsmiling mouth. Suddenly it seemed crucial to convince Tracy that this was possible. Or, was she just trying to convince herself?

"Anyway, I think he likes me too. That's whose call I'm waiting for."

"Oh," Tracy said. She shook her head slowly now. After a moment, she added, "I didn't know you were into all that."

"I'm not really... well, I wasn't, but don't you think those people—Christians—seem happy?"

"No, not particularly, no more than the rest of us."

Should she tell Tracy about the church singalong? What she had seen, the ecstasy that the group seemed to experience. Could she even describe it? No, she would keep it to herself. What would she have thought, even a week ago, if someone had told her that they had been to an event like that? This conversation was new territory for her. Tracy wouldn't understand; she didn't really understand that much yet herself. Now that she and Tracy were speaking again, it was probably better to quit while she was ahead, so she stood to leave the room.

"I hope you're not going to go all weird on me," Tracy said, as Annette walked towards her bedroom.

Although it was more of a statement than a question, she suspected that Tracy would have appreciated some reassurance. Annette didn't respond. There was only one thing she could be sure of right now. And that was that something needed to change.

***

The phone rang later that evening while Annette was in her room getting ready for work. Her breath caught in her throat again, just like it had every time the phone had rung since Sunday. Tracy answered and Annette was grateful that Alex hadn't picked up. With her breath still raggedy, she opened her bedroom door and looked hopefully at Tracy.

"Yes, I'll get her." Tracy winked at her. "It's for you," she said, handing her the phone.

Alex had his back to them, watching TV. He seemed oblivious to the exchange.

Annette carried the phone into her bedroom and pulled the phone cord under the door so that it could close. She sucked in a nervous breath and sat down on the bed to answer.

"Hello."

"Hi, is that Annette? It's Mark, from the bus and the singalong."

"Yes, it's Annette."

"How did you enjoy Sunday night?" he asked.

"I've never been to anything quite like that before. The music was good and your talk... well, it was interesting."

"*Interesting*, thanks, I'll take that. Better than boring." He chuckled, then continued, his voice light and friendly. "Hey, I've called to ask if I can visit you sometime this week?"

"Do you mean here? At my place?"

This didn't sound like a date. Annette wasn't sure what it was, but she hadn't forgotten how he'd looked at her.

"Yes, that's fine. Can you hold on a minute?"

After covering the mouthpiece, she opened the door a little and motioned to Tracy to come into the bedroom.

"Are you home tomorrow?" Annette whispered.

"I'll be out for a few hours in the afternoon. I've got a hairdresser's appointment at two o'clock," she said.

"Thanks," Annette said, and gently pushed her back out of the bedroom.

Tracy waved goodbye, as she mouthed soundlessly, "See you at work."

Annette closed the door behind her and took her hand off the mouthpiece.

"You can come over around two, tomorrow afternoon."

Trying to sound casual, she added, "If you want."

"That works for me. What's the address?"

Annette gave him the address and they said their goodbyes. Excitement was prickling her all over. She walked out into the lounge room and replaced the phone, smiling to herself. That was, until she noticed Alex looking directly at her.

"Who was that on the phone?"

Annette paused; she felt a sting of guilt. Hadn't she done her best to make it obvious that their relationship was over? Well, this might finally give him the message that they had nothing in common. Might as well tell him the truth, well... some of the truth.

"It was a minister; he made an appointment to come and talk with me."

Alex stared at her.

"Bullshit!" he stated matter-of-factly, shaking his head. "Who was it?"

Then, he seemed to check himself. "No, it's okay, of course you don't have to tell me. You do what you want, Annette."

Alex walked into the kitchen. This really was none of

his business. Besides, it didn't matter what he thought of her now. She followed him into the kitchen anyway.

Facing the open fridge, Alex stood with one hand on the door, his shoulders slumped.

"Just leave me alone, that's obviously what you want," he said, not turning around.

His voice was unsteady, the sadness, unmistakeable. An urge to put a hand on his shoulder, to comfort him almost won out, but that would be stupid. They'd probably end up back in bed and she didn't want to be that person any more. Still, it was hard to see him so vulnerable. Particularly knowing she had caused his pain.

"It is true. Why wouldn't you believe me?" she said to his back.

He closed the fridge door and turned to face her.

"Why would *you* talk to a minister?"

"I don't know, it seems to me that people who believe in something, are happier than everyone else. I just want to understand more about that."

Would she really want to find out more about God, if she wasn't so keen on Mark? It did feel good to be talking to Alex this way though. It was as if she were reaching for something higher than he was.

"You are serious then," he sighed heavily, then shook his head. "My mum was religious... You didn't know that did you?"

Annette had never met his family. Assuming it was because he didn't consider her good enough to meet them. And then she never examined that assumption further—never asked him about it.

"No, you haven't told me that. I never met your parents. Remember?"

"Well, I don't speak to her anymore, that's why I never took you there," he said slowly.

Well, this was new information. She softened, maybe it wasn't all about her inadequacies.

"Why, what happened?" she asked.

"If I'd wanted to talk about it, don't you think I would've by now?" His voice took on an uncharacteristic, harsh edge. "Let's just say that my experience with religion has turned me into a devout atheist."

His face relaxed and he smiled at her. "Yeah, well good luck with the minister, but be careful hey." He gave the warning gently, his concern for her obvious.

Then he grabbed his keys and went out.

She was left puzzled. Not only by the warning, but also because there was clearly a lot she didn't know about Alex.

***

After changing several times, Annette pulled out a T-shirt picturing Queen Elizabeth, eyes and mouth covered by the words, *God Save The Queen and Sex Pistols*. It was over-sized for her, but she had liked wearing Alex's T-shirts. He'd said she could keep this one.

Reluctantly, she put it back in the drawer. Aware that she might never wear it again. Now her fingers ran across another one Alex had given her. An ACDC *Highway to Hell* T-shirt.

A memory came to her of Alex, in this same T-shirt standing on the bed, playing air guitar with ACDC blaring out through the stereo. Her, sitting cross-legged on the floor laughing at his antics. No, she shook her head, not for her, not anymore, she was getting off the highway to hell.

Finally, she settled on moderately tight jeans and a plain T-shirt. Mark knew she was no saint, but today she wanted to show him she could do better—be better. That she wasn't attached to her old life.

Mark was due to arrive soon and now that she was ready, time started to drag. She jumped up and checked her makeup again and was happy with the result. The special care she'd taken with the eyeliner and the addition of a touch of metallic blue on her eyelids made her eyes look even bigger than they were. Her freshly washed hair smelled of green apple shampoo. She ran the brush through it one more time and then wandered from room to room checking that things were tidy. There were stray potato chips on the floor, so she picked up the biggest ones. An open Cleo magazine was on the phone table. She grabbed it and took it to her room and stuffed it under the bed.

Annette looked around her bedroom, slowly appraising it, imagining how it might look to Mark—posters of heavy metal bands on the wall—the stained carpet. She pulled the doona up and straightened it more carefully than usual. When was the last time she'd washed the sheets? A long time ago... With a jolt, she checked herself. Don't be stupid. Mark is a minister. Of course, he won't be seeing this room.

And there it was, she couldn't deny it, she longed to be like those girls at the singalong. The happy, carefree virgins. *Their* boyfriends would respect them—if they even had boyfriends. *Their* boyfriends probably didn't even ask, let alone expect, anything from them. Maybe just a romantic goodnight kiss. She wanted that for herself so badly, but it seemed impossible. They were light, she was dark. They were day, she was night. She sat down on the bed. What was this heaviness that was always with her? Why did she feel so different to everyone else?

The doorbell rang. She flew off the bed. Her legs were a little wobbly and her chest was pounding. After one slow deep breath to calm herself, she opened the front door.

Mark greeted her with a warm smile, looking just as

good as she remembered. He wore a dark blue T-shirt that made his eyes seem even bluer. The thick, dark waves of his hair were not too short, but also not too long, reaching just below his collar.

"Come in." With a wave of her hand she invited him into the lounge room.

He sat on the couch and leaned back, looking relaxed. Bolt upright in the armchair opposite him, she wondered whether she was having any success at all in hiding her nervousness. He didn't seem nervous at all. Why would he be? She was the *troubled* one.

"Well, what've you been up to today?" he asked.

Annette didn't want to tell him she'd slept until eleven, even though that was not as late as she usually slept.

"Not much," she said. "How about you?"

"Well, I like to get up early to spend time with God, to find out what He wants for me for the day. So, I spent an hour in prayer and Bible study, then I went for a walk, then I wrote a letter to my mother..." He hesitated for a moment, and then continued in the same easy flowing tone, "She's overseas for a while. And then I made a few visits, one over lunch, now I'm here," he concluded.

It did sound like he'd done a lot already and it was only 2 o'clock.

"Hmm, busy day so far," she reflected.

"I'm here to talk about you though, not about me."

He sat forward. "Tell me all about yourself."

What was there to say? She could try to impress him. The way she was living was a dead giveaway though, so that probably wouldn't work. Another option was to drop her defences, at least a little, and take a risk.

"What do you want to know?" Then, more quietly, she said, "I don't like my life much."

"Why not?" he asked gently.

Suzanne Swift

Annette shrugged and looked down, suddenly close to tears. If she tried to speak, she knew she would lose control, so she stayed silent. He too was silent, for a short time, for which she was grateful.

When he spoke again, his voice was soft and comforting. "There is something better for you and all you need to do to have it, is to invite God into your life. To let Him know you've done bad things—sinned..." He paused. "...as we all have, and that you want to change your life."

Mark gazed at her intently. She felt he was looking deep into her soul. That although he could see all the bad there, he still thought she was worth saving.

She wanted so much to believe him, wanted so much to find an escape from the drinking and the sex that always left her feeling empty, dissatisfied and guilty. Was this what she needed? Could the love of a divine being, one that she couldn't see, feel, or touch, fill the space that nothing else could? Her head said no, but she had to listen to her heart, to her soul. At the singalong, when Mark had read from the book of James in the bible, she had learned that

...one who doubts is like a wave of the sea that is driven and tossed by the wind.

Did Mark see her that way—as a doubter? She wanted to feel strong and secure in her beliefs like those young people the other night. If they didn't have any doubts why should she? Besides, Mark believed these things, Mark had studied these things. Annette wanted to trust Mark so badly. Wanted her life to change. Wanted the hollow void inside her to be filled. She didn't want to be stuck in a chasm of doubt —a state between belief and disbelief. So, she crossed over quickly, dispelling any lingering uncertainty, because she wanted what was on the other side.

Tears fell freely now. Mark slid off the couch and knelt on the floor. "Are you ready to take Jesus as your personal saviour?" He held out his hand towards her.

She nodded. Then took his hand and knelt opposite him. Still crying, but feeling, oh so hopeful. This was going to be a new beginning.

"Repeat these words of repentance and acceptance after me. Dear Lord Jesus, I know that I am a sinner and I ask for Your forgiveness."

"I believe You died for my sins and rose from the dead. I turn away from my sins and invite You to come into my heart and life."

"I will trust and follow You as my Lord and Savior."

As instructed, Annette repeated the sinner's prayer after Mark as he led her through the steps to her rebirth as a Christian. Her voice was shaky with emotion as she prayed for the very first time. This felt wonderful and the process was so simple, yet so profound. In only a matter of minutes, she had forged a personal relationship with a new father, who would always care for her and would always protect her.

Alex's words of foreboding floated somewhere on the periphery and, those words—along with her own doubts—threatened to spoil this moment. She pushed them aside, she had to believe Mark, had to have faith in the promise of the prayer, because what else was there for her, if not? Just let go and trust, that was all she had to do.

Mark said, "Amen", in a celebratory tone and hugged her to him. He lingered there just a little longer than she would have expected. Was he praying again? She refused to consider the alternative, after what had just happened. As he had said in his prayer, she was now a new creature, pure in heart, a perfect lamb of God. And so, of course, was he.

Chapter 4

Annette had the night off work. Mark was arriving soon to pick her up for a Bible study. She was apprehensive and, as usual, didn't know what to wear. Did it matter though? Wouldn't she be accepted anyway? Now that she was one of them. Well, that's what Mark kept telling her during their phone conversations of the past week. She didn't quite feel it inside yet.

He'd asked her to church on Sunday, but she'd said she wasn't sure she could be ready for the 9am pickup after working the night before. That wasn't the only reason though. Church attendance seemed like a huge step—too daunting. The Bible study might be more manageable. Mark had said it would only be a small group of young people.

Again, she had taken special care with her makeup and hair and Alex must have noticed.

His eyes widened. "You look good. Where are you off to?"

There was no choice but to tell him. Mark would be here any minute. Now, she was more than a little worried about Alex meeting Mark.

Since the night before her conversion, she and Alex hadn't spoken. Alex hadn't asked what had happened, but still... she could have told him. Why hadn't she? Or, Tracy, for that matter? Shouldn't she be proud of her new self? There was nothing to be apologetic about. How would they respond though? She was pretty sure they wouldn't understand.

"I'm going to a Bible study," she answered, and waited for the expected negative reaction.

He sighed, letting the breath out slowly, as he shook his head.

"What?" she challenged him, with her hands on her hips. "Aren't you glad I'm doing something positive with my life?"

"And I suppose all your sins are forgiven and you're like a new person and nothing that happened before matters, etcetera, etcetera," he said, still shaking his head.

Well, this was a surprise. Alex understood the way to salvation. Why then, was he so cynical— despite that? Perhaps he'd never experienced it for himself. Was he hanging on to whatever happened with his mother—letting that get in the way? Maybe she could help him find what she'd found. Wouldn't hurt to give it a shot.

"Well, yes," she said. "That's right and I believe it too. I feel... different, better."

"Hmm, whatever," he said. Then turned his attention back to the book he was reading.

"Why are you acting like this? I know you're upset because we're not together, but couldn't you at least be happy for me?"

He dropped the book into his lap and looked directly at her.

"You're right, I am still upset that we're not together. But I've realised that trying to make it work with you was messing with my head. It's impossible to know what you want and just when I think I do; I still screw up. I know I'm a long way from perfect, but I did try."

Annette's gaze dropped to the floor. She knew in her gut that what he was saying was true. No matter how hard he tried, there was always going to be something that wasn't good enough. Didn't matter now though. They could never be together anyway if he didn't believe in God. They were headed in different directions.

"Alex I'm sorry it didn't work out between us, it's probably for the best though." Although she tried her best not to sound patronising, judging by Alex's expression, she wasn't sure she'd succeeded. Taking a breath, she forged ahead, "I don't know what happened with your mother, but maybe you should give God another try, I feel hopeful for the first time in a very long time..."

Alex's face darkened with anger and his lips tightened into a thin line. He stood up.

"Please don't preach to me, you know nothing about religion, and I know too fucking much!" The words spat out of his mouth as he leaned towards her.

Annette recoiled from him.

At that moment there was a light tap on the door. Alex was still glaring at her. Lifting a finger to her lips, she silently shushed him. When she opened the door to Mark, he looked first at her and then at Alex. After a few seconds, he stepped inside and gave them both a tentative smile.

"Hi, I'm Mark."

He held out his hand towards Alex. Alex hesitated, but then hurriedly shook Mark's outstretched hand. When Alex responded, his voice still didn't sound completely under control.

"Yes, I know who you are."

With that, he grabbed his keys and stormed out. Annette stood there shocked, but also curious. What on earth had happened, to make him so bitter?

"Bad timing?" Mark asked.

"Uh-huh." Annette nodded. "Let's go."

As they walked out to the car, Annette felt breathless and excited. She hadn't had anything to drink that day because she was trying to be good. Now though, she wished she'd had something to take the edge off.

Mark followed her to the passenger side of the car. Her hand was on the door handle when she noticed Mark standing behind her. Suddenly, it occurred to her that he wanted to open the door for her. Quickly she withdrew her hand and stepped back. Such a gentleman! The gesture made her feel even more heady, as did the scent of his expensive aftershave when he leaned across in front of her.

Mark's car was littered with the paraphernalia of his calling: tracts, notepads, songbooks, several Bibles. He picked up a pile of papers to make room for her and shoved them over onto the back seat.

"I need to tidy up in here," he said.

He looked a bit older than her. Was it okay to ask him a personal question? Asking his age should be fairly harmless. Even more interesting to her though, was whether he had a girlfriend—perhaps even a wife—but surely, that person would have been at the singalong if he had.

"I thought you would have to be older to be a minister. Perhaps you're older than you look though?"

"I'm twenty-three—straight from high school to seminary. I finished studying the year before last. How old are you?"

She hesitated for a moment, really wanting to say she was a bit older, but not wanting to lie to him.

"Eighteen."

"So how long have you been living out of home? If you

don't mind me asking?" He added, with a slow, measured tone.

No wonder. Annette remembered her angry response to this line of questioning when they were on the bus. Things had changed a lot in that short time. Now, she felt a hunger to be vulnerable and open to him.

"About a year and a half."

"Wow, that must have been hard for you."

The openness was short-lived. She really didn't want to talk about this. She just wanted to shut it down.

"Do you see your parents often?"

Silently, she willed him to leave it alone.

"No, not often," she lied, with a sharper tone than intended.

Annette didn't see her parents at all. Did either of them ever think about her? Wonder what she was doing? No, neither of them cared about her, both had proved that.

"Hmm..." was all Mark said, before changing the subject. "We have the Bible studies at different youth group member's homes. Tonight, it's at Julie's house. Her parents will stay upstairs so that they don't disturb us. If you have any questions, feel free to ask as we go along."

An *upstairs*, equalled wealthy. She had never been into a house with an upstairs before.

The landscape was changing, tree lined streets, more expansive houses. The properties all seemed well kept. They were driving into the affluent suburb of Kew.

"Hope you're not nervous, they're all great kids."

"No, I'm fine, thanks," she said, lying again.

The car pulled up outside a two-story house. Mark rifled through the papers on the back seat. Then, shaking his head, grabbed up the whole sheaf and two Bibles.

"Here's a Bible for you to use tonight," he said, and thrust a heavy, leather-bound Bible into Annette's hand.

"Thanks," she said. She ran a finger over the embossed gold cross on the cover.

By the front porch light, she could see the perfectly manicured gardens. The path was lined with a low border of square hedge. She would have liked to have spent more time looking at the garden, to settle her nerves, but the doorbell was answered promptly.

Julie greeted them with a bright smile. Annette recognised her from the singalong. Perfect hair, perfect clothes —again. She took them into the dining room where two teenagers were already seated at the large table. Julie introduced Annette to them. The pimply-faced boy was there, his name was David. The conservative young man, called Tom, was also there and was again wearing a shirt and tie. Two cheery girls were in the kitchen organising soft drinks for everyone. The girl in the tie-dyed skirt seemed not to have made it.

Mark sat at one end of the table with David and Tom to one side. Annette took the empty seat next to Mark on the other side. Although she felt nervous and out of place, she also felt privileged to be part of this elite group. Her intention was to take this education into righteousness seriously.

When they were all settled, Mark encouraged them to ask questions, to air any doubts they might have. She did have questions. Some of the things Mark had said at the singalong about God were confusing and didn't seem to make sense.

Mark told them that the Lord loves the wicked as much as he loves those who are born again, but that those who don't repent are lost unless they turn to God.

Would that be the fate of Tracy and Alex? She felt sad for them.

"If he loves all of us, why are some going to heaven and

some going to hell?" The question came from the boy in the shirt and tie.

"Ahh, good question." Mark said with an approving smile. "Do you think somebody who loves sin and is unrepentant could be happy living forever with God?"

The three Christian girls were slowly shaking their heads.

"That's right." Mark acknowledged the girls with a nod. "Of course, they wouldn't be happy. They make their choice. God won't force people to do anything they don't want to do."

Tom nodded his acceptance of the explanation.

Mark's answer seemed logical, but Annette didn't feel convinced. A couple of weeks ago, she hadn't given God a second thought. What if she hadn't met Mark? Would she then have gone to hell? It all seemed a bit random.

"Now let's turn to..." Mark looked down to find a passage in the Bible.

He was about to move on, and the moment would be lost. Spurred on, but with her heart hammering in her chest, Annette asked, "How can a God of love punish people by sending them to hell if they don't accept him?"

Warmth flooded into her cheeks. Everyone looked at her. Mark didn't smile this time and she immediately wished she hadn't spoken. Was he a little irritated with her? No surely not, he had invited them to ask questions.

"The answer is much the same as my response to Tom's question. God doesn't send anyone to hell. If they choose to reject him, then, they are choosing hell. I can see that we need to explore this a little more."

Mark then asked them all to turn to verses that proved this. Annette and the other two new converts fumbled around trying to find the verses. The others helped them. They took it in turns to read. The biblical evidence seemed plausible.

During the study, Julie and her two friends had no questions but chimed in with verses that backed up what Mark was saying. They appeared to be completely confident in their beliefs.

"If it's wrong to drink alcohol, why did Jesus turn the water into wine at that wedding?"

This question came from the other new convert, David. Annette was also puzzled about why these Christians weren't allowed to drink. Catholics drank wine; her Catholic grandparents certainly enjoyed a tipple or two. While she waited for Mark's wisdom on this one, she secretly hoped there was no proof that drinking alcohol was wrong.

"Let's turn to Joel 2:19."

They all found the relevant passage in the Bible and Julie read it aloud.

"Jesus didn't turn the water into wine, he turned it into unfermented grape juice," Mark said. "In the first chapter of Joel, the Hebrew word, *yayin*, means fermented wine. God tells the Israelites, through the prophet Joel not to get drunk or to do all the other bad things they are doing. And that they won't be able to get drunk anyway because the locusts have eaten their vineyards. Here in chapter two though, the translation is *tirosh*, which means unfermented wine —grape juice. God is replacing the bad with the good."

David sounded sceptical, "Really? Grape juice? Why would wedding guests get so excited about grape juice?"

Mark went on to expand on this idea of unfermented wine, by discussing the original Greek meaning as well, and the traditions of the day.

Annette wasn't listening any more though, she was reading ahead in the chapter.

And I will restore to you the years that the locust hath eaten, the cankerworm, and the caterpillar, and the palmer-

worm, my great army which I sent among you.

I will restore to you... The words appealed to her, to a deep and hidden away part of her.

"What does this mean, in verse 25?" she blurted out, pointing to the verse.

Mark gave her an odd look.

"Well, it's what I've been saying: In Chapter 2, God says he will restore the harvests that have been lost when the Israelites turned away from God."

"I know a locust is a grasshopper, and I know what a caterpillar is, but what are the other two things?"

"We don't really know for sure, but we believe the palmerworm is the locust larvae."

"And the cankerworm?"

"Scholars believe that the cankerworm is the stage in the locust's life just before its wings open. It still does enormous damage, destroying everything around it, before its wings develop and it flies away. The Bible says in Nahum 3:16 ...*the cankerworm spoileth, then fleeth away.*" Mark inclined his head towards her. "Anything more, or can we move on?"

***

Annette arrived home feeling as though she was floating on air. Light and carefree, a sense of being part of a community, having a sense of purpose. These were all new feelings for her.

Tracy was sitting on the couch with Sam, the man she had met a few weeks ago at the bar. There was a half empty bottle of bourbon and an empty bottle of coke in front of them. Annette had come home to similar scenes before and not thought twice about it. Tonight, was different though. Her life was different.

"Hi, Annette you remember Sam," Tracy's words were a bit slurred.

Annette nodded.

"Do you want a drink?" Tracy asked.

There was a horror movie on the TV. Blood gushed out of a shoulder socket from which the arm had been severed. The background music was harsh, grating. Annette looked away.

"No thanks," she said.

Tracy turned the TV volume down.

"It was flat out at work. A good night not to be there." She paused, then asked, "So where did you go anyway?"

Annette was now determined not to shy away from sharing her new insights.

"I've been to a Bible study group with Mark, and some other young people."

Sam and Tracy looked at each other. Sam covered his mouth to stifle a laugh, then turned his attention back to the TV.

"Really?" Tracy said. "I'm confused, I thought you wanted to see him because you liked him. I didn't think you'd take that other stuff seriously." She paused and raised her eyebrows. "You don't, do you?"

"Yes, I think I do. It makes a lot of sense to me, and... I feel good about making changes in my life."

It suddenly registered with Annette that the bedding on the other couch where Alex usually slept was gone. As were his pile of clothes that had been folded in a heap in the corner.

"Where's Alex?" she asked.

"He told me he was going to leave this afternoon. I guess it finally sank in that he wouldn't get you back, especially now that you've gone off in this new direction."

There was more than a hint of accusation in her tone

and something else too, sadness perhaps? Maybe Tracy had realised something that was only just occurring to Annette —that their friendship might not survive this change.

Annette wanted to believe she didn't feel anything for Alex or Tracy now except pity. Pity because they were unsaved souls. The idea of feeling pity for others because they didn't have what she had, made her feel elevated, better than, for the first time in her life. Was she fooling herself though? Was it was more than just pity?

"So, are you sure you don't want a drink? There's more coke in the fridge."

Annette did want a drink; she very much wanted a drink. However, tonight, Mark had confirmed that it was wrong.

"Maybe just one."

Tracy smiled, a smug little smile. It crossed Annette's mind then, that maybe she should be setting a better example. The thought was fleeting and didn't stick. She went to the kitchen got a glass—a big glass—and the bottle of coke, came back with them and poured herself a drink. Heavy on the bourbon—well, she was only having one.

Sam yawned and patted Tracy's leg.

"I'm getting a bit tired," he declared, and gave Tracy a meaningful look. "How about you?"

"You go ahead, I'll just have a drink with Annette, and then I'll be there."

With a loud sigh, he shuffled off to Tracy's room. Clearly, not the response he was hoping for.

Annette downed most of her drink in the first few minutes and a warm, gentle, glow soon settled over her. The scene in the lounge room which had seemed so alien to her new way of life, just a short while ago, now seemed more familiar—comforting even.

Tracy walked over and flipped the TV off. Then she sat

back down on the couch, looked directly at Annette and asked, "What's going on?"

All Annette's bravado was disappearing fast. She poured herself another drink. The bourbon—its harsh bite tempered by the coke—slipped down her throat easily. Who was she kidding? This was her actual, real life. Living in someone else's flat. Working as a waitress. Not making it through secondary school because she couldn't stand her stepfather. Drinking bourbon on the couch where her ex-boyfriend had so recently been ensconced. She couldn't even make it work with him. What did they fight about anyway? They had so much fun at the start. Why had it deteriorated so quickly? Alex had looked as though he hated her when he'd stormed out earlier. And Mark, well, that was a joke, she was just another convert to him, another victory for Jesus. He would never be interested in her, not in that way. And even if by some miracle he was, he wouldn't be if he knew the real Annette. The real Annette is bad, bad to the core. She has sex with strangers.

Flashbacks came to her in quick succession: Getting pounded in the back of a panel van parked at St Kilda beach at 2am. Scrambling to find her undies under a stranger's single bed. Pushed up against a wall in a toilet cubicle. And the latest one, in South Yarra. Disgusting! She was disgusting! Even once while she was still with Alex, she'd had it off with a diner she'd met at the restaurant. Went home with the guy, got pissed with him, fucked him and lied about it later to Alex. The guy must have been about forty. What was she thinking? Well, usually she wasn't thinking, she was too drunk for that. And, now, here she was drunk again.

Annette realised Tracy was still looking at her, waiting for an answer. Should she confide in Tracy about how fucked up she was? How she didn't deserve to be with someone like Mark anyway? Mark had said God would forgive everything though. That she was made new. She couldn't lose faith. Couldn't let herself drown in the self-loathing. That old life was over, she mustn't dwell on it.

Annette poured herself another drink and sculled it, before responding.

"I don't know. I'm a bit confused. I do like Mark, but I don't think he has any interest in me."

"I'm sure he does like you. Why wouldn't he?"

Annette was taken by surprise to hear Tracy's reassurance. Tracy didn't even know Mark. Was she just being kind? Nevertheless, Annette felt a tiny spark of hope return.

Tracy finished her drink and poured herself another —there wasn't much left.

After emptying the bottle, she sat back.

"But what I don't understand is, why you would be interested in him? He's a pastor. I know he's good looking and all that, but it just seems a little... weird. What have the two of you got in common?"

Annette immediately went on the defensive. Even though, she had wondered what they had in common herself. The bourbon was really kicking in now.

"You think I'm not good enough for him," Annette said.

"That's not what I said. I'm just not sure why you'd be attracted to somebody like that." Tracy paused, as though deciding whether to say more or not. "I mean, it's not that I don't believe there's a God. I do think there's something greater out there, but I don't see the need to go to church or to Bible bash other people."

Bible bash, the words grated. Hadn't Annette used them herself in the past though? Is that how people would view her now, as a Bible basher? Is that what was in store for her if she continued along this road?

"It's only because they care, because they don't want others to be lost." Annette was faltering. Was she really in a position to preach? The explanation sounded patronising. Mark would do a better job of explaining it to Tracy. He could convince her.

"You're sounding just like them now." Tracy's voice rose sharply. "Is that how you see me now? Now that you think you're so high and mighty, as though I'm lost? I'm not lost, I'm doing just *fine and dandy* thank you very much."

Even through the alcohol-induced fogginess Annette sensed that she should stop. Tracy was seeing her attempt at explaining Christianity as judgement. A message that she wasn't good enough. This was harder than Annette had expected. Well, it might have helped if she had stayed sober. What to say though? Annette couldn't agree that Tracy didn't need to change; she didn't believe that anymore. If Tracy didn't repent and follow God, she would burn in hell.

Closing her eyes, she silently prayed for some words of wisdom.

"Are you alright?" Tracy asked. "Oh my God, you're not praying, are you? Shit, I can't deal with this."

Annette opened her eyes. Tracy was halfway to the bedroom. When she arrived at the door she turned around and glared at Annette. Then went into her room and slammed the door shut.

"Goodnight," Annette called out feebly after her.

Suddenly, feeling very sorry for herself she burst into drunken tears.

After a while, Annette stopped snivelling and blew her nose. Then she picked up the phone and dialled Mark's number.

"Hello..." He sounded sleepy.

"Sorry, did I wake you up?"

"Ah... yes. Who is it?"

She didn't want him to suspect she'd been drinking —or crying for that matter. So, she spoke slowly, enunciating each word carefully.

"It's Annette."

"Are you okay?"

"I just wanted to tell you that I don't think I'm cut out to be a Christian. I really think—"

He interrupted, "Annette are you drunk?"

"Umm, not really... Well, maybe a little."

"Annette, I think the best thing we can do is get you out of that environment. It's clearly not good for you. I'm sure you wouldn't be having those thoughts if you hadn't been drinking. Let me make a few calls tomorrow and I'll get back to you as soon as I can." His voice was now brusque and business like.

"Ahh, okay."

"Great! Talk to you soon. Go to bed now and get a good night's sleep."

Before she could respond, he'd hung up.

What was he talking about? Did he want her to stay with him? That didn't seem plausible given he was a pastor. Nevertheless, she began to feel excited. Maybe things would work out well for her after all.

As she fell asleep, she imagined herself in his arms. His hands running gently through her hair, caressing her, taking care of her, comforting her. Loving her.

Chapter 5

Annette had just popped some bread in the toaster when the sound of the phone ringing made her jump and her heart start to beat faster. Was it Mark?

Even though her head had been aching, and her mouth was dry, Annette had still woken up with a pleasant feeling. That sensation of not being fully awake, but knowing something good had happened, or, was about to happen.

After the bathroom, she'd gone to the kitchen for Panadol and a glass of water and noticed through the window that Sam's car was gone, but that Tracy's was still there. With a sinking feeling, Annette remembered Tracy storming off in anger last night. Mark had told her others may scoff and criticise her decision and he'd been right so far. Why was she so worried about what Tracy thought anyway? This new direction was the right one. Tracy's opinion was not even relevant.

Then, she recalled the reason she felt so happy when she woke up. The conversation with Mark. He was going to take her away from all this. He would call soon.

Annette stood in the shower for a long time, letting the

warm water run over her. She thought about Mark's body. Visualising what he might look like under his casual wind-cheaters and jeans. She lingered as she soaped one of her breasts and closed her eyes, imagining it was him touching her. Her excitement rose.

"I need to get in there sometime today!" Tracy's voice cut through the fantasy.

Tracy was still angry; she had never complained before about Annette's long showers. Annette had to work with her tonight. That wasn't going to be much fun.

Hmm... work, her first and only job as a waitress. And, there were no prospects of anything better. How different might her life have been if she had stayed at home with loving parents and continued her education? She had always done well in school—didn't get into trouble, usually did her homework. Even though she didn't think she was particularly smart, her marks were always high. It was possible that she would be in her first year of university now, instead of being stuck in this dead-end job. The fact she hadn't finished high school—well, that was just another reason to resent her mother.

A blurred image from the past flashed into her mind, not quite formed. Just as quickly the memory faded, before she could fully grasp it. Nevertheless, it left her feeling unsettled and uneasy.

Annette ran from the kitchen to pick up the receiver. Thankfully, the shower was still running so Tracy wouldn't be able to overhear her.

"Hello."

"Hi, is that Annette?"

It was him.

"Yes, it's me. Sorry I called you last night, I was just a bit confused."

"No, I'm glad you did," he said. "Annette, have you

ever thought about living in the country?"

What was he talking about? The country?

"Ahh... no, not really."

"I talked to my sister Esther, this morning. She's happy for you to come and stay with her—in Pleasant Valley. It's a small town about 100 kilometres from Melbourne. There is a church there and Esther will help you find a job." His words came out rapid fire, as though this was already settled.

Annette's head was spinning. Didn't Mark live in Melbourne? Why would she want to live with his sister somewhere in the bush?

"Oh, when you said last night that I should get away I was thinking you meant..."

She stopped, realising she was being ridiculous. Of course, she was never going to be staying with him, he was a pastor and no doubt he saw her as just another wayward adolescent. Now that he'd helped her get saved, he was cutting her loose—dumping her. Not with just anyone though, but with his sister. Surely that meant he wanted to keep a connection with her.

"I know you probably thought I meant somewhere in Melbourne, but really I'm not sure that's the best thing for you. I feel convinced you would be better off down there, with good people around you. You'd have a better chance at life."

A better chance at life. That was what she wanted.

"Anyway," he continued. "She's coming down to Melbourne on the weekend. You could come and have lunch with us after church on Sunday and meet her," he said. "You are coming to church on Sunday, aren't you? I'll pick you up at 9.30am."

"9.30am," she repeated obediently. "Yeah, I guess so."

This seemed to all be happening very fast. When Mark

spoke again it was as if he could read her thoughts.

"It might seem as though things are changing quite quickly, but Annette, you must have faith in God's plan. He only wants the best for you."

Back in her bedroom, she sat down on the bed and tried to make sense of the conversation she'd just had. Couldn't she just trust that Mark knew what was best for her? But she didn't know his sister. It wasn't as if it was easy for her to make friends. What if his sister hated her? And the country, what did she know about living in the country?

When she was a kid, the country meant long, hot trips in the old, Ford Falcon. Her mother and father chain smoking in the car, making it hard to breathe, even with the front windows down. There was the inevitable argument between them about where to go, or why it took so long to get going, or whatever—it didn't take much. Their fights made Annette nervous and kept her on edge until her mother backed down, as she always did.

The trip seemed to take forever, even after they left the city, her father continued down long, winding dirt roads. Annette knew better than to ask how much further. And it was so hot in the car. Sweat and road dust were plastered all over her face by the time they finally arrived at their isolated destination—her father didn't like to be anywhere crowded.

They'd find a spot under the shade of huge gum trees. The blanket—made lumpy by tufts of native grass—was spread out on the reddish coloured dirt. Ted would crack a longneck beer from the esky. Rose would pour sticky soft drink—slightly warm because the ice had melted—for herself and Annette. Her father would cook sausages over a small gas hotplate. The flies—already irritating— would descend in swarms when the food appeared. The three of them would eat the sausages wrapped in white bread with tomato sauce. Annette did enjoy those sausages and the sticky soft drink after the long trip. Even with the constant waving away of the flies between each bite.

Her parents sometimes called a rare truce on these outings. They would talk easily with each other and with Annette. They would all settle down under the trees with full bellies, and, for a short time, Annette felt safe and happy, and that all was right with the world. She would explore a little, and then, her mother might help her make a dirt garden decorated with tiny wildflowers.

As the day progressed and her father drank more and more longnecks—even though he was the driver—those happy feelings usually evaporated. There would be the sting of a slap or two on her leg, or her backside, for some wrongdoing. Or, yet another argument with Rose.

On some trips though, her dad wouldn't drink as much, and the day would continue in a relaxed way. She remembered one time she noticed a leech clinging to her calf. After she had let out a bloodcurdling scream at the discovery, her father comforted and reassured her as he carefully burnt it off with a lighter.

"See it can't hurt you now," he said. Then he wiped the tears from her reddened eyes. His voice was gentle and kind. No, the memories weren't all bad...

Annette shifted on the bed, as she did, she noticed the corner of an envelope emerge from a crease in the crumpled doona. On the front it said, To Annette. She opened it and scanned to the bottom. The handwriting was quite neat and legible. It was from Alex.

Dear Annette,

I'm not very good at writing letters. Actually, to tell you the truth, this is the first real one I've written since we had to practise in school. So here goes.

I'm really sorry I got so angry the other day. I just don't know how to make you understand about religious people. I'm worried you will get hurt like I did. It can be confusing, but you have to know that not every Christian is a good person, not every Christian is genuine. Some are, but some aren't. I don't know whether that guy Mark is or not, but I want you to be careful.

I've decided to tell you about my experience, not because I want your sympathy, but because I want you to understand. My mother was a Christian, a fundamentalist Christian. Do you know what that means? Someone who takes their religion to extremes, by taking every part of the Bible as fact. How can you do that? The Bible contradicts itself.

Anyway, back to my story. I went to Sunday school from the age of four. The first thing we had to learn was the Lord's prayer. You know the one, it goes Our Father etc. When I tried to say it, I would get mixed up, which is not surprising, I was four years old. The Sunday school teacher would tell my mother that I needed to practise at home. And, of course, my mother did make me practise. If anyone in authority in the church told her something, she acted as though God himself had spoken.

If I couldn't recite what I was supposed to have learned on Sunday afternoon, I would get a belting with a stick and into the hall cupboard I would go with the Bible and a torch, until I could recite it perfectly. After a few hours, she would make me pass the Bible out to her and recite the passage by heart. If it wasn't correct, I would have to come out for another belting and then would be sent back in. You've heard of 'spare the rod and spoil the child'. My mother took that text very seriously. If it was a long passage I had to learn, I might be in there overnight. No dinner, a bucket for the toilet. Which of course, I had to deal with when I came out. As you could imagine, it got more difficult to get it right the longer I was in there. The light was dim, and my eyes would start stinging. I got tired and hungry, so it was hard to concentrate. She would say, 'You'll thank me for this one day'. Well, she was wrong about that, like she was wrong about most things.

As I said though, not all Christians are bad. There was this older lady, she was a Christian too, but not from our church. She looked after me a few days a week, between when school finished and when mum got home from work.

I knew she was a Christian because she would sing songs about God while she was doing the housework. I wasn't used to cheerful believers. She and her husband were good to me. I didn't see him that much, he was mostly at work, but she was a sweetheart. She always had fresh baked Anzac biscuits or some other treat for ready for me when I came into the kitchen after school. At first, if I spilt a glass of milk or something, I would expect a walloping from her, like at home. But she would just say, 'It can't be helped', and she'd clean it up. She was like a miracle to be around, compared to my mother.

My mother always put me in long pants. I guess it was to cover the bruises. One day I had slipped in the mud playing footy at school. I knew I'd be in big trouble when mum saw me. As usual, this lady wasn't angry, she did suggest I take my pants off and she'd wash them and put them through the dryer. She gave me a blanket to wrap around my legs. When I was walking to the bathroom to put my pants back on, the blanket slipped off. It was then she noticed the bruises on my legs. She asked me about them. I was terrified that she'd confront my mother. Mum had made it very clear that I shouldn't tell about what happened at home. I lied that day and said the footy had hit me in the back of the legs. Stupid excuse, I'm sure she didn't believe it. I think maybe she had *been suspicious of my mother all along.*

A few days later, she asked me why I was so good at my Bible verses, saying it was unusual for someone so young. She had often heard me muttering them out loud, practising for Sunday. I often did this without realising—so embarrassing! Got me into some shit at school I can tell you. When she asked me about it, I have to admit, I burst into tears and, because she was so sweet, I told her about the cupboard. I was nine years old at the time.

Turns out it was a good decision. She called Social Welfare and they contacted my father and I went to live with him and his new wife.

You know, I never saw that lady again but to this day I'm still grateful to her for getting me out of that hellhole. I haven't seen my mother either since the day after she got dobbed in. The day I left the house with the social worker. I remember she was outraged that the social worker was questioning her methods. I thought she was going to come after us with the stick. But in the end, she just stood there rattling off verses, at the top of her voice like a crazy woman.

I know I haven't told you about my father before either, have I? You can see that my story is not that easy to tell. And I didn't want anyone feeling sorry for me, especially not you. I don't blame my father for not staying with her after she became religious. They broke up when I was a baby. Do you know she lied about him to me and to the church? She told everyone he was dead. I think that hurts more than the years of abuse. Thinking he was dead.

Anyhow, life with my dad and Cindy was much better. They have a couple of younger kids and we all got on pretty well. Some hiccups, but the problems were normal problems, you know, not like before. I was a bit of a handful for them though, ran a bit wild. They sent me to counselling—that was annoying—but they did it because they were worried about me. And the counselling did help me understand that it wasn't because I was bad that my mother treated me that way. It's funny how you believe everything's your fault when you're a kid. Having a loving family made the most difference. I settled down after a while. My dad got me the apprenticeship, he's a builder. We're still close and keep in touch.

I guess I still haven't got my act together in the way I'd like, but you know that of course. I do feel like I'm getting there though. I don't even think about my mum much anymore. Until all this came up with you of course. Now, after reading this, maybe you can understand now why I got so angry.

Well, this letter has turned out to be a lot longer than I thought it would. Not bad for a first try.

I'm sorry I didn't tell you all this before. It feels good to get it out. I also wanted to say goodbye. Bit hard to say it face to face. Hope things work out well for you. Please, be careful.

I won't forget you.
Love Alex x

Annette read the letter over several times. Alex said that he hadn't written a letter before and Annette hadn't ever received one. Unless she counted the birthday card sent from her mum last year.

Dear Annette,
Happy Birthday, hope you are well and happy,
Love from Mum and Bob.

Why had her mum even bothered with writing *Love*? Annette hadn't seen the evidence from her mum and as for Bob— well, Annette felt she was just an annoying interruption to him. So, no, she didn't count the card from her mum. This letter was different. Alex had taken the trouble to sit down and write to her. To tell her his deepest secrets. Why? Because he cared about her. That's what he'd said.

Somehow, she had known instinctively that his childhood hadn't been easy. She didn't know how she knew; she just did. Turns out his childhood had been much worse than her own. This was why he was so angry with her. She wished she had known about his history when they were together, then perhaps she could have understood him better. Maybe she would have been less focused on herself.

The guilt she had felt about their breakup had lessened since her conversion. The breakup made sense, out with the old and in with the new. She felt the guilt hit hard again now though. Was it only guilt she felt, or did she miss the intimacy they had shared at first? Again, she wondered, why she had lost interest in him. He really hadn't done anything wrong. Yes, sometimes he got a bit moody. He drank and sometimes he even smoked dope, but it was no wonder, given what had happened to him. And he did recognise he needed to improve his life. He had admitted that to her to when they were together, and he'd said it again in the letter.

She remembered the night they met and how she'd been attracted to his rugged good looks. More than that though, she remembered how he seemed genuinely interested in her. In contrast to other men, whose focus seemed more single minded.

Then, the night she broke up with him. On Valentine's Day they were out for dinner. It had been Annette's idea to go out. She could have waited for him to ask but was scared he wouldn't. They didn't go out to eat very often and it felt like kind of a big deal to Annette. To be the one being waited on, instead of the waitress. She was excited and had high expectations for the evening. Maybe this would bring back the spark they had in the beginning. Together, they had chosen an Italian restaurant in Carlton.

They met outside the restaurant. Alex had bought flowers. A dozen red roses, a little brown around the edges and wilting slightly. Already, she was annoyed. Couldn't he see they weren't right when he bought them? Or, maybe they had been sitting in the sun too long in his van. It had been a really hot day; it was still hot. She smiled anyway when he handed her the roses—still beautiful—but without much life left in them.

"I love you," he said and kissed her.

While they were waiting to be seated, Annette looked around the restaurant. There were lots of couples sitting at small tables. The tables were clad in red and white checked tablecloths. There were candles burning in glass holders, casting a warm glow. Bottles of white wine wrapped in white serviettes rested in tall ice buckets next to some of the tables. Other couples were drinking red wine. To Annette, all but the two of them, appeared to be well-dressed and confident couples. She and Alex were out of place—too young—their clothes not put together as well. Trying to play the part of grown-ups but not really succeeding.

They ordered red wine. Annette didn't like the taste much but drank it anyway. She looked at the menu. There weren't many items she recognised. Luckily there were descriptions underneath. She decided on the veal and asked Alex what he was having.

"Spaghetti Bolognese," he said and closed the menu.

"Why don't you have something different?" Annette suggested. "We're out," she added, by way of explanation.

"I want Spaghetti Bolognese," he said.

"But that's what we have all the time at home," Annette persisted. "I'm having Veal Saltimbocca."

"Good for you," he said drily.

Annette was aware he was getting annoyed, but she couldn't stop herself. Could they not pretend for just one night that they were as good as everyone else? That they were no different to these other people; that they were a normal, happy couple.

"Have you ever tried any other type of pasta?" she asked.

"No, have you?" he snapped then.

"A couple of them. I don't want to eat the same thing all the time."

The waitress came and took their orders. Alex stared at Annette as he ordered the spaghetti.

"I'll have the Veal Saltimbocca thanks," she said, and stared back at Alex.

Why was she giving him such a hard time? She considered apologising, but decided to change the subject instead.

"So how was your day at work?" she asked.

"Oh, it was alright, we worked on a huge house in Toorak. The ceilings were fifteen feet high."

Alex lifted his arm to indicate the height of the ceilings and exposed a damp, oval patch of sweat under his arm. Annette shook her head slowly.

"What, what's the problem now?"

"Did you put deodorant on? We're out for dinner on Valentine's Day and you didn't put deodorant on. I can't believe it!"

Alex looked stunned. "Yes, I did this morning, I didn't have time to go home for another shower. I just got changed at work. I don't know if you've noticed, but it's bloody hot outside."

She knew she was being ridiculous—again though, she couldn't stop herself.

"I really don't matter to you, do I?" she said quietly, on

the verge of tears.

"Oh, for God's sake, it's really not that big a deal," Alex pleaded.

The couple at the next table glanced across at her and Alex. They looked away again when she caught them. How pathetic are we? She sighed heavily.

Their meals arrived and Annette realised after the first mouthful of veal that she really would have preferred the Bolognese.

"How's your meal?" he asked.

She didn't respond. The meal continued then in stony silence, until they left the restaurant and Alex drove them home. The weight of her crushed hopes for the evening felt unbearably heavy.

They were still in Alex's combi van, sitting in the driveway, when she said, "That's it we're finished."

Alex didn't speak but got out and slammed the van door. She went into their bedroom, got his pillow and a blanket and threw them out into the lounge room.

"I don't get what just happened," he yelled at her closed bedroom door.

Later when he was asleep, she crept past the couch where he slept and went out the back door to the van. She collected up the roses he had given her. In the kitchen she filled a jar with water and took the roses and the jar back to her room. Then, she carefully arranged them in the jar, one by one, feeling again, that strange mixture of relief and loneliness that came with separation.

In the days that had followed, it had come as somewhat of a surprise to Annette that she felt very little about the breakup. It was like a door in her heart that she had left slightly ajar, was now slammed shut again. This feeling was more familiar, somehow more comfortable. They had been together for three months.

Annette carefully folded the letter and put it under the base of her bedside lamp. She stood up from the bed, and, just like shutters closing in front of a window, she shut off any regrets about Alex. Even shook herself a little to help shake off all the thoughts and feelings that didn't match her plans. Did Alex think she was an idiot? She was an adult and could make good decisions.

Alex was just a boy when all that happened, he had no choice. Besides, she reasoned, his story had a happier ending than hers. He'd ended up with a loving family. Didn't he want her to be happy? Just because his mother was a raving lunatic didn't mean that Mark was too. Alex had said it himself; *some Christians are good people.* It seemed like Alex had just been very unlucky. Unlike her—her luck had changed for the better.

Chapter 6

When they arrived at church on Sunday morning, Mark left Annette at the door to attend to his duties as youth pastor. That was unexpected—she hadn't thought it through—but of course, he couldn't stay with her.

This church was very different to the plainer hall next door where the singalong had been. It had huge ceilings, and row upon row of comfortable looking chairs were set out on the thick carpet. The chairs faced the darkened stage upon which musical instruments were set up. At the back of the wide stage was a massive white cross back-lit in purple.

Annette found a seat near the back where the chairs were sparsely occupied and watched as the congregation filed in. She recognised some people from the singalong and the study. There were a lot of young families. A few older people, but not many. Annette wasn't the only one on her own, nevertheless, she still felt very uncomfortable. As though, someone might question her presence at any moment. No use dwelling on whether she should be there or not, this was her direction in life now. There could be no turning back.

Coloured lights came up on the stage after people had settled in. It looked more like a concert than a church service. The musicians walked out and took up their positions and their instruments. Mark wasn't one of them—where was he sitting? She couldn't see him.

A hushed air of expectancy came over the room. There was silence for a few moments, then, an attractive, young woman began to sing unaccompanied. She had a crystal-clear voice that seemed to have a hypnotic effect on the congregation. After the first few verses, the musicians joined in and people began to rise to their feet as the young people had done at the singalong. Those that she could see around her closed their eyes. Soon, very few were still seated. Annette felt conspicuous, so she stood up too. People began to sway and sing. This went on for quite a long time and there were lots of "Praise the Lords" and "Hallelujahs" as each song ended.

A middle-aged man walked onto the stage as the last song finished. A spotlight trained on him. He was dressed in a suit but without a tie. The man raised one hand, closed his eyes and asked the congregation to pray with him. No-one knelt, they just stood there, heads bowed, eyes closed. Annette did the same. The preacher finished praying and then cracked a joke. Then he began to speak and the more he spoke, the more animated he became. He paced across the stage as he talked. His voice increasing in volume in direct proportion to the intensity of his message.

Annette had been to a Catholic church with her grandparents a few times when she was young. The priest had been dressed in long, flowing robes and stood behind a pulpit to preach—not moving at all. Not until it was time to walk across to where the congregation were lining up to drink the wine and eat the bread. There was no band at that church—no coloured lights—just an organ playing and altar boys singing. Back then, Annette pretty much tuned out completely, except that she liked to listen to the clear, sweet tones from the altar boys. The rest was very boring. She was supposed to stand, sit and kneel when everyone else did. Usually, she lagged behind because she wasn't paying enough attention. Also—when it was time to kneel—the rail on the wooden pews was so hard, it hurt her bare knees. Her grandparents, and everyone else, seemed to know when and how to respond to the priest.

The priest would say; *The word of the Lord*, and all would respond; *Thanks be to God*. Then, he would say; *The Lord be with you*, they all said; *And, also with you.*

How did they all know what to say and when to say it? It all seemed a bit robotic to her at the time.

This service was much less orderly. People were yelling out, "Praise the Lord", and, "Amen". It seemed to happen randomly—whenever they felt like it. At first, Annette was more interested in what was going on around her than the man on stage. There came a point though, when he captured her attention. He spoke about how Jesus called sinners to follow him. He read from the Bible about a lost sheep, a lost coin and a lost son. The preacher talked about how Jesus hung around with sinners: prostitutes and tax collectors —those spurned by their community. It was confirmation that there was a place for her with God, it really didn't matter what she'd done in the past.

"Salvation is conditional though," he said. "When you turn away from being a sinner and turn towards the Lord God, you must live a sanctified life. You must turn your heart from the old ways."

Watch what you put into your body, because it's the temple of God. Eat only healthy food. Do not consume alcohol.

Think about what you allow your mind to dwell upon, banish impure thoughts.

If you must watch television, limit what you watch. Don't allow your eyes to see licentious acts and mindless violence.

Be humble, think more about others than yourselves.

Pay tithe to the church regularly. Give back to God.

Give to others when they ask you.

It seemed like a long list, but if everyone else here was able to live a pure, unselfish life, then why couldn't she? Didn't the preacher just say that, with God's help, sinners could turn their life around?

In her mind's eye, she saw again, the words scripted in Alex's careful handwriting.

Taking it to extremes... taking every part of the Bible as fact.

This wasn't extreme, it all sounded feasible and reasonable—even if still a little alien to her. What had Mark said about doubt? She didn't want to be a doubter, tossed about like the wind tosses the waves of the sea. The sermon had inspired in her, a strong, new determination to do the right thing.

After the service she stood in the queue and shook the preacher's hand. He smiled just as warmly at her as he had at the person before her.

"Glad to have you here," he said, giving her hand one firm shake. Then, as he let go, he moved his attention to the next person in the line.

Annette went out onto the front lawn and stood in the shade of a tree. It was Autumn, but the weather was still quite warm. The leaves were turning to a reddish brown, some had fallen and were swishing around in flurries on the grass. She positioned herself to keep an eye on the door, so that she could see Mark when he exited. It took a few moments until she became aware of furtive glances in her direction. Some of the younger men were watching her—and a couple of the older ones too. The wind was whipping up her thin summer dress. She plastered it down onto her thighs with the palms of her hands. Hurry up, Mark.

"Pretty dress." A voice came from behind her.

Annette felt her face flush. The woman who now stood beside her, had come from the direction of the carpark, not the church, so Annette hadn't noticed her until she spoke.

"Hmm, wish it would behave itself though," Annette mumbled, still struggling to control the flimsy material. "Did you hear the service?" Annette indicated towards the pastor still shaking hands on the steps.

"No, actually I'm here to meet someone."

The woman smiled a warm smile. Her face was free of makeup. Her hair—dark brown and wavy—ended in thick curls that fell loosely around her shoulders. She wore a long, flowing, brown skirt, brown calf length lace-up boots and a white, peasant top. She looked vaguely familiar to Annette, but Annette couldn't remember having met her before. Mark emerged from the church at that moment and walked across the lawn towards them.

"Annette, I see you've met my sister." He looked confused. "How did you find each other?"

"A lucky guess I suppose and besides... you told me she was pretty."

Esther smiled and offered her hand to Annette.

"Hello, nice to meet you."

Annette looked away; her face flushed again. Embarrassed, but also excited. Mark thought she was pretty.

She took Esther's hand and shook it, "Hi."

"I looked for you during the service. Were you hiding somewhere?" Mark asked Esther.

"No, sorry, didn't make it to the service, I was running

a bit late."

A look of annoyance flashed briefly across Mark's face and just as quickly he replaced it with a smile.

"Not sure that's the best example for our young friend here," he said, still smiling.

Esther didn't flinch. "What did you think of the service Annette? Did I miss much?"

"Well, I didn't follow everything, but I did like the part when the preacher said Jesus cares about people who are lost. He talked about a father who had one son who was good and the other who went out drinking and partying. Then, after the bad son had wasted all his money, he came home, and his father still welcomed him..." Annette paused. Unsure whether she should say how much she related to the parable. She decided against it, it was probably obvious.

"Ah, yes the prodigal son. It's a good story, but I have heard it quite a few times before, so maybe I didn't miss much. Glad you enjoyed it though." She smiled at Mark. "Shouldn't we go and eat? I'm starving."

Esther's attitude towards Mark's obvious displeasure was making Annette more than a little nervous.

***

The three of them were at a trendy cafe in Hawthorn, not far from the church. After they had ordered, Esther began the conversation.

"So... you two met on the outreach bus."

"Yes, we did. I believe God brought Annette to us that night."

"Hmm," was Esther's only response. It seemed like there was friction between Mark and Esther. Annette wondered whether they were always like this, or whether something had happened.

"You should come down one weekend and see what we do, maybe help out."

"Not sure we'd see eye to eye on what's best for the lost," Esther said.

Then she gave Mark a meaningful look. His face darkened with annoyance again. What was wrong with Esther? Couldn't she see that her brother was so self-sacrificing? He spent his Friday and Saturday nights helping young people get saved.

Mark ignored Esther and turned to Annette. "Do you like your burger?"

"Yes, it's great."

Annette was relieved at the change of subject. Her burger was good, and so were the chips, not oily, nice and crisp. She considered his meal, a chicken salad. Esther had a large bowl of lamb and vegetable soup. Both of their meals looked much healthier than her choice. Maybe she should have ordered a salad?

"So, Mark tells me that you would benefit from coming to live in the country," Esther said.

What was that in Esther's tone—sarcasm—disapproval? Did Esther think it was a bad idea? Was it a bad idea? What alternative was there now though? Annette didn't want to stay where she was. Still better to act as though she didn't really care either way. At least until she knew what was going on with Esther.

"Ahh... I haven't really thought about it much."

Esther sat silently for a while. When she spoke again, her face relaxed into a warm smile. "Of course, you are more than welcome to come."

"I'm not sure what I'd do there..."

"Don't worry, Mark told me you're a waitress. There's a cafe I used to work in when I was at high school. They are looking to hire at the moment. If I tell them I know an experienced waitress from Melbourne who's looking for work, they will put you on for sure. If that's what you want?"

Annette wasn't used to kindness like this, it was a little overwhelming.

"Oh, thank you!"

She paused, fumbling about trying to find her next few words. She felt drawn to Esther but wanted to let Esther know she was from a different world, a way less perfect world. To warn Esther, so that she wouldn't be disappointed with her when she found out.

"Mark mentioned that I could live with you, but you don't know me. I mean, I'm only just starting to learn about God and what to do and... everything."

The words came out a bit lame—pathetic even.

"Well, I've known about all of this..." Esther threw up her hands, "for years and I still don't get it right."

Her voice held a hint of sadness, regret. Esther's confession was like a warm, gentle spa easing away Annette's self-doubt and confusion. She felt a sudden rush of emotion. Excusing herself, Annette made her way to the toilets, wiping away a tear as she went. No tears for ages, then floods of tears coming without warning. What's happening to me? Is this what happens when you're converted, the ice inside starts to melt?

Luckily, the restroom was empty. She blinked into the mirror, trying to compose herself, then wiped off a small wet, smear of mascara and took a deep breath. Although, she didn't have much interest in moving to the country when Mark first mentioned it, now—such a short time later—it seemed like her only hope. And Esther seemed so nice, so understanding.

On her way back to the table she could hear that Mark's voice was raised. He had his back to Annette, so he didn't see her approach. Esther was looking down at her soup. Annette hesitated, turned sideways and pretended to inspect the cake cabinet.

"What's going on with you? Maybe this was a bad idea. First you miss church, then you act like being a Christian is a burden. If I didn't know better, I'd think you were trying to sabotage her salvation."

Esther was still staring into her soup. "Well, I'm not going to pretend, it isn't easy being a Christian. And, I told you from the start, I'm not sure we're doing the right thing by her. Taking her away from her life here."

"You know you're the only option at this stage. I've put a lot of time and effort into this and you've got to do your part." He shook his head as he spoke.

In the pause that followed Annette took her seat. They all continued to eat in silence, as though that task needed their complete and undivided attention. Annette could sense that her chance might be slipping away.

She sucked in another deep breath and spoke slowly, "I would like to give it a go."

Both siblings looked up, eyes fixed on Annette.

"I would like to come and live with you. You know —we could just try it. If it doesn't work for you, then... I'll leave."

Mark shrugged and lifted his hands looking first at Esther and then to Annette, "You know, neither of you need to worry. This is God's will, and he knows what's best for all of us better than we know ourselves."

"Are you're sure that's what you want? Won't you miss your life here?" Esther probed gently.

Annette didn't hesitate. "Yes, I'm sure it's what I want. And no, I won't miss my life here at all," she said, with conviction.

Both Esther and Mark smiled at her.

"Okay then," said Esther. "When would you like to come? I could pick you up next Saturday morning if that suits you."

"Sounds good," Annette said.

The tension in Mark's face relaxed and he let out a just audible sigh. He seemed very pleased with Annette's decision; her wellbeing was obviously very important to him. She felt herself unwind too. She could relax, knowing that God, and these people cared about her, and only wanted the best for her.

***

Once Mark had confirmed that Annette had a job waiting and that the plan was going ahead, Annette told Tracy the news. She was much more upset than Annette had expected. At first, she seemed flabbergasted, baffled. She bluntly told Annette that she was crazy.

Later in the week, though, Tracy's attitude seemed to shift to one of genuine concern.

"You don't even know these people. You've only known Mark a few weeks and you've met this woman, what, once? What if it doesn't work out, what then? You don't even have a car. You'll be stuck."

Annette could see that Tracy didn't understand how kind these people were. She tried to convince Tracy that she was making a good decision, but eventually she gave up. Mark had warned her that non-believers would find it hard to understand her choices. Tracy wasn't a Christian and she was, so, why bother? They were like chalk and cheese now. These were the kind of sacrifices she would have to make on her journey along the higher road she was following.

Annette worked up until she collected her pay on the Friday night. When they arrived home, she asked Tracy to let the boss know that she wouldn't be coming back to work. Tracy moved towards her and hugged her tight.

"I'll miss you. Come back if it doesn't pan out," she said, her voice cracking a little.

She sniffed back tears as she let Annette go. Annette was surprised by the display of affection. And even more so, that Tracy had offered to have her back. She couldn't think of how to respond because couldn't even say for sure that she would see Tracy again. Her life was moving in a different direction, there would be no turning back.

Yet, they had shared some good times together. Usually alcohol was involved, and all that went with it. The one-night stands, the failed relationships, the hangovers, the drunken parties, the bars, and the clubs. Not for her, not anymore.

"Thanks for having me here," she said.

Chapter 7

There wasn't much to pack, just a few clothes and makeup. Annette hesitated over her records. Flicking through them, she came across the first album she had ever bought. It was Janis Joplin's Greatest Hits. Released in 1973—three years after Janis died at the age of twenty-seven from a heroin overdose. Annette had bought it second-hand with her first pay. There were just a few light scratches on the vinyl. They were hardly noticeable against the rawness of Janis's voice belting out her songs of love and pain, over the electric guitars.

Janis, seemed to be another lost soul, like Annette had been. Also, like herself, Janis had a strong relationship with bourbon. Annette breathed a prayer of thanks that she had never used hard drugs. Maybe one day she too would have ended up like Janis, dead from an overdose, if she hadn't found Jesus.

She picked up another album that Alex had left behind. She found herself singing the words from Black Sabbath's, 'Paranoid', out loud, *Happiness I cannot feel and love to me is so unreal.*

Well, she thought, that may have been true in the past but not anymore.

It seemed that her taste in music was not really suitable for church life. *Welcome to my nightmare* by Alice Cooper jumped out at her, as being inappropriate at the least, positively evil at the worst. Still, she couldn't leave her collection behind. She wasn't quite ready. She carefully wrapped them in clothes and lay them in the bottom of her suitcase. In a trade-off with God, she left a half-melted candle stuck in a Jim Beam bottle and her heavy rock posters behind.

***

Next morning, she sat alone in the flat waiting for Esther to pick her up. Misgivings about the move were starting to nag at her. She did like Esther, but it was true, they had only just met. Although she had tried to defend her decision, Tracy was right. What if it didn't work out? Annette would be stuck. Well, it was no good second guessing her situation now, she would just have to trust God—and Mark and Esther.

She felt much better when they were travelling along in Esther's cute, yellow Datsun.

It was as though the weather had been especially designed to soothe her nerves. It was a perfect, sunny Autumn day. They soon left the outskirts of Melbourne. The hills and paddocks were beginning to green up after a long, dry summer. Contented looking cows and sheep ambled around or stood grazing in the sun. As they drove through small towns, autumn leaves put on a rust coloured show.

Annette spotted a wallaby at the edge of a state forest. It stood stock still and watched at her as they drove past. She felt herself softening towards country life by the minute. They drove past some apple orchards and Esther told her they had just been harvested.

"You haven't tasted a real apple until you've tasted one fresh off the tree," Esther said.

Esther chatted for a while about the other crops that were grown around Pleasant Valley, along with some of the other farming industry in the area. Soon the conversation shifted to Esther's life in the country. Annette discovered that Esther had started work as a primary school teacher this year after finishing her course the year before. She was teaching at a church school, twenty-six kilometres away, in a larger town called Wellspring.

"Unfortunately," Esther continued with a sigh. "Pleasant Valley is too small a town to have a church school. It helps with the finances though, that I still live in the family home."

Annette's attention had been drifting, but now it snapped back to the conversation. She hadn't considered the possibility of other people living in the house; people she hadn't even met. What would Esther and Mark's parents be like? Mark had said his mother was overseas—he hadn't mentioned a father.

"Oh, I assumed you lived alone. Will your parents be there?"

She glanced at Esther, who was shifting in her seat and sucking in her top lip.

"They've been away for a few years working at an orphanage in Thailand. They run the place. It's funded mainly through donations from the Pleasant Valley church."

Esther's tone was different—it had an edge now. What was with the change in mood? Maybe Esther didn't get on with her parents. She couldn't imagine why not, they sounded very selfless. Like Mark, these people cared so much about others. Leaving Australia to work in an orphanage...

"He's not our actual father. Our dad died when we were quite young."

"Oh," Annette tried to think of something sympathetic to say—but couldn't.

Esther continued on, "He's a good man though, my mother's husband. He turned his life around. Used to be an alcoholic. He's completely devoted to helping others. "They come home a couple of times a year. Meantime, I look after the place."

Esther looked sideways at Annette. Annette nodded to show she was listening, but she wasn't really anymore, she was distracted. She was wondering the same thing that she'd been wondering since that day in the cafe. When would she see Mark again?

"Does Mark come back to Pleasant Valley much?" she asked, keeping her voice light and casual.

"Yes, of course. He comes and stays sometimes. He helps a little with the garden and jobs around the house. He's not that into gardening though." She laughed. "And not particularly good at maintenance either, for that matter."

"Very often?" Annette asked, trying hard to keep her excitement hidden.

"Pretty regularly actually, about once a month. He runs a youth service at the church, it's part of his role as youth pastor in the city. There's no youth pastor at our church, so that's the arrangement he negotiated so that he could support the young people here."

Annette sat back in her seat and gazed out the window. She couldn't keep the contented smile from broadening across her face. This was very good news.

***

Finally, they drove down the main street of Pleasant Valley. It was a quaint little town, with the verandahs of the aged buildings reaching out to the kerb's edge. Once, long ago, horses would have been tied to the posts.

Annette gasped with pleasure, "Oh, it's so pretty."

"Yes," Esther agreed, "Most of these buildings are preserved by heritage laws and can't be changed on the outside."

"Well, I'm glad about that,"

Esther indicated the cafe where Annette would work. It was a two-storey building made of old rough red bricks. The verandah—with its curved, corrugated iron roof—jutted out from the middle of the building creating shade over the outdoor tables.

"I'll take you to meet them tomorrow," Esther told her.

A few kilometres after leaving the town behind, they turned into a long driveway lined with tall, silver birch trees, with their yellowing leaves and white trunks. The gravel driveway widened as they pulled up outside the old house.

Esther announced, "This is it." Then she busied herself taking things out of the car.

Annette stood for a moment taking it all in. The same rough, old red bricks that she'd noticed at the bakery formed the bottom half of the big square posts that supported the verandah. The lower half of the house was also brick and weatherboards lined the top half. The paint on the old cream coloured boards was flaking and bubbled in places, but the overall effect was still lovely.

The front garden took Annette's breath away. Two large camellia bushes with their pastel pink flowers looked so pretty situated on either side of the front steps. Even at this time of year, there was huge variety of colour. Paths with sandy coloured stepping stones wound through the beds. Plenty of weeds, but beautiful, nonetheless.

The house was as lovely inside as it was on the outside. The bay window in the lounge room was framed by delicate, white curtains which billowed gently inwards when Esther opened the windows. Against the adjacent wall stood a piano.

"So, do you play?" Annette asked, as she ran her finger along the polished woodgrain. A photo of Esther and Mark as adolescents caught her eye among the many on top of the piano. They were on a small stage, Esther, playing piano —looking a bit like a hippy with a long, floral flowing dress and her hair in plaits. Mark—sitting on a stool playing guitar —opposite her.

"Yes, I guess it's part of growing up in the church... being involved in music."

Another photo of two young children sitting on the grass, on either side of a woman. She was smiling at her children rather than the camera; she looked kind. Esther and Mark with their mum, she supposed.

"Is this you and Mark with your mother?"

"Yes, it is. I love that photo," she said.

There was only one photo of a man and it was a very old photo. The man looked very much like Mark. Best not to ask about that one.

"Are there any photos of the orphanage in Thailand?"

"Ahh, yes... but I keep them somewhere else. I'll show you another time. Come and see your room now," Esther said, her voice a little brusque. Then she disappeared down the hallway.

Esther left Annette in the bedroom at the back of the house while she went to the kitchen to make them sandwiches. This was to be her room. She went to the large window and took in the view. She could see the back garden from here, and again, there was a myriad of late colour. Annette opened the window and breathed deeply. What was that smell? A climber with small, bell-shaped flowers —honeysuckle. The scent reminded her of her mother's garden.

Annette grew up in a suburb where all the streets had tree names—Oleander Way, The Oaks, Eucalyptus Drive. She lived in Frangipani Court. The names sounded idyllic; the irony had escaped her until now. They were sad housing commission settlements, for those who couldn't afford better. If you turned left out of Frangipani Court and crossed the main road you would find the infant welfare centre. The sign pushed over and left lying on the ground, by some local skinheads. Annette had seen them do it. The houses were nearly all the same. Concrete boxes with their cold interiors in winter. While Annette couldn't remember too much about the inside of their house, she did remember the water dribbling down the inside walls as the sun warmed the concrete in the morning. Running her fingers through it, making drawings.

Yes, her town was a rough, harsh place. That was, except, for Rose's garden. She hadn't been included when Rose gardened. It was a solitary pursuit for her mother. At her grandparents' house Annette had spent many happy hours working in the garden. She'd had her own little weed bucket and fork and worked alongside her grandparents. Her grandmother had taught Annette a lot about plants and how to identify which were weeds and which were not.

Annette didn't really care that her mother didn't let her participate though. She was content to watch and play while Rose worked alone.

She still had a vivid picture of the honeysuckle against the shed wall in Rose's garden. It created a backdrop for the tall hollyhocks with their rich crimsons, purples and pinks. In front of the hollyhocks were the snapdragons. Annette would pick one and put her thumb and forefinger inside the petals and move them to make them talk. Rose would shake her head in mock anger. And, then—the new moons of her fingernails black with dirt—she would take a snapdragon too and they would play together.

This place and the town of Pleasant Valley felt like safe havens. She sighed deeply, relieved to have escaped her old life, just as the garden had been an escape when she was young. For her and, probably, for Rose too.

***

The rest of the day went quickly. After lunch Annette unpacked. Then Esther took Annette to the bakery. It was closed. While Annette was wondering whether they should come back later, Esther was already walking around the back and up the staircase that led to the owner's premises. He and his wife turned out to be a chubby, friendly couple. They introduced Annette to their daughter, Daisy and their son, Andy. Daisy didn't look up when she was introduced —she seemed very shy.

Jack sat down at the old wooden dining table with Annette while his wife, Jane caught up with Esther in the kitchen. Jack seemed happy with Annette's responses to his questions. He presented her with an apron with *Our Daily Bread*, emblazoned across the front and asked if she could start at 9am Monday morning.

Then Esther and Annette made a quick trip to the supermarket before it closed and stocked up. Annette offered to pay half, but Esther told her to wait until she had settled in.

By the time they arrived home it was time to eat again. They ate dinner and talked for a while. It wasn't long after they'd cleaned up that Esther said she was tired and went to bed. It was only 9.30pm.

Annette wasn't really that tired but there didn't seem to be anything else to do but go to bed. She sat in her room. It was so quiet. After the constant noise in the city, the silence was a little unnerving—spooky even. She would get used to it. This was her new home; she could hardly believe it. And her new employers seemed great. No more dealing with the cranky, French chef. She smiled, remembering the fun she and Tracy used to have joking about him.

Yes, she had a lot to be thankful for. It occurred to her that she should pray. She should thank God for all these positive changes. She felt guilty for not thinking of it sooner. Mark had told her how important it was to keep talking to God. He'd assured her that praying would soon be as natural to her as breathing.

Praying silently, she said, "Thank you Lord..." No, that's not right. Don't be so lazy, do it properly. She got out of bed, careful not to make any noise that might wake Esther. There was a small rug right next to the bed that seemed like it might have been placed there for the purpose of kneeling. The floorboards would've been much more uncomfortable.

She began her prayer again, repeating what she'd heard Mark say. "Thank you, Lord for all your blessings. I am so grateful for all your mercies...."

A low murmuring sound crept into the silence. Her eyes snapped open. Was God speaking to her? No, that was silly. The sound was coming from the hallway.

She rose from her knees and walked to the door. Still not able to decipher the sound clearly, she opened the door a few inches.

Now, she could hear snatches of Esther's voice. Who was she talking to? When no other voice responded, Annette realised she must be on the phone.

Esther spoke in a loud whisper and her tone sounded urgent. It was hard to make out much. Annette heard just a few isolated phrases,

"...if she finds out..." "...need to tell her. I can't keep this up."

Silence for a time, followed by, "Okay, as soon as possible then, bye."

Then the sound of the phone clicking gently back into its cradle.

Annette closed the door and returned to bed. Now she was even more sleepless than before. Was this all really as straightforward as it seemed? Had she been crazy to trust these people? Then again, maybe she was being paranoid. Maybe Esther wasn't even talking about her. She couldn't even be completely sure about what she had heard. What had Mark said? That she shouldn't worry, this was all part of God's plan. After what seemed like an eternity, she finally fell into a restless sleep.

Chapter 8

The next morning, Annette pulled the pillow behind her to sit up in bed. The sun streaming through the window and the view of the garden, both warmed and calmed her. The whisperings of last night seemed unimportant now. She was worrying about nothing. Nothing could spoil the promise of a perfect morning in this wonderful place.

It didn't take long for her uneasiness to return though, when Esther asked over their breakfast of scrambled eggs and toast, "Are you sure you want to go to church today?"

What? Why didn't Esther want her at church? What was wrong?

Esther didn't wait for her to respond.

"It was a busy day yesterday, you might just want to hang around here," she said

"Don't you want me to go?" Annette knew this sounded pathetic, but she badly needed some reassurance.

Esther paused, then her frown relaxed into a smile, "Of course, of course I want you to. Don't be silly. We need to get going soon though, if you're coming."

Relieved, Annette asked, "What time does it start?"

Esther had already showered and was now quite dressed up. Annette, however, was still in her pyjamas.

"10 o'clock, but I have to be there a bit early because I play piano for the service."

"Oh, okay."

Annette pushed the remainder of her breakfast away. It was already a quarter past nine.

"I'd better get a wriggle on then," she said cheerfully.

***

Annette was struck by the stark, plainness of the church building compared to the quaint heritage buildings she had seen so far. It was set back from the road on the river side, not far from the bakery. At the front of the building were a few, sparse, straggly shrubs. Out the back was a bare, grey gravel carpark, surrounded by a wire fence. Off to one side was a concrete toilet block and a tin shed. Behind the fence were the redgums that lined the river.

She was feeling anxious—as always—about meeting new people. This was worse though. This morning she would be meeting new people en masse. It wasn't quite so important at the city church because she would probably never see those people again. Besides, she was mostly concerned with what Mark thought of her then. Here, it mattered very much what people thought of her. She wanted to be accepted, because—as Mark had said—this was going to be her new church home.

When they walked into the church, a middle-aged woman disengaged herself from the group she was talking to and rushed towards them. She was quite tall and thin, and her smile didn't really serve to mask the determined expression on her face.

"Esther, I've been looking for you." The woman paused when she noticed Annette following behind. She looked Annette up and down, "Well, hello. Welcome to Pleasant Valley church."

Esther provided a very simple introduction. "This is Annette. Annette this is Carmel."

Annette smiled at Carmel; Carmel smiled back. There was an uncomfortable moment during which Carmel pursed her lips and raised her eyebrows. She seemed to be waiting for more information about the newcomer. None was forthcoming though, so Carmel gave up and turned her attention back to Esther.

"Where is the photo board of the orphanage, Esther? It was right here near the door last week."

"Oh, sorry I didn't tell you... Umm... I took it home to update it, they sent me some more recent pictures."

"Well I guess that's okay. It might be a problem though, when the offering plate goes around, and visitors can't see what they're donating to."

Her finger—which was in close proximity to Esther's face—jabbed at the air, punctuating her words. "You will bring it back during the week though. So that it's here for next Sunday."

Without waiting for a response, Carmel asked, "How are Grace and Edward doing anyway?"

Esther grabbed Annette's arm. "They're fine. Look sorry Carmel, we're in a bit of a hurry. I need to find a seat for Annette, then I've got to check my sheet music. Come on Annette."

Esther didn't have to drag her away; Annette found Carmel a little intimidating and was also eager to move on.

The church was much smaller than the one Annette had attended in the city. There were maybe only fifteen rows of pews. Pews—rather than comfy chairs. Standing at the end of a pew—in the middle section of the church—Esther stopped and introduced Annette to a woman around Esther's age.

"Annette, this is Violet."

Shiny long black tresses, pale skin, penetrating green eyes. Violet wore a forest green velvet skirt and a black shirt. She was stunning. Annette could hardly drag her eyes away.

"Hi Annette, Esther told me you were coming to stay with her."

"You'll look after her, won't you?" Esther said, and then directed Annette to slide into the pew next to Violet. Annette wasn't sure *what looking after her* meant, but Violet had a warm, open smile and Annette was glad not to have to sit alone.

"Of course, off you go," Violet clasped Esther's hand for a moment, and dropped it just as quickly. Esther sucked in a breath, before thanking Violet. Then, walked away and disappeared out of sight behind a curtain at the front of the church.

As the people filed in and seated themselves, the portly couple from the bakery made their way towards Annette.

"Hi, great to have you here." Jack gave her hand a vigorous shake.

He was followed closely by Jane, who leaned down and gave Annette a kiss on the cheek. Annette didn't even know these people. Yet, they had given her such a warm greeting — it was as though she belonged here. She felt the tiny, prick of a tear, which she blinked away quickly, hoping they hadn't noticed.

"See you tomorrow," Jane said. Then they moved away to find a seat.

"I'm starting work at their bakery tomorrow," Annette explained to Violet.

"Yes, I know, Esther told me."

"Oh, did she?" Annette said.

"Don't worry, Esther and I are good friends. You don't have to be concerned that everyone will know your business, Esther's not like that," Violet said, and then she sighed. "You are in the country now, though. It's not quite so easy to have a private life as it is in the city. You do have to be a bit careful who you confide in."

Annette was used to the anonymity of the city. Until this moment she'd taken it for granted. Was that one of the costs of having a church family? Still, better to be part of this new family than a nameless face in a crowd like she was in Melbourne.

A hush came over the congregation then. Esther and a young man came out onto the small stage at the front. Esther began to play softly. The rich tones of the piano swelling slowly and blending perfectly with the young man as he began to sing. Though Annette was no expert on music —especially this kind of music—she could recognise Esther's skill and sensitivity with the piano.

"She's amazing, isn't she?" Violet whispered, turning to Annette who nodded in agreement.

People began standing and waving their arms in the air. By end of the third song, most of the congregation had risen from their pews, their eyes were closed. They swayed to the music as though spellbound. Annette decided she would try it. She felt a little silly at first, but before long, she too was swept away. The music was intoxicating. Or, perhaps this was how it felt to be filled with the Holy Spirit. It was a wonderful feeling, like the world outside this place didn't matter. These people were filled with love. God loved her.

The pastor—who had been standing at the front row —moved onto the stage. He was not as flashy as the city preacher, voice and movements, not as animated. It didn't matter though, she still listened with rapt attention. She was ready and open to hear whatever God wanted to say to her.

At the end of the sermon, men began to walk to the front of the church with offering plates.

The pastor asked them to, "Give without thought for tomorrow, as Jesus himself tells us to do."

The offering plates were sent along the pews. One man passing it to the first person in the pew, then another man collecting it at the end and moving it to the next pew.

"Remember too, the orphanage in Thailand and be thankful for what you have," the pastor, reminded them.

Annette could see the plate now and was amazed to see the large notes that were being piled on top of each other. She fished around in her purse. All she had were two twenty-dollar notes. It was hard for her not to baulk at giving such a large amount. Forty dollars represented more than four hours work at the restaurant. Besides, it was all she had left.

The preacher went on to talk about how Jesus gave his life for all of them. How their sacrifice was so tiny in comparison. How could she have hesitated for even a second? She dropped the two notes into the plate as it came down the row.

***

They didn't stay after the service even though there was a 'potluck' lunch. Esther made apologies for them saying they had things to do, as they shook the pastor's hand at the door. Annette didn't think she had anything else to do and the lunch might have been nice. Neverthelesss, she trailed obediently out to the carpark after Esther.

On the drive home Annette was full of questions. During the sermon she had learned a new list of sins to guard against. And, if she could avoid sin, it would enable her, ...*to be a pure lamb of God*. The congregation had nodded and amened in agreement with everything the pastor said. Annette tried to suspend her niggling uncertainties. She wanted to remain in that state of pure joy she'd experienced during the singing. It didn't work though. Although, the pastor had been diligent in backing up everything he said with a text from scripture, some of the requirements just didn't seem that relevant to the '80s.

"I didn't really get why we can't eat pork or seafood," she said.

"You can eat seafood. Well, you can eat fish, as long as it has scales," Esther answered.

"I don't understand though, if it's so important to God, why do so many people from other Christian faiths eat whatever they want?"

When she stayed with her Catholic grandparents, they never skimped on the bacon with breakfast and she had loved to help her Nana cook the Sunday pork roasts with apple sauce.

Esther took a breath and began what sounded like a well-rehearsed spiel, "The Bible is very clear about unclean foods, there are texts in Leviticus and in the New Testament —remember, the pastor read them. The reason other Christians don't follow the Bible properly anymore is because they've lost their way. They've watered down Christianity and put God into a box that they only open on Sundays. Or, sometimes, only at Christmas and Easter. At our church, we try to live the way that the Spirit directs us in our everyday life," She paused, and took her eyes from the road, looking directly at Annette, "You don't want to be a half-baked Christian, do you? Doing whatever you feel like, as long as you get along to church each week?"

Annette was taken aback, she hadn't expected another sermon, especially not from Esther.

"No, I guess not. I do want to do God's will... um... all the time."

Esther was disappointed in her, that was clear. No point asking any more questions then. She was surprised at her new friend's reaction. It seemed at odds with what Esther had said, just a week ago, that she herself, didn't always get it right.

***

They ate a healthy lunch of salad and chicken washed down with orange juice. Neither of them talked much; Annette was still feeling the sting of being chastised in the car.

Esther announced she was going out to visit a church member. She didn't invite Annette to come along. Annette felt relieved; she would be glad of some time alone. This wasn't going as smoothly here as she'd hoped. Maybe she should apologise? These were Esther's heartfelt beliefs that Annette had questioned. From now on she would save her questions for Mark.

After Esther left, Annette washed the dishes then wandered out into the garden. There were weeds running rampant through the garden beds. The old Annette probably would've felt bored and lonely on a day like this— in a place like this. The old Annette would need to find a distraction—TV, alcohol, going out. She was reborn though, and gardening seemed like an appropriate pursuit, more in keeping with her new life. She would make herself useful.

There was a small shed out the back and in there, Annette found some gardening gloves, a large bucket to hold the weeds and a small garden fork. Choosing the large patch of garden near her bedroom window at the back of the house, Annette pulled out those that she remembered for sure were weeds and anything else that didn't look like it was meant to be there. She dead headed the roses and the agapanthus. The sun felt good on her back and she worked solidly for more than an hour. Every now and then, she emptied the bucket of weeds onto a pile of old sticks and other green waste at the back of the property. She paused absentmindedly to push her hair behind her ears with her dirty gloved hand. How nice it was to be focused only on what she was doing. Not worrying about a million things, like she usually did. The country life was good for her.

At this point she noticed a small patch of pansies. One was a perfect specimen. So pretty, in purple and white. She thought of the pansy in her dream—drenched in water. It had been the same colour. It made her feel even more hopeful to see this pansy alive and thriving. Maybe it was a sign... She weeded ever so carefully around the delicate flower.

When she'd finished, she stood back and surveyed the weed-free bed with pleasure, surprised that she'd enjoyed the process so much. She pulled off the gloves and put the tools back in the shed where she found them, looking forward to relaxing inside with a cold drink.

As she was leaving the shed, she noticed a pushbike leaning up against a large flat object covered with a sheet right at the back of the shed. The bike looked like it would be okay to ride. Perhaps Esther would let her use it to ride to work. She was about to pull the door shut when she remembered the conversation between Esther and Carmel. Was that flat object the board that Esther had taken from the church? She probably shouldn't investigate—it was like prying—but she was curious about the orphanage. Surely Esther wouldn't mind. She dragged the sheet off the board. Just then she heard the Datsun pull up in the driveway.

Chapter 9

Annette stared at the large pinboard. It showed pictures of the children at the orphanage. There was a colourful, cardboard banner pinned across the board diagonally—Suchada Orphanage, Bangkok, Thailand.

What grabbed her attention though, was a photo on the right-hand side. In it were two westerners, a middle-aged man and woman, seated on the floor surrounded by children of various ages. The woman had Mark and Esther's wavy, dark hair. Annette recognised their mother, Grace, from the photo inside. She was reading to the children. But the man, the man was unmistakably Annette's father.

In shock, she kept trying to comprehend what she saw, but it didn't make sense. She moved away from the board, stumbling backwards against a large terracotta pot. To stop herself from falling over, she grabbed the edge of an old wooden workbench to steady herself. Her heart was racing, a wave of nausea swept through her. This couldn't be a coincidence. Why would they trick her this way?

Esther appeared in the shed doorway. Her face dropped when she saw the board was uncovered.

"Oh, Annette..."

Annette shook her head and threw up her hands.

"I'm so sorry... I didn't want you to find out this way. We were going to tell you, we just wanted you to be settled in first."

The nausea increased in intensity and Annette thought she might vomit. She stared at the photo again. He looked older, his hair—greying at the sideburns. He was smiling broadly at the camera.

"I... I don't understand."

"You don't look well." Esther moved forward and held her arm. "Come inside and sit down. I'll explain everything."

Annette's instincts told her to run, to pack her suitcase and leave right now. But where would she go? Back to her old life, back to Tracy's flat. She snatched her arm away. How could she be so naive? Thinking they cared about her, when obviously there was another agenda. She tried to slow her breathing, so she could think clearly. Her hand still gripped the bench.

Esther was pleading with her now. "Please Annette, we just wanted to help you and... Ted."

Help me! How? He'd abandoned her and Rose ten years ago. Only when he was gone did she feel like she could breathe again. What could possibly be helpful about this situation? She looked at the board again. At the top was a Bible text in a child's handwriting. *"For I know the plans I have for you," declares the Lord "Plans to prosper you and not to harm you. Plans to give you hope and a future." Jeremiah 29:11* Could this be part of God's plan too? Surely neither Mark nor Esther would ever do anything to hurt her. She should at least hear Esther out. She let go of the bench and followed Esther into the house.

***

Esther phoned Mark straightaway. After the call, she told Annette that he planned to drive there as soon as he could to help explain things. Esther wanted to wait for Mark to arrive so that the three of them could talk together.

Annette then spent an hour and a half in her room. Various possibilities catapulted around in her head—each one more confusing than the one before. Up until her discovery in the shed, Annette had hoped to see Mark as soon as possible. Now she felt like disappearing and never laying eyes on either Mark or Esther, again. The trust she had allowed to grow was so delicate—like a fledgling bird on its first flight—it could so easily be crushed. In fact, maybe her lack of trust in the past, had served her much better.

Finally, Annette knocked on Esther's door and told her she couldn't wait any longer. They seated themselves in the lounge room. Annette curled up on the comfy, floral sofa with a cup of tea in her hand. Esther sat opposite her on a leather recliner. Annette's chest was still tight, but her stomach had settled now. She took slow, deep breaths while she waited for Esther to speak. The hot, sweetened tea was comforting.

Esther sipped her tea. Then, keeping her eyes on Annette, she began to speak, "We met your Dad about five years ago, not long after he moved to town. He and Mum met when he came to the house asking if she had any handyman work for him."

Esther paused, had another sip of tea and went on. "Mark and I were still at school; I was in Form 11 and Mark in Form 12. Anyway, we were at school that day. Mum gave him a coffee on the verandah. They talked for a long time and Mum invited him to church the following Sunday. He probably only came to church because he was interested in Mum, but he kept coming along each week, kept visiting Mum regularly."

The tight coil of tension in Annette's chest loosened its grip just a tiny bit. The apple doesn't fall far from the tree, it seemed. Why had she gone to the singalong if not to be around Mark? No, it was more than that. It was the promise of something better. Maybe her father felt that same hope when he met Grace. Perhaps that's how you see the promise first, you see it in the kind eyes of a believer.

"Of course, Mum made it clear she wasn't interested," Esther said. "She would never have a relationship with a non-believer. It was obvious she liked him though. He came for dinner, got to know us. Both Mark and I were wary at first. Well—for that matter—most of the congregation were worried about Mum getting too close to him. Of course, they didn't say anything to him. Mum got plenty of warnings though, about him being an unknown quantity. At that stage, only Mum knew he'd been an alcoholic."

Annette straightened in her chair. That was a surprise. That he would admit to having been an alcoholic. He'd always denied it when Rose had accused him of having a drinking problem.

Esther dipped her head towards Annette, "That must have been hard on you growing up... his drinking."

Annette felt the strange mix of anger and its underlying companion, fear, rising in her as the memories flooded back. What could she say? *Hard on me,* yes, you could say that...

There were many nights she'd lain in bed listening to her parents in the middle of a raging argument, too scared to move. One of those nights was when she was about seven years old. She'd heard something hitting the wall with a clang, followed by several sharp whacks. Then the sound of his heavy footsteps moving away. A door slamming, and, afterwards, only a terrifying silence.

Annette hopped out of bed and, being careful not to

make the floorboards creak, she crept out to the lounge room where she could see into the kitchen. A dented biscuit tin lay over to one side of the room, its lid on the other side. Her mother was crying softly as she swept crushed biscuits off the floor. Half her hair had escaped from her long plait and fell loosely across her face, but the strands didn't hide the red welt and the tears on her cheek. Annette crept back to bed. Somehow, she knew that Rose would be hoping she'd had slept through it all.

What could she say to Esther about a life during which both she and Rose walked on eggshells around her father waiting for the next inevitable explosion? Annette said nothing, so Esther continued.

"One day—it was such an emotional day—Ted gave his heart to Jesus at the church. Right in front of everyone. I remember Mum had tears in her eyes, she was so happy. Then he admitted to the whole congregation that he'd been an alcoholic in the past and that he was very regretful about that, but that he'd changed and, with the help of God and the church, he would never touch a drop again. After that day, it seemed like he never looked back, he learned everything he could about our beliefs and became a respected elder in the church."

Never looked back, hey, what about me? Annette thought. Did he never think of her? Or, her mother? Although, for years, she had been glad he was out of their lives, now she was hearing about how wonderful he was in this new life, she felt that old familiar sting of self-doubt and shame. What was wrong with her? Why couldn't he have stopped drinking back then? Suddenly, she was impatient with this story.

"So, what's this got to do with me? Why am I here?"

"I'm getting to that. Just give me a minute," Esther took a deep breath and sighed it out, "They got married about twelve months after they first met. It was a lovely ceremony. We all felt sad for him though because he had no family there. He had told us his parents were both dead long ago. We assumed there was no-one else."

Esther glanced at Annette, her face holding an unspoken apology. So, he hadn't told them about his first marriage, or that he had a daughter. She wondered, how he had explained the years before he and Grace met?

"Anyway, of course he moved in. We all got on okay... considering he's not our father. Not long after, Mark moved to Melbourne to study. But then, there was this one night..."

Esther's eyes were focused on some indiscriminate spot ahead of her and she sat quite still. When she spoke again, her voice was shaky.

"One night, he got drunk. We'd never seen him drunk. He was yelling at Mum and me... It was awful."

Until this moment Annette had only been concerned about herself and how this all affected her. Now, she began to feel anxious for Esther. This part of the story was sounding much more familiar to Annette, more like the Ted she grew up with.

"What did he do?" she asked Esther gently, as though speaking to a frightened child.

"Oh, he didn't hit us or anything. It's just that my own father never yelled, and of course he didn't drink, I wasn't used to it. We were both scared, but Mum kept saying to me that the devil drink had taken control of him and that he didn't mean what he was saying."

"What was he saying?"

"Stupid things, unfair things. He said Mum had trapped him into joining the church and then trapped him into marrying her. He was rambling a lot, but he talked about other women and how they'd treated him in the past as well. Then he threw one of Mum's statues of Jesus at the wall. I remember it smashed into about ten pieces; fragments of Jesus's body scattered all over the floor. I had my car by then and I wanted to leave the house, but I was scared to leave Mum alone. I tried to get her to come with me, but she wouldn't. She picked up all those little pieces of Jesus and sat on the floor with them in her lap praying, while he kept swearing and storming around the house."

Esther was now staring at a spot on the floor as though she could still see the image of her mother from that night.

She roused herself and continued, "Anyway, that was the night Mum and I first heard about you. While he was ranting about the other women. We didn't know he'd been married twice before, or even that he had a child, before that night."

"Twice before?"

"Yes, twice." She looked uncertainly at Annette. "I guess you couldn't have known anything about what happened after he left. He was ranting about her too, that night, his late wife."

Annette was shaking her head, incredulous, "She died?"

"Yes, a fall down the stairs."

At that moment there a knock on the front door and they both jumped. The front door opened, and Mark's voice travelled down the hall, moving towards them.

"It's just me. Is it safe to come in?"

His nervous smile was disarming. Annette tried not to smile back—without success. She so wanted him to stay the person, she thought he was. Kind, gentle, caring... So wanted to keep her guard down with him. It was rare for her to be able to do that with anyone, but she trusted Mark —well, up until now, she had. And, besides, she'd forgotten how blue his eyes were, the easy way he held himself.

Esther seemed glad of the interruption, "Actually, you've timed it well. I was about to tell her about the morning you came up and the three of us confronted Ted about getting drunk." She rose as she was speaking, "Let me get you a cup of tea, though." And with that she disappeared into the kitchen.

Mark had an overnight bag with him. He dumped it on the floor and flopped onto a chair.

"It's been a long day," he said with an audible sigh.

Annette realised it had grown dark outside. It occurred to her that it was Sunday, and he may have had more important things to do besides rush up here. Despite her anger and confusion, she was glad he had. Esther came back with a cup of tea for him.

Taking it from her, he said, "Thanks, I don't suppose... could you get me some toast or something? Haven't had a chance to eat since breakfast."

Esther nodded. "Yeah sure," and disappeared again.

"I hope she told you what a great asset to the church Ted is. We couldn't keep that orphanage running without him."

Annette could feel her defences rising,

"Yes, she did. She also told me that he got drunk, *and,* that he was abusing your mum, *and,* that your mum and Esther were scared of him."

"Yes, that's all true, but the next morning around the breakfast table he explained himself. He was crying, the poor man, he was so sorry, begged for our forgiveness. He said it was because he felt like such a failure. That—because of his drinking—he'd lost custody of you. He told us that his first wife, Rose, wouldn't let him have access. She wouldn't let him see you. That she returned all the letters he sent you unopened. He said he wasn't angry with her. He couldn't blame her. He said, because of that, he gave up drinking. Soon after, he met a wonderful woman and married again. Then, he found his purpose in life, working alongside her to help unfortunate children, but he still couldn't forget you."

"What do mean, what sort of work did he do?"

"He worked in some sort of children's home, he said, his wife was already working there as a house mother when they met."

Annette shook her head. *Unbelievable!* This person was sounding like a completely different person to the one she remembered.

"Then one day his second wife died—just like that—no warning. Their future together stubbed out. After he had worked through the grief of his second wife's death, he found that he still couldn't get over the loss of his daughter. It was so hard on him that you were still alive and he couldn't see you. He said that you were the reason he had relapsed."

Annette found this hard to accept, Rose had always maintained that she'd never heard from him, didn't know where he was—didn't care for that matter. Why would she lie?

"We prayed about it, asked God's forgiveness for him. He didn't talk about you again after that, but it was still on our minds that he was hurting. It wasn't long after that the orphanage project was started. When, he and Mum volunteered to go and run it, the church was more than happy for him to head it up. He had been doing such great work as an elder. And besides, he already had experience working with underprivileged children. He was perfect for the job. A few months after they left, Mum wrote to me and asked me to find you. She was worried about Ted. In her letter, she wrote that he was becoming more depressed and withdrawn each day. It was impacting the work they were trying to do there. Some days he would disappear and not come back until late at night. We all thought the best thing that could happen would be for the two of you to be reconciled."

Esther had come back in while Mark was still talking. She placed a pile of toasted cheese and tomato sandwiches on the coffee table. Then sat on the recliner, shaking her head.

Mark corrected himself, "I should say that when I got Mum's letter, I agreed with Mum that it would be for the best. Esther wasn't convinced. I think what happened that night made her lose perspective. But you can't judge someone too harshly for one lapse. Jesus said, 'forgive seventy times seven'. What He meant was, that we should never stop forgiving. I do realise Ted had a drinking problem before, and I'm sure that impacted you, but we can't dwell on the past. We're all made new in Jesus."

Annette was still struggling with the deception. They should have told her. She thought about the times she had seen the bus sitting there. Quite a few times, over a period of months. It was disturbing to realise she'd been watched for so long.

"How did you find me anyway? I'm not in the phone book."

"You filled in a tax declaration for work, didn't you? Let's just say I only had to explain the situation to a sympathetic church member who works in a particular government department..."

Mark seemed pleased with himself, "We park the outreach bus in the city anyway, I thought I'd just park near your work, watch you for a while and see what happened. The rest is history."

He casually picked up a sandwich, as if he'd just given directions to the shop, rather than disclosed a covert operation. One that included obtaining personal information about her, which—for all she knew—was probably illegal. It just didn't seem like an appropriate activity for a pastor.

"You've got to admit you're much better off here. You can't have been happy. If I hadn't watched you, going into that bar every weekend, writing yourself off. Or, going home with... well, you know. I might have had second thoughts, but for me it became a mission to save you from yourself, as well as to help Ted."

Annette was torn. Should she feel patronised or rescued? No use pretending, it was true that she wasn't happy with the life she was living. Mark could see that. And it was true, he did save her, but he'd also deceived her.

Esther had been quiet for some time. When she spoke, her voice was quiet, but assertive, "We should also tell her about this weekend."

Mark stared at Esther, clearly irritated. "Don't you think this is enough for her to take in right now?"

Esther ignored him. "You should know that Mum and Ted are coming home this Friday," she said.

Chapter 10

Esther dropped Annette off at the bakery on her way to work in Wellspring. It was too early to start, so Annette decided to explore a bit. Esther had told her that if she walked down the street next to the bakery, she would find the river. It wasn't far from the main part of town and the area around the river was pretty. A fountain created the centrepiece for the tidy garden beds which were surrounded by lush lawns. Further down towards the river, the lawns thinned out and became patchy when they reached the huge-trunked redgums that lined the river itself.

Annette sat on a park bench overlooking the river. She could see a mother duck and her three babies creating their rippling wake in the otherwise still water. The early morning sun glistened on the tiny waves they left behind. She was glad she had decided not to leave last night. The prospect of a new job and a new start motivated her, but the thought of being close to Mark motivated her even more. She smiled —only for a moment, then lapsed back into turmoil over yesterday's events.

Esther had headed off to her room to do some preparation for her classes the next day as soon as the discussion about Ted had wound down. Annette and Mark were left alone to talk. He seemed different to when she'd spent time with him in Melbourne. After they'd told her everything, he visibly relaxed, sinking back into the chair. He talked about life in the city and how he preferred living in the country. How he couldn't keep up with all the parishioners. Sometimes he couldn't even remember everyone's name, he'd said. Couldn't get around to visiting all the young people as often as he'd like. That was a real concern for him. Annette couldn't imagine how anyone could remember the names of that many people. And why would he need to visit them all anyway? Weren't they already on the right path? She listened in rapt attention though, it was like a veil was lifted for her into his private world. She had gone off to bed with a renewed hope that something wonderful might happen between the two of them.

If only that was all she had to think about, but no... the prospect of seeing her father again loomed large—like an unexpected cloud blocking the sun. He had left when she was eight years old. He hadn't said goodbye, he was just gone when she returned home from school one day. Rose sat her down and placed a glass of orange juice and a chocolate chip cookie in front of her. This was unusual for Rose. Most days, when Annette asked for something to eat after school, the answer was, "wait for dinner". This day felt very different. This day, Rose had a large band-aid stuck on her face lengthwise, just to the right of her mouth. It crossed Annette's mind that it was an odd place to need a band-aid, but her mother's behaviour was so strange that day that she just sat waiting, without asking questions. Not even touching the drink or the cookie. Waiting to find out what was going on first. She was used to unpredictable events and so began to steel herself against whatever was coming.

"Your dad's gone," Rose said in a deadpan voice. The band-aid gaped open to expose a cut lip when she spoke, then flattened again as the silence descended once more.

Annette didn't ask how long he was gone for, or when he would be home. She knew what her mother meant. Her mother and father—each of them in turn—had threatened so many times to leave that she wasn't really surprised to hear that it had actually happened. She was relieved that it was her father who had left, not her mother. Was she so unimportant to him, though, that she didn't even deserve a goodbye? Maybe, he would come back and say goodbye.

"Will he be coming to visit?"

"No, I don't think we'll ever see him again." Rose's voice cracked, and a tear made its way towards the band-aid, which was working its way loose. Rose touched it with her finger to push it back in place. She sucked in her breath in pain. "Ow... Bastard!"

Annette was shocked, her mother never swore. Then, Rose threw her head back, brought both hands to her face and began to sob. Annette made her way around the table towards her mother to try to comfort her.

Before she could get there, Rose stood up and said, "I'm taking you to Nana's for a while. Go and pack your duffle bag. Make sure you take everything you need for school too."

Annette stayed at her grandparent's house for two months. She didn't hear from Rose during that time. It wasn't so bad, she liked being with her Nana and Grandpa. Her grandmother fussed over her and gave her lots of hugs and concerned looks. Annette didn't understand though, exactly why she'd had to leave home.

"Nana, why did I have to leave just because Dad left?"

"Your mum's upset, she just needs a bit of time to sort herself out."

When Rose finally picked Annette up and they arrived back at home, Bob was sitting in the lounge room drinking coffee and watching the news. Annette decided her mum couldn't have been that upset. In fact, Rose seemed happier than Annette had ever seen her. A few weeks later Bob moved in.

The ducks swam by again and the mother duck flapped her wings against the water. Annette snapped out of her reverie and checked her watch. *Shit!* She was going to be late on her first day!

***

The day went smoothly. She was busy, so didn't have much time to mull things over. Interactions with Jack and Jane consisted of them each in turn instructing her on their way of doing things. They were patient with her, and she was a quick learner. It seemed like very little time had passed before she was waiting out the front of the bakery for Esther to pick her up. She wished she could just feel satisfied with her day's work and look forward to this evening, but the disturbing thoughts returned to her like a spider crawling around in her gut.

"How did your first day go?" Esther asked.

"Pretty good. They're nice people."

Annette made no effort to extend the conversation. She still wasn't quite sure how to feel about Esther. Esther had obviously wanted to tell her what was going on all along, but she hadn't. Why not? Annette felt so connected to Esther when she first met her. Now she felt betrayed, as if by a close friend. So stupid! She should have listened to Tracy. Why did she let Esther in so easily? And even to those few in the past that she had let in, the door was only opened a crack, never was it wide open like this time.

Esther spoke again, breaking the silence. "Mark called me at work, he's decided to take a week off and stay with us. I picked up leg of lamb for dinner. Hope you like lamb?"

Annette relaxed with a sigh. She hadn't expected to see Mark again so soon. And, he would be here when her father arrived...

She turned to Esther and smiled. "I love roast lamb," she said.

Annette helped prepare the vegetables. Esther cooked the lamb until it was almost falling off the bone. They arranged the lamb on a platter surrounded by the roast potatoes, pumpkin, carrots and peas. This was accompanied by a jug of thick gravy. Mark didn't appear until he was called for dinner. He explained that he'd been working on next Sunday's sermon.

"The senior pastor has given me the okay to preach here next Sunday," he said, while he stood and carved the lamb.

He served it to the girls first, then himself, "This looks great. Look how tender it is."

Mark and Esther seemed to be acting as though nothing untoward had happened. Annette fought the urge to do the same. She felt her stomach twist as she gathered the courage to speak.

"I don't know if I'll still be here by then."

"What are you talking about?" Mark sat down with a thump.

"You've just started a new job," Esther chimed in.

"Well, I wouldn't have chosen to see my father again. I really don't think I want to."

"How can you say that? About your own father." Mark shook his head. "Are you going to continue to condemn him for the sins of the past? What if God did that with you? Where would you be? Can't you find forgiveness in your heart, just as you've been forgiven?"

He paused, waiting for an answer. She really didn't think she could forgive Ted, but clearly, that wouldn't have been the right response. She looked down at her empty plate.

Mark continued, "Not to mention that I spent months praying and waiting for the opportunity to help you, and now, you're saved. You've given your heart to God. You have a new life in Christ. We've offered you a home and Esther's found you a job. Why would you throw it all away? Just because you can't forgive him?"

Annette was ashamed. How petty was she? God had forgiven her. Mark had seen what her life was like and he had accepted her. How could she be so harsh? She couldn't bear for Mark to be disappointed in her, so she didn't say more. But the questions hadn't gone away. Had her father really changed? The man had left and never contacted her again. Would this just end with more hurt? And, Mark did deceive her, even if it was for what he believed was a divine purpose.

There was a part of her that was outraged. Part of her said that it was crazy to trust these people or to ever trust her father again. That part of her thought she should have packed up and left as soon as she'd heard the whole story last night.

But maybe that was just her old self talking. Perhaps she should listen to the other part of herself that was trying to be heard. Maybe God was directing her not to react in the old ways. Telling her to remember how lost and alone she was before and that she wanted this new life so badly. Reminding her that she was so ready for change and how much she wanted the acceptance that Mark had promised her. Yes, it involved being vulnerable. Yes, it meant trusting what Mark was saying. And yes, it meant forgiving her father and believing that he had changed.

What an idiot she was being. She had chosen the higher road and was now baulking at the very first test of her Christianity. Of course, Mark was right, she had to choose forgiveness, she had to be vulnerable. There was no alternative, only to go backwards. She didn't want that.

She sighed heavily, as she picked up a golden, roast potato and popped it on her plate.

"I'm so sorry Mark, I am very grateful that you found me," she said with heartfelt conviction.

***

Friday night came around a lot faster than Annette would have liked. Esther had stayed late in Wellspring, so she could pick up her mother and Ted from the train station there. Annette and Mark were alone in the house. They were in the lounge room. The TV was on, but she was hardly aware of it. The old fear of her father was threatening to take over. However, she was determined to put the past firmly behind her. She would accept Ted, just as she had been accepted by God. No judgements. Despite her good intentions, her stomach wouldn't stop churning.

It wasn't just Ted she was worried about. She also had to meet Grace, Ted's wife. Mark and Esther's mother. How would she treat Annette? She was after all, the daughter of another woman. In the photo on the piano, Grace looked kind, but then, so did Ted, in the photo. No, stop being silly. It will be okay. God is in control. And besides, Mark was there with her.

Mark was watching the news. An ad break came on and he turned the TV down.

"Are you excited?" he asked, as he eased himself off the recliner and stood to face her.

"More nervous than excited," she answered honestly.

"Hope you're not worried about Mum. She'll love you, I'm sure of that. And your dad... Wow, is he going to be surprised!"

Annette's eyebrows shot up and her mouth opened wide in disbelief. She wanted to scream at Mark, *What the fuck?* But she swallowed her words. Better to be careful around him now that she understood just how bad she could feel when she disappointed him.

"What... what do you mean surprised?" Her voice thinly controlled, quiet.

"Well, it's a surprise for him. You, being here. I thought you realised that."

"No, no, I didn't realise that. I thought he wanted me here."

"Of course, he does, I have no doubt about that. When he sees you again, he'll be thrilled. You don't understand how important you are to him, the way he talked about you that morning. How sad he was because he couldn't see you for all those years."

Shit, shit, shit!!! She knew she wasn't supposed to swear, even in her mind, because of course, God knew her thoughts, but this was unbelievable. She had made a commitment to herself to accept Ted, but he didn't even know she was here. How would she react?

A car pulled into the drive. Mark came closer and squatted down in front of her, he put his hand on her knee.

"Don't worry, it's all in God's hands."

He stood up and went out into the hall towards the front door. She stayed seated on the couch. Even Mark's touch couldn't distract her from the intense anxiety she was experiencing. Her heart was racing, she was already feeling the old fear that used to accompany her father's homecoming. Now, that was heightened even more with the news that Ted didn't know she was here. Fear was turning into sheer panic.

She heard sounds of greeting at the door—including her father's—still she didn't move. Then, the clatter of multiple footsteps coming down the hall towards her, and Mark's voice saying, "We have a surprise for you Ted."

Suddenly, she galvanised into action. Without further thought, she jumped up and walked quickly towards the kitchen and the back door. She stood with her hand on the brass door handle, poised to turn it. Her hand dropped to her side. Wasn't this what she wanted? To be part of a loving family? She'd never had that. Mark had assured her that her father had made a profound change. She just had to trust that was true.

"Oh, there you are. Come on in." Mark put his hand on her back and led her into the lounge room.

Her father was thinner than she remembered him, his light, summer shirt and shorts hung loosely on his once solid frame. He still made a tall, imposing figure in the room, just as he always had.

Right now, though, he looked puzzled, but was still maintaining the charming smile that Annette remembered so well.

"And who is this lovely young lady?" he asked.

Mark's face fell. "You don't recognise her?"

Both Esther and her mother said nothing. They all seemed dumbfounded by Ted's question. For some reason Annette couldn't comprehend, she began to laugh. She didn't want to, but she couldn't help it. Clapping her hand over her mouth, she tried to stifle what was threatening to become that kind of hysterical laughter that was impossible to stop. They were all staring at her as though she had become slightly unhinged. All except Ted. His smile had disappeared now, his eyes were crinkled in confusion.

"Annette?"

She managed to gather herself and stop laughing when he spoke.

"Yes, it's me."

Her cold sounding response—so quickly following the laughter—served only to increase the bizarre quality of their meeting. In the long pause that followed, Annette could sense the tension in the room rise even higher than before, when she was laughing. Why doesn't he say anything? His eyes moved to the left, then to the right. Annette wondered what was running through his mind.

Finally, he spoke, "What are you doing here?" He still wasn't smiling.

"We knew how much you missed her and how happy you would be to see her, so I sought her out in Melbourne." Mark sounded a lot less confident than he had up until now. "And not only that, the best news is that she's saved, she's come to Jesus."

It wasn't lost on Annette that Mark seemed to be trying to convince Ted that his daughter being here was a good thing. It was probably obvious to everyone in the room, that Ted was way less than delighted to see her.

"So, how long are you here for?"

Again, Mark answered for her, speaking quickly, "She's living here Ted, Esther found her a job at the bakery, and she comes to church..." His voice trailed off as Ted's expression darkened.

Ted looked at his wife. "Did you know about this?"

"Yes, it was my idea." Grace's voice was strong, assertive.

Ted shook his head. "You should have told me." His voice barely under control.

He turned to Esther.

"Where are the keys to the Valiant?"

Esther headed towards the kitchen.

"What are you doing Ted, we just got home? Your daughter is here—your flesh and blood." Grace indicated towards Annette, her eyes wide, brows drawn together in confusion.

Esther returned with a set of keys and handed them to Ted. She was clearly frightened by his reaction. Without another word, Ted left the house. Grace followed him outside.

Esther walked across the room and put her hand on Annette's shoulder. "I'm so sorry."

At Esther's touch, Annette broke down and wept. Esther held Annette close as she sobbed.

Mark spoke, but his voice lacked conviction, his face, crestfallen. "Don't worry he's probably just tired from the trip."

Annette became aware of the sounds of a car engine trying to turn over. Eventually the engine caught. Then, the sound of it roaring out the drive. Grace came back inside. Annette sniffled and composed herself.

"Oh, you poor dear. You mustn't get yourself too upset. It was just a shock to see you. He hasn't been himself lately either, but don't worry, I know he loves you. Look, let's all have a cup of tea and a Bible reading and then we'll go off to bed. Things always look better in the morning."

The three sat with a cup of tea. Grace read from the Bible, "For I know the plans I have for you, declares the Lord, plans to prosper you and not to harm you, plans to give you hope and a future." Then Grace asked them to kneel and hold hands as she prayed a soothing, comforting prayer.

It was the same verse as she'd seen on the orphanage board. She felt better. God kept reminding her that He was in charge. This was a shock for her, so maybe it was for Ted as well. Perhaps Grace was right and it would all be okay after all.

***

Things weren't any better the next day though. Ted hadn't returned, and everyone was very subdued over breakfast. Annette hadn't slept well and still felt quite fragile after yesterday. She was also annoyed again. Grace and Mark had acted on a whim. Even if it was out of kindness, it had obviously still been a bad decision. Did they think about how this might affect her? Or were they only worried about Ted? Why am I still here? She kept asking herself this question even though she knew the answer. She really liked Mark, but it was more than that. There was that aching void inside her, nothing else had been able to fill it so far. Even with all that had happened, she was still hopeful that her life would become less isolated, less meaningless.

The sound of a car pulling into the drive made her sit up straight in her chair. The tension around the breakfast table rose. Annette heard footsteps come in through the unlocked front door, walk into the bathroom and close the door. The four of them stopped eating and waited. Soon after, Ted came into the kitchen. He looked dishevelled, perhaps he'd slept in the car. He smiled and then walked around the table giving each of the women a kiss on the cheek, including Annette. She stiffened as he approached. He smelled of toothpaste.

"Good morning everyone," his voice was cheerful. "Sorry about last night, it was a long trip and then seeing Annette... Well, I guess it was a bit of a shock. I just wish you'd told me."

Annette hadn't forgotten how Ted's moods could shift

dramatically from one extreme to another, but even she was amazed at how happy he seemed this morning.

"Yes, we're sorry too. We just thought it would be a nice surprise, but I can see now we should have let you know." Mark's relief as he spoke was obvious.

Grace was still silent. Annette wondered what she made of her husband being away all night.

"Anyway, I don't really want to interrupt breakfast, but would you mind if have a few words with Annette... alone."

He put his hand on Annette's shoulder and she stiffened again. Grace looked as though she was about to say something, but perhaps thought better of it. The three of them left their half-eaten breakfasts and filed out the door. Mark went through last and closed it behind him.

Ted walked to other side of the table and continued to stand, resting his hands on the back of a chair. Annette was relieved that his hand was gone from her shoulder, but now his relaxed, carefree expression was replaced by a more forbidding one. His smile had vanished. She felt like she was five years old again.

"Why are you here?"

"Mark told you, I'm here because he introduced me to God and Esther found me a job. They wanted a better life for me. I didn't know you were here when I made the decision to leave Melbourne."

"I find that hard to believe," an unpleasant sneer moved across his lips.

"I'm telling the truth. They didn't tell me either, not until I'd moved here. I only found out last Sunday."

"Hmm," he shook his head slightly. It seemed that he didn't believe her. "So, what have you told them about me."

"Nothing really, why would I? Apparently, you've already told them about your..." She hesitated, not wanting to make him angry— Rose was never allowed to mention it.

Maybe it was okay now though, since he'd admitted it himself. "...your drinking."

His face relaxed ever so slightly. "And do you plan to tell them anything else?"

"Do you mean the..."

He focused intently on her. Annette realised she was shaking but was still determined to say the words. It was unacceptable for him to pretend that nothing had happened now that she was an adult.

"...the physical violence? That you bashed Mum?"

He sighed. Then he smiled a wide smile. What an odd thing to do.

"Oh, they know about that too," he said, still smiling.

"I heard you got married again, after Mum. Did you bash her too?"

"No, of course not." He looked a little irritated now. The smile was more forced. "It was the devil drink that made me do it. And I quit after I left your mother. I've never laid a hand on anyone since."

She smiled. Maybe, he had changed.

"So, I guess you're not here to make my life difficult after all?"

"No, of course not. I want to be forgiving. I don't want to live in the past."

Annette was confused, what was he talking about?

"Well your mother has a lot to answer for too you know... Anyway, I agree, I'm all for leaving the past behind. Let's get everyone back in here and tell them how glad I am that they found you."

When everyone was settled back in their chairs, Ted lead them in a prayer of thanksgiving for the return of the prodigal daughter.

As they lifted their heads, he said with a jovial tone, "What's a man got to do around here to get a feed?"

Grace made him breakfast and they all finished the meal together, talking about the orphanage in Thailand, the local village and the food. Now, it was almost as though there had been nothing unusual about their homecoming. Annette should have been used to her father acting as though nothing had happened. And his ability to jolly and charm others into the same belief, but the sequence of events last night and of this morning still felt quite surreal to her. Especially in this pretty house, with these good, Christian people.

Chapter 11

The sense of unreality continued for her over the weekend. The proximity of her father, his strange questioning of her in the kitchen Saturday morning. Then, seeing the congregation fawn over him at church —all so pleased to see him and Grace—it all added to the dreamlike quality of those first days.

Annette was relieved to get back to work on Monday. The bakery was not overly busy—people didn't usually have to line up—customer traffic was constant though, throughout the morning. Most of the locals were friendlier than she was used to in the city. They would often have a chat with Jack or with Jane or both. There wasn't that sense of being in a hurry that there was in Melbourne. There was time to talk.

She was taken aback by the interest people took in her. Some would ask her name and where she was from. Still, she would give minimal information and only her first name. She wasn't used to telling strangers her business.

Even when Jane commented, "I didn't realise until we were at church yesterday that Ted was your father." Annette just nodded her head, affirming that he was, but didn't elaborate. Jane was obviously waiting to hear more, but what could Annette say about their relationship? Although, she had made a decision to let the past go, she hadn't forgotten it. Perhaps she was harsh, cold and unforgiving. The church people—including Mark and his family—seemed to see Ted as a truly wonderful human being. She didn't see him that way, as much as she may have wanted to. Her mother's pain was still too clearly etched in her memory.

Late in the afternoon, the bakery was empty except for Jane and Annette. Jack left the bakery after the lunch rush. He went home at that time to sleep each day, so he could rise early to do the day's baking. Annette was busying herself cleaning the glass display shelf. Daisy came into the bakery, shuffling her little feet. Andy and Daisy had come after school most days last week too, but Annette had been so focused on learning the job she hadn't really paid much attention to them. Besides, Andy went straight out again after he'd wolfed down some food. And, Daisy... well, she was so quiet, it was easy to forget that she was there. Daisy came around the counter and said hello to her mother. She didn't look at Annette.

"Say hi to Annette, Daisy." Jane's face took on a drawn quality that Annette hadn't noticed before.

"Hello, Annette." Daisy said dutifully, with her face still lowered.

"Hi, Daisy," Annette was struck by the girl's almost expressionless face.

"How was school?" Jane's happy persona had now completely disappeared.

"Same."

"Where's Andy?"

Daisy sighed, as though it was an effort to speak.

"He's got footy practice."

"Oh, that's right, I forgot. Do you want something to eat?" Jane asked.

"No, thanks."

Daisy left them and went and sat at a back table that was reserved for staff and family.

Annette noticed as she walked away how thin she was. Her legs stuck out from under her school dress like white sticks. Daisy took out her coloured pencils and a sketchbook and began to draw. Jane sighed and shook her head.

"Is she okay?" Annette asked in a whisper.

"No, she's not really." Jane's voice cracked a little. "She's been like this off and on for a long time now, but she seems to be getting worse again. It's like she's never particularly happy, not like Andy. So quiet and withdrawn, can't concentrate at school. I tried taking her to a counsellor in Wellspring, but it was a waste of time. I don't think she said much to him. We really don't know what's wrong. It's worrying though." A tear formed in the corner of Jane's eye. She quickly brushed it away.

"Sorry, look do you want to take a break. Maybe see if you can get her to eat something," Jane suggested.

Annette was surprised by the display of emotion.

At that moment a group of three young teenagers came in, laughing about some joke or event they'd just shared. Jane's cheery smile was quickly planted firmly back on her face as she served them.

Annette had been told she could eat whatever she wanted while at work, so she took a jam donut off the shelf and placed it on a plate along with a knife. Then, she grabbed a can of lemonade from the fridge and went over to the table where Daisy sat, immersed in her drawing.

"Do you mind if I sit here too?"

Daisy shrugged her shoulders, not looking up. Annette

sat a few chairs away from the child. Not wanting to seem as though she was hovering.

"This donut's so big. I can't eat it all. Would you help me and have half?"

Annette cut the donut in half. Then, she took half in her hand and pushed the plate with the remaining half towards Daisy.

"No, thanks," Daisy repeated.

The half donut sat there between them, bleeding jam. Annette ate her donut, sucked up her lemonade through a straw and wondered what else to say. This was a bit uncomfortable. She wasn't used to talking to kids. Daisy was so sad though, and that sadness drew her to the girl.

"What are you drawing?" Annette asked.

"Aw, nothing really," Daisy said, hardly moving her mouth, voice barely audible.

"Can I see?"

Daisy looked directly at Annette, as if deciding. Slowly, she pushed the sketch book towards Annette. The drawing was all in black, grey and red. The background was grey and swirly like storm clouds. A large, grotesque figure was in the centre of the drawing. Its body was elongated, ethereal, hands like claws. One hand was gripping a heart that dripped red. The heart had a bite out of it and more red globules were hanging from the grinning mouth of the monster.

Annette gulped. She was shocked. The picture was terrifying. Now, she really didn't know what to say, but she didn't want to upset Daisy.

"Well, you're good at drawing... it's a bit of a scary picture though," Annette said, with mock fear on her face, trying to make light of it.

"It's the church monster," Daisy said softly, but with a stubborn look that defied argument.

"What do you mean? There are no monsters at church."

"It's the church monster, I've seen him," she repeated with emphasis.

Then she turned a new page and began to draw again. The conversation appeared to be over, so Annette went back to the counter.

"Thanks," Jane whispered as Annette was putting her apron back on.

Annette was puzzled for a moment until she followed Jane's gaze. Daisy had pulled the plate across and was slowly eating the donut.

***

From then on Annette made a habit of exchanging at least a few words with Daisy when she saw her. It was more difficult when Andy was there, he was loud and demanded attention. Fortunately, he could only sit still long enough to have his snack, then he was off to play in the backyard or kick the footy with his mates. His mother would call out, "Don't forget your homework." Annette guessed that the reminder fell on deaf ears.

In the quiet moments Annette and Daisy had together, Daisy didn't say much, but she seemed to grow a little more comfortable with Annette each day. Annette would share her snack with Daisy and Daisy would eat—usually only a bite or two. Annette was happy though, to be making even a tiny difference in another life. She felt good about herself.

At home things were not going as well. Annette was finding she didn't really know what to say to her father. Maybe if Mark was still there, it would be easier, but he had left that Saturday afternoon after Ted and Grace's return a few weeks ago.

There was a divide between herself and her father that she didn't know how to cross. She wasn't even sure that she wanted to. It was next to impossible to relax around him. A legacy of the past perhaps? She felt guilty for feeling this way. Did it mean she couldn't forgive?

He certainly didn't seem interested in improving their relationship either, didn't seek her out. In fact, if he found her alone in a room, he would make an excuse to leave. Annette had made a commitment to herself to stick it out though. God—and Mark—had promised her a better life. And she was still hopeful it would turn out as well as Mark had led her to believe. If only Mark were here though, to reassure her.

Grace was kept very busy visiting the elderly and the sick in hospital and attending and running Bible studies. It seemed that her services had been sorely missed while she was away. She was sweet to Annette and they had a common interest in the garden. Grace had been delighted to discover that Annette had been responsible for weeding the back beds. Now, Grace had started to get the rest of the garden into shape. Annette helped her on the weekends. Ted did the mowing and the edges but expressed no interest in plants.

"I have a black thumb," he said.

Annette wasn't sure what he did with his time during the week when she wasn't there. Except that he went to Melbourne a few times on "church business". He went to one weeknight Bible study with Grace and a men's only Bible study. On Saturdays, he spent some time working on the car in the shed. And of course, Sundays were taken up with church. Later, he would read the Bible and other religious books. There had been no talk of him getting a job. So, Annette didn't know whether he and Grace planned to stay here or not. It would be rude to ask so she would have to just wait and see.

The transition from being out at nightclubs or working at night, left Annette a bit lost in the evenings. The nights when the four of them were home, they would gather for Bible study in the lounge room. Someone would read something from the Bible, or from a devotional book. Then Grace, Ted or Esther would lead in prayer. This ritual felt quite strange to Annette at first, but at least it was something to do. After the study though, the long evenings stretched ahead of her. Grace encouraged her to read the Bible, but it was hard going, and she grew bored quickly. She found herself reading a passage over and over—not taking much in. Although she tried to persevere, she couldn't stick at it for more than short periods. She used to enjoy watching TV, but even that was limited now, because there were so many programs considered unsuitable for Christians.

And, as she wondered a hundred times a day, when would Mark return? Boys, rock music, alcohol—they had been the antidote to loneliness and boredom. None of those options were available now. This way of living was tough, but it was what she wanted, so she would force herself to get used to it.

It was Friday afternoon and Esther was due to pick Annette up from work. Annette had ridden the bike to work all week, so this would be a nice change. And, both Ted and Grace would be out at their Bible study tonight. They usually ate dinner with another couple before the study and so had left before she or Esther arrived home. Annette was looking forward to it being just her and Esther for a change. She hoped Esther wasn't going out. Maybe they could do something together, play a game, watch a movie.

Esther was still very much an unknown quantity to Annette. Although Esther seemed to have forgiven Ted for his transgressions, Annette didn't think she completely trusted him. In fact, Esther seemed to be out more and more since Ted and Grace had returned. Even when she was home, she tended to stay in her room mostly, saying she had students' work to correct. Annette wasn't so sure.

Esther pulled up out the front of the bakery and Annette jumped in. The aroma in the car made her immediately hungry.

"Something smells amazing," Annette said.

"I picked up takeaway in Wellspring. Do you like Chinese?"

"Yes, I love it."

"Hope you don't mind but I thought we'd have dinner with Violet."

"No, I don't mind at all."

Even better, she liked Violet.

Violet's apartment was beautiful—just like Violet. Although there was an assortment of furniture that looked like it might have been gathered from second-hand shops —it was put together tastefully. The colours were vibrant. A rich red sofa was central in the lounge-dining room and two cross-back chairs stood on opposite sides of a charming old round dining table nearer the kitchen. Every wall was hung with artwork. Annette scanned the room and realised the paintings and prints were all of females. Women and girls from various, different cultures. Annette could see into the bedroom where a chipped, but pretty, cast iron double bed was laid with a deep green and purple satin quilt. On the bedroom wall, Annette could see a painting of an African woman with her breasts exposed. There was another picture that she recognised because she'd seen it a pub in Melbourne. Chloe! Yes, that was it. The famous full length portrait of a young naked woman that she'd seen at the Young and Jackson's hotel on Flinders Street.

"Do you like my artworks?" Violet asked.

"Yes, they're lovely." Annette didn't want to be rude, but she had to ask, "Is it okay to have pictures like those..." She indicated towards Chloe. "...when you're in the church?"

Violet laughed, "If someone from the church comes around, I usually shut the bedroom door, just in case they don't appreciate great art. You're not offended, are you?"

Still smiling, she lifted her eyebrows, a little mischievously. A naked painting wasn't something Annette would have thought twice about before, but these days she found herself questioning her attitudes about a lot of things. It was getting more and more difficult to know what was okay and what wasn't. Hadn't the pastor read a verse the Sunday before last about not being seen naked in front of others? She would have to look that up and check.

"Of course not," Annette said. Even though she wasn't completely sure whether it was okay not to be. "What do you think?" she asked Esther.

"Well, I think they're beautiful." Esther appeared to be weighing her words. She put a hand on Violet's shoulder. "I wouldn't have them on my wall though."

The tenderness of the gesture didn't seem to change the harsh impact of Esther's words. A cloud moved across Violet's face and a look passed between the two of them that Annette couldn't quite fathom. Just as quickly, it was gone, and they were both smiling again.

"Let's go and eat," Esther said, as she moved towards the kitchen door.

Chapter 12

Annette was excited. Another week had dragged by and finally, finally, Mark was coming home for the weekend to run the youth service on Sunday. Mark was picking her up on his way through and she could hardly wait. At last, time alone with him, so that they could talk.

At 5pm exactly, Annette stood waiting out the front of the bakery. Daisy ambled out and sat down at an outdoor table near her. Daisy didn't usually say anything except a thin, "Bye," when Annette stepped onto her pushbike or climbed into Esther's car. And then, she would duck back inside. Today she seemed to have picked up on Annette's mood.

"You are very smiley today," Daisy said.

"Am I? I didn't realise."

"Yes, since I got back from school, when I look at you, you're smiling, and there's nobody there."

Annette was a bit embarrassed and hoped no-one else had noticed. Maybe it wouldn't hurt to confide in Daisy about the source of her happiness. It wasn't as though Daisy talked to anybody else much.

"Mark's coming home tonight to stay for the weekend. He's picking me up."

"Is he your boyfriend?"

"No, of course not, he's a pastor."

"Hmm," Daisy said.

Sometimes, Daisy seemed way older than her ten years. The car pulled up then and Daisy waved goodbye—her mouth curved, ever so slightly upwards.

Annette had forgotten how gorgeous he was. When he smiled his wide, warm smile she just wanted to melt into him. Fatigue was showing in the dark circles around his eyes, but that just made him more appealing to her. He was a such a tireless worker for God. How she wished she could run her fingers through his hair while he kissed her hard right now.

She wanted this to be a Friday night that they were going home together to their own cosy house. There, she would cook him steak, mash and peas and they would talk together about their day. After that, they would cuddle on the couch, eat ice-cream and watch a movie. When they went to bed, they would make love for hours. It would be sweet but also amazing because, with Mark, sex would feel passionate and safe and wonderful all at the same time. All of this ran through her mind in the fraction of a second before he spoke.

"Hi, great to see you. You look good," he said, then quickly added. "I mean you look well... that's what I mean."

Mark looked away with a slight shake of his head, but Annette didn't care, she flushed with pleasure at his *faux pas,* glad she'd taken the time to freshen up her makeup and hair before leaving work.

"Thanks, you too. You also look good—and well," she said. Made brazen both by his words, and by the way he was looking at her.

***

They were all home for dinner that night and when they were all seated Mark announced that he had some news. Annette was instantly apprehensive. What now?

"Do you remember Pastor Dean was taking a month off to visit the Holy Lands? Well he's decided to take twelve months and make it a long sabbatical instead. He realised he needs a longer break—well, I think his wife had something to do with that. Anyway, he's leaving in two weeks. So..." He paused looking at each of them in turn. "...I applied to be his replacement, and I was successful." Mark was positively beaming.

Grace was the first to react, "That's wonderful sweetheart. I'm so proud of you," she said. Then she stood up from the table and went over to kiss him on the cheek.

"I'm sorry I didn't say anything before, but we're not really allowed to, not until it's official."

"Good for you," Esther chimed in. "It'll be great for the youth to have you around more often."

Annette was thrilled. He would be coming back here to live. Her mind was racing ahead again to their future together.

Ted cleared his throat, "Uh-hum..."

Mark glanced across at Ted. His expression a little less excited now. "And that's not the only news. The church board had some concerns over me being so young." His smile was gone. "They wanted an older person to work alongside me. An experienced elder, they said. They suggested Ted, and I was agreeable to that. So, Ted will be my assistant, in a lay pastor role. It will be announced at church on Sunday, but hey, you need to keep it under your hats until then."

Grace's eyes widened, taking in Ted's pleased look.

"You didn't tell me this. So, I suppose that means we're not going to go back to Thailand?"

"As Mark says, we aren't allowed to discuss the selection process until it's finalised." His tone held a warning.

Annette recognised it and felt the old fear. She hoped Grace could hear the steel in his voice too.

"I mean, it's wonderful news, but I'm your wife. You couldn't tell me?"

"I didn't see the need to discuss it. You understand that as the head of the house, it's my decision," his tone was getting even darker.

Grace hesitated, then backed down. "Yes, of course, darling. I'm sure you're following God's will and that's always the best way."

The atmosphere relaxed immediately. Annette became aware she'd been holding her breath, and now she released it in a silent sigh.

"I'll receive the same stipend I received in Thailand, so financially I'm in the same boat. You might have to look for part time work though. Perhaps you could get your old job back at the nursery?" he suggested to Grace.

"Well, I'm sure we'll work things out. But right now, I think we should celebrate. I'm going to get a bottle of sparkling grape juice that I've been keeping for just such a special occasion," she said. Her voice was cheerful, as though the last few moments had never happened.

***

Esther went out shortly after dinner, saying she would be back late in the morning as she was staying at a friend's overnight. Shortly after she left, Ted and Grace went to their Bible study. At last, she and Mark were alone.

"Well, how is it all going?" Mark asked.

Should she tell Mark about the continuing tension between herself and her father? No, Mark would be disappointed to hear that. Besides, everything would be better now that he was coming here to live. She settled for safer topics; work, helping Grace in the garden, learning more about God. She also told Mark about her blossoming friendship with Daisy, expecting him to be impressed by her efforts to help the young girl.

"Daisy is such a sweet kid. I don't know why she's so sad all the time, but she is talking to me a little more each day."

"What has she said to you?" he asked, seeming instantly alert.

So lovely to hear his concern for each and every church member, young and old.

"Oh, she doesn't talk much, but she draws... the most awful pictures. I mean, awful, as in frightening. 'It's the church monster,' she told me," Annette followed this with a little chuckle, not wanting Mark to think she took it seriously. She cut it short, however, when she saw the dark cloud move across Mark's face.

"Hmm..." He seemed caught up in thought.

Then, abruptly, he chuckled too. "Poor kid! Maybe, we shouldn't describe the devil so graphically all the time, when we really don't know for sure what he looks like."

Of course, that's who Daisy meant. Why hadn't she thought of that? What a relief. Now she could talk to Daisy about it and set her mind at rest.

Mark shrugged then and shook himself a little, as though removing a heavy jacket.

"Let's talk about happier things. What do you think of my news?"

"I think it's brilliant; I'm very happy for you," she hesitated, "I'm just not so sure about my father being a pastor... a lay pastor you said?"

"Yes, that's a pastor who hasn't been to seminary. Why, what's the problem?"

The question of whether Ted really had changed as much as they all seemed to believe still remained for Annette. After reading lots of verses that talked about the way Christians should behave, she wasn't sure that Ted was making the grade.

Not wanting to upset Mark, she measured her words carefully.

"I'm not sure whether he has his anger under control. Doesn't the Bible say, 'For a man's anger does not bring about the righteous life that God desires'. Shouldn't he be..." She hesitated, watching Mark's face carefully. "...I don't know, less moody, if he's going to be a pastor."

Mark looked impressed when she quoted the Bible, but that changed quickly.

"There you go, sitting in judgement again. The Bible also says, 'None is righteous, no not one.' None of us are perfect, we all err, because we're all human."

Yes, he was right, she was so judgemental. As if she was perfect herself. Mark's face changed again; he was watching her intently. She couldn't read his expression.

"Take me for example, I was looking at you in a way I shouldn't have this afternoon."

Annette's heart started to hammer in her chest. Well, this was unexpected. In that moment she became conscious of how she might appear, sitting opposite him with her summer skirt ridden up just above her knees, legs slightly apart. For the first time, he was admitting he was attracted to her. At least, she thought that was what was happening. It would be nice to be sure.

"I don't mind, Mark... I like you that way too."

Mark's tongue slipped out of his mouth and came to rest on his lower lip. Annette became conscious of the warmth rising between her thighs.

"Sometimes it's really hard to do the right thing," his voice was husky and low.

As he stood up, he said in the same low voice, "I'd better go and do my study."

Now his tongue was sliding over and moistening his top lip. He continued to stand there. Annette waited on the couch, torn, she wanted him so badly, but she didn't want to cause him to sin. And, she didn't want to sin either.

"No, don't go," she said softly.

That was all it took. He pushed her down on the couch. His hands were everywhere at once. Squeezing her breasts, pushing her skirt up, pulling her pants down. Rubbing her. It wasn't quite how she'd imagined it, but she was still glad it was happening. Now, he was undoing his belt, releasing his cock. She pushed her hand in between their bodies and grabbed his penis and held it firmly, it felt good and hard. She pulled it a few times. Mark groaned, then shuddered, and suddenly her hand and stomach was sticky and wet.

"I'm sorry, I'm sorry... I shouldn't have done that," he stammered. He shook his head as he lifted himself off her.

Annette pushed her skirt back down over the stickiness and went to touch his hair with her clean hand. Quickly, he moved his head away and stood, holding his pants up.

"I shouldn't have done that," he muttered again.

"No, neither of you should have."

Annette and Mark looked in the direction of the voice.

The voice belonged to Ted, who stood in the lounge room doorway, glaring at them. Grace stood beside him. Her eyes were downcast.

"Mark, how could you?" she said, her voice low and

laden with disappointment.

"It takes two to tango Grace, I'm sure it wasn't just his idea." Ted raised his eyebrows and looked directly at Annette. "It seems that it was providential that our study was cancelled. You two clearly can't be trusted to be alone together."

Annette didn't like what she saw in his eyes. Suddenly, she felt dirty and ashamed. She flew off the couch and strode quickly to her room.

Ted's voice called out behind her, "We'll discuss this more in the morning."

Annette slammed the door with frustration as the tears welled up. What's to discuss? I'm an adult, he can't tell me what to do. Shaking with anger, she paced up and down the room, a scathing monologue running through her head. That bastard, he wasn't there for her for so many years and now he's all pious and righteous. What does he know about relationships? Look what he did to Mum!

She loved Mark and she would be with him. No matter what her father said. He might be able to control everyone else in this family, but he wouldn't control her.

Finally, when her anger had run its course, she sat down heavily on the bed. Beneath the anger there was hurt, disappointment. It wasn't just Grace and Ted's unexpected arrival that had ruined everything. The whole event hadn't gone as she'd hoped. It was all so fast—not romantic at all. Though, she couldn't imagine that Mark didn't care about her. It must be because he's inexperienced, doesn't know exactly what to do. Nothing about how it happened fit with her fantasies of him as a lover, but it did make sense. He might even be a virgin. Hmm, yes, that was probably why. They would just have to get used to each other.

Another possibility though—and one that she really didn't want to entertain—was that they may not get another opportunity. Mark seemed to really regret his actions, even before he knew Ted and Grace had seen him. Maybe he would ask her to leave. Or Ted, or even Grace might throw her out? She couldn't bear the thought of not seeing Mark again. On the other hand, if she did stay how could she face everyone? Her father had made her seem like a dirty slut. What would Esther think of her now? The weight of their actions began to sink in. How would this affect Mark's role as pastor? Would he be sacked? The possibilities kept tumbling around, one on top of the other, until the early hours of the morning when she must have finally fallen asleep, still fully clothed.

***

The clean, freshness of the new morning, didn't match Annette's mood the next day. Still feeling ashamed and dirty, she showered and put on clean clothes, but that didn't help. She passed Mark in the hallway on her way back from the bathroom and he didn't look at her or speak to her. Why hadn't she let Mark leave the room when he wanted to? She shouldn't have asked him to stay. This was all her fault. Back in her room again, the regret deepened. She knelt and prayed for forgiveness for herself and for Mark. Asked that Mark not suffer any consequences because of her actions. The responsibility for what had happened sat squarely on her shoulders she said to God and then promised Him that she would leave if she had to, so that Mark's ministry wouldn't be affected. She acknowledged how sinful and wrong her actions were, and that she would stop herself if she ever found herself in this situation again. From now on she would wait until she was married to have sex. That was her commitment to her Lord. When she stood up from the prayer, she felt much better—felt cleansed of her sin.

Annette hovered in the kitchen doorway. Ted and Grace were seated at the table. Ted had the Bible open in front of him. Mark looked sheepish, he glanced up at Annette and gave her a quick smile, and then looked down again. It was as though they were two naughty schoolchildren in the principal's office. Ted had a very serious face on, Grace looked dejected.

Annette had repented and was determined to be good from now on, but as much as she trusted that God had forgiven her, she wasn't so sure about her father. Her chest tightened and breathing became more difficult.

"Take a seat," Ted instructed.

Annette took her time sitting down, desperately trying to calm herself. Reminding herself that she was an adult now. But she didn't feel like an adult, she felt like a frightened child.

"We've been discussing the implications of the events of last night," Ted began. "Do you understand that what you did was wrong?" He directed this to Annette.

"I understand that the Bible says you shouldn't have sex before you're married..." Annette said. She wanted to sound matter-of-fact, like he couldn't control her. Like it was none of his business. It didn't come out that way, her voice was shaky and hollow. Not confident at all.

"I keep telling you we didn't have sex... we didn't actually do it," Mark said. His voice had a pleading quality to it.

Ted shook his head and said, "Mark do you think we're stupid? We saw you. Please, don't keep saying that, neither of us believes you. You're making a worse fool of yourself."

Grace continued to stare at the table, saying nothing.

"Mum, you know I wouldn't lie about something so serious. Please believe me, Mum."

"Be a man, son. Own up to what you've done." Grace looked at Mark as though her heart might break.

Annette wondered whether she should speak up and verify what Mark was saying. It seemed hopeless though. Ted and Grace seemed immovable. And, she didn't want to be accused of being a liar too. Besides, she was pretty sure that they would have had sex, if Mark hadn't climaxed so fast. It really did seem like Mark was splitting hairs.

"So, Annette, I can see you're a bit unsure about all this. Let's clear things up for you. What do you think marriage means?"

Where was this conversation was going? Why were they talking about marriage?

"Marriage is when a couple have a wedding ceremony —"

Ted interrupted, "Ah, now that's where you're wrong. A marriage is nothing to do with a wedding. The wedding is only the outward celebration."

Annette's fear was giving way to frustration. Just get to the point Ted. Were they going to throw her out or not?

"Well, you can't be married without a wedding," she said, feeling as though she was stating the obvious.

"Well, actually you can. Let me read to you from the Bible—Genesis, Chapter 4, verse 1: 'And Adam knew his wife Eve, and she conceived and bare Cain and said, I have gotten a man from the Lord.'"

Annette looked at Mark, then at Grace. Both were looking down—no clues there. Ted must have realised that she still had no idea what he was talking about.

He sighed, then continued, "When the Bible says 'Adam knew his wife' it means they had... intimate relations. This was obviously the case because she, Eve, became pregnant afterwards. Do you think they had a wedding in the sense that people do now?" He didn't wait for an answer. "No, of course they didn't. There were no religious rites for weddings in the Old Testament. They had wedding feasts to celebrate, but the way they became man and wife was by having sex, and then, of course, they had children."

What was he getting at?

"So?" she asked, still mystified.

"Let's look at the New Testament. In 1st Corinthians, the Bible says: 'Do you not know that your bodies are members of Christ himself? Shall I then take the members of Christ and unite them with a prostitute? Never! Do you not know that he who unites himself with a prostitute is one with her in body? For it is said, the two will become one flesh.' The Bible is clearly talking about a man having sex with a prostitute and, when they have sex, that unites them. When you have sex with someone you 'become one flesh'. Both in Genesis in the Old Testament and in Ephesians in the New Testament, the Bible states that a man shall become one flesh with his wife. Are you starting to understand now—the implications of what you've done?"

She looked at Mark. Again, he gave her a weak smile.

"Of course, according to the Bible if you weren't a willing participant, you would have the right to refuse to marry Mark, but it's pretty obvious that you were just as guilty as he was. So anyway, there really is no sex before marriage in the eyes of God, if you have sex with someone you are simultaneously joining with them—marrying them."

Marry Mark!!!

He was still talking, but Annette wasn't listening, the words 'marry Mark', kept repeating over and over in her head until finally they sank in. That's what this was all about. It was ludicrous. People don't get married just because they've had sex. If that were true, she would have been married a lot!

An unexpected laugh rumbled up from her belly interrupting Ted, who was saying that they needed to keep themselves from the sin of adultery now by staying together for the rest of their lives.

"You can't be serious. We're living in the 1980's," She was shaking her head.

No-one else was laughing. Mark breathed in deeply and then sighed the breath out heavily before he spoke.

"I'm a minister Annette. I have to do what I would expect anyone else to do in this situation. We must honour the commitment we've made with our bodies. It is *true* that *we didn't actually have sex...*" he looked at Ted as he said this, then back to Annette, "but... the intent was there. In God's eyes, it's the same. I'm sorry if you weren't ready for this, but we have to do what's right before God and the church."

Annette wanted to be with Mark, and she knew he liked her, but this was a huge step. And it wasn't happening at all how she had imagined a wedding proposal would happen. This felt more like a punishment for being bad, than something to celebrate. On the other hand, she had done the wrong thing. As usual she hadn't said no, even though now, she had known it was a sin. She probably deserved whatever fate God dished out to her. And besides, she had imagined a perfect future with Mark and here it was being handed to her—without question—she would be married to him if she went along with their craziness. The whole situation was bizarre, but the idea was quickly beginning to grow on her. Grace was talking now about a wedding, an actual proper wedding ceremony in the church. Annette would be a bride.

"Of course, there will have to be a wedding service in the church. We'll have to have it soon, but not so soon, that it seems like it's been rushed for any reason."

Mark turned to his mother. "Whatever you think Mum, I'll leave you in charge of that side of things," his voice was flat, defeated.

He didn't sound at all pleased with the situation. That was a bit unsettling. Maybe it was just the shock, like it was for her. He would get used to the idea. They would be great together.

Ted, however, looked quite smug and self-satisfied.

"You do understand you can't talk about the circumstances of your engagement to anyone. Not that you would, I guess. But now that you are to be a pastor's wife, there is no talking to anyone about your personal business. You can't say anything that might reflect badly on the church or our family. You do understand that, don't you?"

Oh, so that's why he was so happy. He didn't want her telling anyone in the church about how he'd treated her mother. Not that she'd planned to, but it was annoying that he was so focused on himself in this situation.

She nodded, "Yes, I understand."

"And, of course, you two will want to get a place of your own," Ted said, with an even wider smile.

Mark nodded his agreement, his head still down.

So, Ted would get to keep her quiet and also, get them both out of the house. It was quite the coup for him. She didn't mind though; she would be setting up house with Mark—just the two of them.

Grace rose from the table and got a frypan out of the cupboard to start breakfast. Her face much brighter now, as she prattled on about the wedding.

"We'll make the church so lovely with flowers and candles. Esther will play, and we could ask young William to sing some songs that are fitting. Oh, and we'll have to get you a dress Annette, I've seen some gorgeous ones in the bridal shop in Wellspring—" She turned suddenly. "Oh, my dear girl, I've just remembered that you haven't been baptised yet! We'll have to do that privately, just the family, otherwise it might raise some eyebrows."

Annette continued to sit in stunned silence as the arrangements for her future were made right in front of her.

Chapter 13

This was not a fairy-tale engagement by any stretch of the imagination. Nevertheless, Annette was happy. Happier than she could ever remember being. Soon she would be Mark's wife, his partner, his lover, his friend for life. She daydreamed constantly about her wedding day and the wonderful life that lay in front of them. The date was set for two months' time.

Esther didn't seem to be aware of the real reason for the marriage. Although she commented about the speed of which it had happened, she said she was happy for them. She did ask Annette though, whether she'd considered what it meant to be a pastor's wife. Violet had responded in a similar way. With kind concern in her eyes, Violet had wondered out loud how Annette might feel about being married to a pastor.

How strange that someone like her, could end up in such an important position. Still, it was a perfect example of God's grace though, that He wouldn't penalise her for her past, or even for her recent sin with Mark, but would still heap blessing on her. Besides, the current pastor's wife seemed happy enough. Her smile was pretty much a permanent fixture on her face. And, she seemed to always have a kind word for all the church members. The pastor and his wife appeared to be loved and respected. The congregation reacted with sadness to the news of them leaving in two weeks. Why wouldn't she want to be a pastor's wife when the couple were treated so well?

Despite their disappointment about losing their old pastor, the church responded with much congratulations and excitement both to the news of Mark being their local pastor for twelve months and to the announcement of the couple's engagement. Of course, they didn't know how long Mark and Annette had been together. Or, that she was a brand-new Christian. Since they had both been living in Melbourne, nobody questioned the timing. They probably assumed that the two had been courting for a long time and had just kept their relationship quiet.

Everybody seemed pleased about Ted's appointment as well. Although some asked questions about who would represent the church at the orphanage now. Ted responded that someone from Wellspring Church had expressed an interested in volunteering, but that the appointment hadn't been finalised yet.

Things were going so well for Annette that she floated blissfully through the days. The ever-present empty feeling that had plagued her in the past was quickly becoming a distant memory. Yet, a twinge of apprehension lurked in the background. How did Mark feel about her and the impending wedding now?

Mark had returned to his work as youth pastor in Melbourne, until the transfer occurred, so she hadn't seen him since the Sunday afternoon when the announcement was made in church. She'd heard Ted on the phone in the hallway, talking to Mark a few times since. Mark hadn't asked to speak to her. Maybe he was still embarrassed about what had happened. Hopefully, that was the reason he hadn't spoken with her.

Mostly though, she managed to put her doubts aside by remembering the way he'd looked at her that day and how much he'd wanted her. Of course he might be a bit hesitant at the moment but soon they would see each other again and then the reason for their sudden engagement wouldn't matter anymore. He would look at her with that hunger in his eyes and hug her and kiss her. It would all go more slowly next time—more like she'd imagined. They would be happy together. All she needed was for him to be there with her, and it would all work out. Clearly, it was what God wanted for them both.

In her enthusiasm, she had even rung Tracy. Tracy sounded cheerful—like she was happy to hear from Annette. That was until Annette told her the good news. Of course, she should have expected that Tracy would have misgivings—still, it would have been nice if Tracy had been a little more positive.

"Really? You've known him such a short time though."

"I was hoping you'd be happy for me."

"I am happy for you, if you're sure. But marriage is so... so final. You don't think it would be better to wait for a while, to be sure?"

"We are waiting, the wedding's not for two months. And don't worry, I am sure. Well as sure as anyone can be, I suppose... I would like to send you an invitation. Do you think you would come?"

"Of course, of course I'll come. I'd love to come. Congratulations."

Tracy was the one person Annette might have been able to tell how she came to be engaged. However, she doubted that Tracy would understand. She'd had trouble with the concept at first herself. Actually... Tracy would probably laugh —much as she had done. The idea that seemed so ludicrous in the beginning, now made perfect sense. She couldn't expect an unbeliever to comprehend God's laws the way that she could now.

It would be good to see Tracy again though. There was no-one really that she could talk to here—not like she could talk to Tracy. To make a good impression on people she couldn't really be herself. Not the self that still craved alcohol and fatty fish and chips on a Friday night. The self that missed the nightlife of Melbourne, the bands and the dancing. The self that had wanted to have sex with Mark even when she knew it was wrong. Tracy would understand those urges. What she wouldn't understand is why Annette wanted to stop them. Should she ask Tracy to be a bridesmaid. Probably not, Tracy wasn't a Christian, so it wouldn't be appropriate.

Another problem was whether or not she should invite Rose. Should she even tell her mother about the wedding? Annette hadn't discussed this with Grace or Ted. How would they feel about seeing Rose? It would be easier not to invite her, but although she wasn't the best mother in the world, she was still her mother. It would be weird, wouldn't it, to be married without Rose there?

She hadn't given Rose her phone number. Not when she lived at Tracy's, and definitely not here. In fact, Rose wouldn't even know where she was living now. Perhaps—if she knew—Rose would even be proud of the new life that Annette had found for herself. That was highly unlikely though, when Rose had practically thrown Annette out of the house.

Funny though, the more time Annette spent around Ted, the more she empathised with her mother. It was hard not to bend to Ted's will. And, even though he was a Christian, Annette still felt intimidated by him. Bob must have been a welcome change for her mother, he wasn't scary at all. He didn't drink. She was starting to understand why her mother wanted to be with someone who made her feel safe.

The last time she had seen her mother and Bob was at Christmas. Her mother had cooked a turkey and was cheerful and happy when Annette arrived. Annette, however, sulked throughout the meal. Even though both Rose and Bob tried hard to make conversation with her, she answered only in monosyllables. By the time Annette was ready to leave, the old sadness had returned to Rose's face. Thinking back, Annette knew she was responsible for that sad look. She could've made a bit more effort with them, she supposed. Maybe, she would call Rose after all. Sometime soon, just not right now.

***

On Monday morning and Annette arrived at the bakery at 9am, glad of the distraction the workdays brought. Time was dragging now; she couldn't wait to see Mark. Friday night—five long days to get through and then he would be home for good. A twinge of excitement coursed through her as she tied her apron on.

She busied herself helping Jack serve the few customers in the store.

"Where's Jane?" she asked, when the bakery had emptied, and they were alone again.

"She's upstairs," he said. His eyebrows drew together. "She actually asked me to send you up there, after the rush. That is, if you don't mind? It's Daisy."

Worried now, Annette took her apron off.

"What's wrong, is she okay?"

"Not really." He shook his head and then went out to

the kitchen.

Jane opened the door to Annette's knock and came outside to join Annette on the porch, closing the door behind her.

"I'm at my wit's end with that girl. She was getting better, I'm sure she was. The time you were spending with her was helping, but now..." Jane spoke in a hushed tone. "She won't go to school, she won't eat and worst of all she won't say what's wrong. She's been like this since we got home from church yesterday. She was okay when we left the house. I just don't understand what's happening."

"Is she sick?" Annette asked.

"No, she says she's not sick, but she looks sick. When I suggest going to the doctor, she gets frantic. I know I shouldn't be involving you in our problems, but she does like you. Would you talk to her? See if you can find out what's wrong?"

"Of course, I will."

Jane led Annette into Daisy's bedroom.

"Look Daisy, Annette's come to visit you."

Daisy didn't respond, didn't look at either of them. Her eyes were fixed—with a vacant stare—on the wall in front of her. Jane looked as though she might cry. She gave a soft sigh and turned her head away.

"Well, I'll leave you girls to it then, I'd better go and give Jack a hand."

"Hi Daisy, can I sit down?"

Still no response. Annette took a seat on the bed.

Daisy was pale, beads of sweat on her forehead, seemingly unaware of Annette's presence. Annette was really concerned now.

"Daisy!" she spoke sharply, trying to get her attention.

Daisy shook her head as though waking from a bad dream. Now, she looked dazed and confused. She began to sniffle and then to cry.

Annette moved towards her to give her a hug. Daisy stiffened and backed away as though she didn't know Annette. Then as recognition dawned, she moved forward again, lay her head on Annette's shoulder and sobbed. Annette held her for a long time until the heartrending sounds subsided. Then she held Daisy at arm's length and looked into her eyes.

"Daisy, you have to tell me what's wrong."

"I can't." Daisy sniffled. She looked terrified.

"Why not? What are you so scared of?"

Daisy averted her eyes. Annette followed her gaze and noticed the sketchbook on a small chest of drawers in the far corner of the room. She smiled at Daisy.

"You don't have to be scared of the Devil, Daisy. He won't hurt you; he has no power over you because you love God."

Annette walked over and picked up the sketchbook and moved back towards the bed.

Daisy whispered in a desperate voice, "No, no, it isn't the devil! It's the monster! Don't bring it near me!"

Surprised by the strength of Daisy's reaction, Annette asked, "Can I look at it over here?"

Daisy sighed. "Yes."

Annette sat on a stool near the drawers, opened the book and leafed through. She found the picture that Daisy had shown her weeks ago—when they had first talked in the bakery.

"Did you see the church monster again? Is that what's upset you?" Annette asked.

Daisy took a deep breath but didn't speak.

"Daisy, I want to help you. Tell me did this monster frighten you?"

Daisy still looked terrified, she nodded slowly.

"He... hurts me."

Annette was confused, this was all familiar somehow. She, herself, had been plagued by night terrors—waking sweaty and frightened from dreams of monsters chasing her. Legs paralysed, unable to escape in her nightmares. Annette recognised the fear, she had felt it too, and not just at night either. Often, she felt it for no particular reason. It came out of nowhere and left her strangely depressed afterwards.

Logically, Annette knew Daisy had imagined this "church monster". Jane had said Daisy was okay before they left for church and was like this when she got home. Nothing out of the ordinary had happened at church. Nevertheless, she recognised that Daisy's fear was probably as real her own fears which had no logical explanation either. Annette couldn't just dismiss Daisy's imaginings—they were obviously having a very real impact. Annette thumbed backwards through the sketch book, coming to an earlier picture.

This picture had the same ethereal nature as the other and this monster was also grinning. Again, the monster had the long claw like hands. One hand was gripping what looked like a tiny doll, squeezing it. The other hand held an elongated finger vertically to its lips. There was a ballooned caption coming from its mouth.

Annette's chest began to tighten. She stared at the drawing and it became harder for her to breathe. Her pulse was racing and she felt sick. The words above the drawing triggered a long-forgotten memory. There was a sensation of heavy weight on top of her and then pain shooting through her. The feeling of intense terror was increasing. As was the burning pain that rhythmically ripped through her. Annette felt trapped, breathless, she tried to move, but was paralysed with fear. Then, as though from a long way away, through a dense fog, Annette heard Daisy's plaintive voice.

"Annette, are you alright?"

The experience was probably momentary, but it felt like it had lasted for ages. She shook her dazed head and looked around the room. Seeing the pretty pink bedspread, and then Daisy's face, she remembered where she was. She felt her chest and gut begin to uncoil and her breath slowed. She still felt sick, confused and frightened, but she needed to pull herself together. What was going on? What had happened to her? No time to worry about that now. She was supposed to be here for Daisy. Annette sighed. It was a long, deep sigh.

"I'm okay... It's just that... seeing those words upset me a bit. Was the monster calling you that?"

Daisy didn't answer.

Annette had to steel herself, before she could say the words aloud. "Why did the monster say, *bad girl*?"

Daisy's head was lowered. She shook her head almost imperceptibly.

"Can't say," she whispered.

"Daisy... is the monster real?"

Daisy looked up at Annette, as though pleading with her to stop.

"Daisy, you have to tell me, is the monster real?"

"Of course he is, but you can't tell my parents about him, you can't tell them... not ever, or..."

"Or what?"

Daisy shook her head. Annette sat down on the bed again.

"It's okay, Daisy, I won't let him hurt you again. I promise."

Annette had no idea how she would do that, but she was determined to protect Daisy from threat, whether that threat was real or only imagined. Deep down though, in a frightened, fragmented, almost completely hidden away part of her, Annette knew that the threat was indeed, very real.

Chapter 14

Daisy had gone to school for the rest of the week. However, she still looked unwell—pale and distant —when Annette saw her in the afternoons at the bakery. Daisy didn't seem to want to talk or interact much, but Annette tried to chat with her a little each day, keeping the topics light for fear of deepening Daisy's distress. Annette had no real plan as to how she would protect Daisy, other than to keep an eye on her at church. That seemed to be the place where she was the most frightened.

Annette was worried about her young friend, but it was more than that. She felt unsettled and couldn't put her finger on what was wrong. The feeling sat just out of consciousness, like a rogue wave at night, unseen, but constantly threatening her.

This evening felt different though. Annette waited with delicious anticipation. Mark would be here soon. Everyone was out, they would have the place to themselves. Ted and Grace were at Bible study and Esther was probably at Violet's.

Esther spent most of her spare time there now. It had

crossed Annette's mind that the two might be lovers. She dismissed the idea again just as quickly. Surely, it wasn't possible when they were Christians. Annette was pretty sure that being homosexual was unacceptable in the eyes of the church. The church here in Pleasant Valley took a strong stance against that particular sin. The pastor had called the practice an "abomination" and had followed up by saying, "It's Adam and Eve, not Adam and Steve". The congregation had laughed at the time and she had smiled right along with them, even though she'd felt a little uncomfortable.

Homosexuality wasn't something she had thought about much. She hadn't met any lesbians—that she knew of—before and it wasn't really talked about in her home. Except, of course, for Ted referring to blokes as *queer* if they didn't drink beer or whisky. What if Violet and Esther were lovers though? She felt a twinge of sadness for them. They had a right to be happy too.

The sound of car tyres crunching on the gravel driveway made Annette leap to her feet. It's him. By the time she opened the front door, he was pulling bags out of the boot of the car.

"Hello. Good to see you," she said as she approached him with a wide smile on her face.

"Hi," he replied, and then stood there for a moment with bags in both his hands.

Why wasn't he dropping those bags, running to her and hugging her tight? What was that uncertain smile about? Should she take the lead? A bit difficult when his were full.

Disappointed, she gave up waiting and asked, "Can I give you a hand?"

He shook his head. "No, don't worry, I'll get the rest tomorrow."

He walked past her towards the house, and she turned and followed. After he had deposited the bags in his room, he returned to the lounge room where she was sitting on the couch. Still standing, he leaned over and gave her a peck on the cheek. Confused—yet glad of even this small display of affection—she jumped up and wrapped her arms around him. He lifted his arms and gave a very brief, light squeeze in return. Then, after just a moment, dropped them again and moved away to sit in the armchair opposite her.

"Where is everyone?" he asked. There was a lightness to his voice that didn't match the uncomfortable look on his face.

Annette was struggling not to cry. This was not at all what she'd expected at their reunion. She breathed deeply and tried to settle herself down. They should be enveloped in each other's arms right now.

"Well, Ted and your mother are at a Bible study and Esther is at Violet's..." A flash of anger towards him whipped through her. "...as usual," she added with a wry smile.

Mark's head cocked to the side, instantly alert.

"What do you mean as usual?"

Did he have suspicions about them too? Annette instantly regretted her words. When she spoke again, she tried to make her voice sound as casual as possible.

"Oh well, they're good friends, I guess it's natural for friends to spend time together."

Annette rolled her eyes. "Not much else to do here in the bush, is there?"

The last comment drew a frown from Mark. Nevertheless, he seemed to relax and accept her assessment of Esther and Violet's relationship, which was a relief. She was still angry though. Why was he behaving as though they were still pastor and parishioner? This wasn't fair, she had rights now—they were engaged.

"What's going on? Have you changed your mind about me?"

"I don't know what you're talking about."

Annette's voice increased in volume. "You're over there, I'm here. We haven't seen each other for weeks. It seems obvious to me that something's wrong with this picture."

"What more do you want, Annette? I'm still planning to marry you. If you expect me to be all over you, that's not going to happen. Our behaviour needs to be completely above board now. I'm a pastor, Annette, don't forget that. I don't ever want to be embarrassed like that ever again. There's a time and a place for everything."

This sounded like a sermon written and recited just for her.

"So, what do you mean? Are we going to wait until we're officially married then?"

"I think it's best to wait. You don't expect us to sneak around, do you? Or, sleep in the same bedroom openly, before we're married? I know what we believe, but we live in a society that makes judgements about those behaviours. Besides, what would Esther think? She doesn't know why we're doing this."

She backed down. Of course, she was in the wrong again. "I guess so, if you think it's better."

Maybe she would try a different tack—safer ground.

In a low, coaxing voice she said, "That doesn't mean we can't at least kiss or hold each other does it?" Then gave him a less than confident smile.

"No, we cannot! That would put us at risk of going further and I think that's a bad idea."

Disappointed, she sat in silence for a while. Wouldn't he even kiss her properly until their wedding day?

"Look, I'll be honest with you. I've had some time to reflect on this whole thing, and even if that..." he paused, and wrinkled his nose before continuing, "...if that unfortunate incident hadn't happened, I do think it's a good idea for us to get married anyway. I think it's important for a pastor to have a family, to have children and to teach them Christian values so that they can be role models for the church. And besides, I do like you and you are learning to be a good Christian."

Like! Was that all he felt? Nothing he was saying sounded particularly romantic. Perhaps she had to get used to that. Maybe that was just the way it would be—being married to a pastor. Or, maybe, it would just take time. Clearly, Mark wasn't used to romance.

"Annette, I understand you can't retrieve your innocence."

Annette was puzzled and it must have shown on her face.

"I mean you can't retrieve your... virginity, but I'm willing to take you on anyway. What have I said about judging the sinner? Jesus forgave even the prostitutes, he even let one wash his feet with her hair. I can do no less than forgive and accept you."

"Are you calling me a prostitute?"

"No, of course not, but I watched you from the bus remember? Let's not pretend you just gave those guys a peck on the cheek and went home alone."

She felt her cheeks redden. But what about his behaviour, the last time he was here? He wasn't perfect either. Best not to mention it though. Mark always seemed to be able to turn things around so that she ended up feeling ashamed. She was already feeling that way now. And besides, she felt pretty sure that his sexual lapse with her would have been a one off for him. Better to change the subject altogether.

"What does the church think of homosexuality?"

His mouth dropped open.

"Oh, Annette, you're not going to tell me you've had a homosexual relationship as well as everything else?"

She shook her head. "No, I'm just wondering about it. I mean, if two people love each other does it really matter if they're the same gender?"

"You're kidding, right?" He threw up his hands. "Of course it matters. You're worrying me now. I would have thought, with all this time you've had to study, that you would be a bit clearer on the word of God."

"Well, it just seems unfair—that's all."

"Isn't it obvious? Homosexuals can't create children, so without a doubt it's wrong. Even if the Bible were not crystal clear, the... anatomy doesn't match, surely you can acknowledge that? Annette, you surprise me."

Annette was confused, she had accepted everything that the church had told her so far. Sin after sin had been expounded upon and verified biblically. Why was she uptight about this issue? It didn't affect her personally. Just let it go.

"Yes, I suppose you're right. Hey, you look tired."

"I am tired, really tired and it's not just that..." He hesitated. "...I've had some concerning news from the orphanage."

"What's happened?"

"I don't know the details yet. There was a letter from Dao, she's the Thai housemother there. My guess is that there are problems because we don't have anyone from here managing it at the moment. There will be a meeting in Melbourne to discuss the letter in a few weeks. Let's not say anything to Mum and Ted until we know what's going on. We don't want to worry them—they love those kids."

Annette didn't understand why, when she heard this, it made her feel sick to her stomach.

***

There was no reassurance from Mark about his feelings for her as the days drew forward. When the rain was too heavy to ride her bike, she would call him, to ask if he would pick her up from work. Those times were really the only chances they had to talk.

She considered asking him if he knew more about what had happened at the orphanage. But every time she thought about it, she got that strange, queasy feeling, so she quickly pushed the thoughts away.

Sometimes, they spoke about other, more mundane church business. When they did, Annette felt included in his world for a short while. More often than not, though, Mark seemed distracted, the conversation was stilted, and they soon drifted into silence.

The rest of the time, he threw himself into the work of the church. He would be in his room studying, or preparing his sermon, or attending to the plethora of demands of the church that needed following up each day. Usually, he only surfaced when he was called for dinner. Then, he would excuse himself to do more preparation before the clearing up started. After that, he was out until late. One night a week he conducted a Bible study for the youth and one night a week for an adult group. The remaining nights he went out visiting. Not only did he visit the sick and the elderly but was systematically working his way through visits to the entire congregation.

Surely, Mark would only be this busy in the beginning. Nobody could live like this all the time. Even Ted was busy with church life. Although he was only getting a small stipend, he was out visiting with Mark three or four nights a week and seemed to also have a fair share of church business to attend to. And he was still running a Bible study once a week.

Annette had suggested to Mark that she attend one of the Bible studies that he ran. However, he didn't seem to want her to go. Apparently, the adult group was a bit too advanced and the youth group were all younger than her. She didn't argue, she really wasn't as interested as she was in the beginning. Besides, sitting there not saying much would be boring. It would be inappropriate to ask questions. All doubts should be well and truly put to rest by this stage. Especially now that she was engaged to the pastor.

Annette silently questioned Mark's busyness. It seemed at odds with the importance of prioritising family life. So often, the message in sermons was to make sure there was time to connect with your loved ones. There was no point addressing this with Mark though. The pattern was that whenever she brought up concerns with Mark, he could find a way to justify whatever he did. Annette always came off as the bad guy. So, she had learnt to keep her mouth firmly shut.

She began to feel more alone than she'd felt when Mark was still in Melbourne. At times, she was nostalgic about living with Tracy in the flat. There were a lot of laughs back then. And memories also came unbidden of the early days with Alex. The fun they'd had learning to cook together. The way he had always slipped his arm around her shoulder when they sat together watching TV. She brushed the thoughts away. That was the past, she was living in sin then. Those relationships, and that self-absorbed lifestyle, were an abomination to God.

***

The same thoughts came back though, that Sunday, as she sat in church. Funny, it was when she watched Violet and

Esther. There was something about the way they looked at each other—there was such an easy warmth between them. Annette craved that so much. Later—after Esther had played the piano for the opening songs—Annette noticed Esther's hand brush across Violet's fingers and pause there for an instant, as she took her seat beside her friend. A tear formed in Annette's eye. Sadness for them, sadness for herself... *Don't be an idiot! You're getting married.* She wiped the tear away hoping no-one had noticed.

Her attention turned to Daisy who was sitting a few pews away—diagonally in front of her. Annette had positioned herself so that she could keep an eye on Daisy. She still looked pale but had managed to give Annette a weak smile when she saw her. Annette felt a bit silly watching for danger like this. It crossed her mind that Daisy might have some sort of mental problem. Maybe she saw things that weren't real while she was awake. Annette had heard about that. She'd seen movies where people in mental hospitals imagined people that weren't there attacking them, or saying strange things to them. No other explanation made sense.

Today was like any other day at church. Ted and another elder had just finished collecting the offering. They both brought the offering plates to the front and lay them on a table in front of the pulpit. One elder returned to his seat in the congregation. Ted returned to his position near the door that lead to the carpark. She guessed that he sat there to welcome any latecomers, because she had seen him do just that.

She didn't know that much about the church. Was that an elder's role, to take up the offering, welcome latecomers? And now that Ted was Mark's assistant, would he have more responsibilities on a Sunday? Was he still an elder? It was hard for her to reconcile the Ted from the past and this

Ted in the present. This Ted sacrificed his time and energy to do good works. But still, was he that different than before? He seemed to resent her presence. It was as though he was just tolerating her. And, he took any and every opportunity to put her in her place. To let her know that he was the head of the household. The emotional distance between them wasn't completely his fault though. She felt uncomfortable around him, uneasy, on guard.

Mark preached a heartfelt sermon on forgiveness and Annette felt guilty—as she did after every sermon. What a bad Christian she was, not forgiving Ted and she was resentful about Mark. Worst of all, she'd been thinking about Alex. The music began, and she rose to her feet along with everyone else.

Everyone stood except Daisy. Jane grabbed Daisy's hand and yanked it gently to get her to rise. Daisy took her mother's hand and pulled Jane down towards her and whispered in her ear. Annette could see the surprise on Jane's face. Jane picked up her cardigan and, in the fraction of a second before Jane got it wrapped it around Daisy's waist, Annette saw the wet stain on the back of Daisy's skirt. Jane motioned to Jack, who was absorbed in the singing. He seemed confused as he followed them out. When they reached the door, Ted greeted them with a look of concern. Annette noticed Daisy draw back away from Ted. Jane let go of Daisy's hand to shake Ted's outstretched hand and Daisy raced out the door. Her parents followed immediately after.

What was wrong with that girl? So, Ted wasn't that nice really, but Daisy couldn't know that because he was always so charming at church. The congregation saw him as a tireless servant of God. A man who had given up a comfortable life here to live in substandard conditions in another country to help children he didn't even know.

Well, all that may be true, but it didn't stop Annette's unease around him. As much as she tried to convince herself he was a good man, she realised she still did not trust him. Did something happen here at church? Had Ted gotten angry with Daisy and frightened her? Annette was sure he wouldn't allow himself to do that in front of everyone. She knew he helped out with the Sunday school class sometimes. Maybe something had happened there.

Stop it!

More evidence of her sinful, unforgiving nature. No more than a few minutes had elapsed since the sermon had ended and here she was, thinking bad things about Ted again.

Of course, Daisy was in a hurry to leave. She wet her pants, she was embarrassed. No more to it than that.

Chapter 15

The next day at work was extra busy at lunchtime. On a typical day, there were regulars and there were tourists. Jane and Jack knew all the regulars and greeted them by name. Annette was getting to know them too. Their orders didn't vary much.

However, the tourists stood out in the small town. They took their time ordering. They lingered over their coffee and tea, as they took out their maps and discussed their next destination. Often, they had questions about the food. "Yes, we have wholemeal bread," Annette would say, as she pulled a loaf out from under the counter where they kept it just in case. Why would anyone want to eat wholemeal anything?

Today, though, the clientele was different again. Not locals—Annette didn't recognise any of them—but not tourists either. Rugged blokes in paint, dust or mortar spattered overalls strode in during the early part of the lunch break. They ordered rolls, sandwiches, meat and shepherd's pies. These men were tradies.

"I reckon they've finally started work on the new hospital,"

Jane said to Annette after the rush had subsided.

Up until now, the closest proper hospital was in Wellspring. The town had been making do with a bush nursing hospital for many years.

Jane was excited. "What a great thing for the town." Then, she winked. "And for the bakery, I might add. They expect it will take six months to build."

Annette stopped listening. Standing in the doorway, she saw a familiar figure. The top of his tall frame nearly reaching the door architrave. He just stood there, staring at her—unmoving. Jane hadn't noticed him yet. What was he doing here? What would Mark think? What would the church members think? Was he stalking her? How did he know she was here? Although, she should be angry, it wasn't anger she felt. She couldn't take her eyes off him. Jane was now following the direction of Annette's gaze. Annette quickly turned to the sink and began busily stacking dishes.

"Hi."

She heard his voice, as he moved closer.

"Can I help you?" Jane asked. There was a lot more curiosity in her voice than usual. Had she noticed something?

"Yes, I think I'll have a hot roast beef roll," Alex said.

Jane went into the kitchen to prepare the roll. As soon as she was out of earshot, Annette wheeled around to face Alex.

"What are you doing here?" Her whisper was as harsh and as cold as she could make it.

"Aren't you even a little glad to see me?"

When he said it, Annette realised that, yes, she was glad to see him. If nothing else, she knew where she stood with Alex. Alex didn't play games with her, not like Mark seemed to be doing. Of course, Mark couldn't help it. He was probably confused about his feelings towards her and he had a lot of responsibilities. Mark had to keep up appearances. Alex, well, he was pretty straightforward.

It was stupid to even think this way. She was going to be married soon. Perhaps, this was just nerves. Yes, she was certainly on tenterhooks about the wedding. And now, Alex's presence here could jeopardise everything.

When he spoke again, he kept his voice low and conspiratorial. "I saw Tracy at the bar, and she told me you were living here now. When this work opportunity came up, I thought, why not? It's good money, and, I get to see you and check out whether you're okay at the same time." He paused, then asked, "So, how are you, Annette?"

They both heard the ding of the timer on the toaster oven come from the direction of the kitchen. Annette needed to end this conversation immediately.

"Please don't say anything about us."

Alex leaned towards her, resting his elbows on the counter. Annette moved back, feeling the cold metal of the bench on her back. Alex could ruin this for her. Very few people here knew about her past. She was going to be a pastor's wife. How would she explain this relationship?

"Meet me after work?" he asked.

Annette stood there mute. She didn't have time to argue. If she said no, what then? Would he try to convince her? In that moment it occurred to her, how little freedom she had. She rode straight to and from work. Didn't really go anywhere without someone knowing where she was. Although, on the other hand, maybe it wouldn't be so difficult? Mark certainly wouldn't miss her.

What was she doing? Here she was trying to figure out how she could manage to see Alex without anyone knowing. Of course, she should say no. It was so good to see him though and she had to tell him something anyway, to make him leave. Later—when she could think straight—she would decide whether to follow through or not.

"I can't tonight. Where are you staying?"

He smiled and said, "At the Tea Tree Motel, room 6."

"Okay, I'll meet you—not tonight—tomorrow, just after 5pm." She paused and waggled a warning finger. "On the condition that you get out of here as soon as you get your roll."

Annette turned back to the sink, just as Jane pushed through the coloured, plastic flyscreen strips that shielded the kitchen.

"Can I have a coke too, please?" Alex asked.

When Jane turned towards the fridge, Alex shot a satisfied smile at Annette. She glared back at him, then put her head down and busied herself wiping the counter. It took an excruciatingly long time for him to find the required coins and pay, but at last Annette heard his footsteps leaving the cafe. She didn't look up.

Jane turned towards Annette. "Do you know him?"

She glanced at Jane, who had raised an eyebrow to emphasise her question.

She didn't hesitate with the lie. "No, why do ask?

Jane paused, searching Annette's face.

"Just the way he was looking at you..."

Annette shrugged, fighting hard to keep a poker face.

***

At home later, Annette was kind of regretting her decision to meet Alex, but her mind was changing from minute to minute. She didn't want to deceive anyone, but they were kind of forcing her to, weren't they? Meeting an old boyfriend, particularly at his motel room, would certainly be frowned upon. And what if someone saw her?

She was also curious about how much Tracy had told Alex? Did he know that she was getting married? Then, the self-satisfied feeling returned. She was getting married, and would live a respectable, Christian life with a pious, selfless man. Possibly a little too pious though. It was hard to be around Mark when he seemed so distant. The cold front he displayed towards her was only to protect them both from getting too close again before they were married. This behaviour was temporary. She was sure of it. Soon they could relax and really be together.

Sometimes questions stole into her mind though. The questions were unwanted and crept in like spiders, crawling in through tiny crevices. Would he be any less busy with the church after they were married? Would he have time for her then? Was she mistaken in believing that he had real concern for her wellbeing? Or was his warmth when they first met, more about converting her to Christianity? Was she living in hope of that caring, responsive, interested Mark returning to her? Was she ignoring the very real possibility that this judgemental and aloof man might be the real Mark? It was confusing. He was wonderful at church. So many times she had watched as he shook hands with people and asked how they were. He seemed genuinely caring. And so, he was with her too... at first.

Was this why she was so pleased to see Alex? If she were to be honest with herself, she was looking forward to being around someone who knew her and didn't seem to think she needed to change. She knew she was nothing special, but it was comforting to think that Alex thought she was okay just as she was. She wanted so much to be better, but in many ways this Christian lifestyle was so hard. It was like trudging up a mountain when the peak kept shifting ever higher. And, it was so easy to backslide. Even when she may have appeared to be doing well outwardly, her thoughts were all wrong. She knew she was fundamentally selfish. Mark's neglect of her was really only because he was working so hard for others. A proper Christian would be happy that he was so earnest about doing God's work— but she wasn't.

There were so many other sins she still committed. Violet and Esther's relationship didn't seem wrong to her. Not only did she not enjoy reading the Bible—worse still —she questioned what she read. She questioned what she heard in sermons—either that—or she was just plain bored with them. She missed seeing bands and yearned for a bourbon and coke. Maybe the worst sin of all was this plan to meet Alex.

His motel was in the opposite direction of home. Yesterday, she had lied to Jane when she said she didn't know Alex. If someone from church saw her riding there, that may require yet another lie. Out of nowhere, a Bible verse came to her, "The Lord detests lying lips". God was speaking to her. Delivering words from the Bible just when they were most needed, to save her from sin. Perhaps she shouldn't go after all. Her heart sank, the excitement that was astir all through her, fell flat and lifeless like lemonade that had sat out too long.

Yes Lord, I am weak, I should have said no. I should have said that my old life is over.

It was too late, though. Alex would probably come back to the bakery. Why did she lie to Jane in the first place? She would just have to carry through with the plan.

This way of life, the sense of not being able to put a foot wrong, was stifling, she needed a break. Some time alone with Alex would be respite from this endless struggle towards righteousness. Besides, it should be okay to see an old friend. Really, she shouldn't have to deceive anyone. It probably wasn't that big a deal. Why not just tell everyone the truth?

***

Because Annette was busy mentally rehearsing what she planned to say, it took a while for her to pick up on the mood at dinner that night. When Ted was at home, dinners weren't the relaxed, fun occasions she had imagined, with everyone sharing about their day and laughing together like on the TV shows. It was better though, when Ted wasn't there. The mood was lighter, and the conversation flowed more freely. Annette herself was careful about what she said in front of him and mostly she didn't say much at all.

Tonight, however, nobody was talking at all. Grace stared down at the food she was shifting around on her plate. Annette's earlier resolve to be honest about visiting Alex was wavering.

Before she lost her nerve, she tried for a nonchalant tone and said, "Wow, we were flat out today with the workers from the hospital, and you wouldn't believe it, but—"

"Are you okay, Mum?" Esther interrupted.

"Hmm, I'm fine," Grace responded. She didn't sound fine.

"Aren't you hungry?" Esther said.

Grace pushed some carrot and peas onto her fork, placed them in her mouth and chewed slowly. A tear slid down her cheek. On her face—a faraway look.

"It's too awful, I can't believe it happened while we were there." She shook her head, and said, "It doesn't make sense."

"What on earth are you talking about?" Esther looked alarmed.

"That's not something you should be discussing with anyone else," Ted warned. He turned to Mark. "You shouldn't have told her, look how upset she is."

"I thought she had a right to know before she hears it at the meeting tomorrow night Ted." Mark's voice was soft but assertive.

"What's going on?" Esther searched the faces around the table for an answer.

"It's the orphanage—" Grace began.

Ted interjected, his voice getting louder, "What, why is it going to the board? These matters shouldn't be discussed that widely. We can handle it."

"I'm sorry, Ted, I know it's an awful thing to talk about, and I understand that you're affected by it too, but it's the board that needs to decide whether to inform the police or not," Mark said.

"Inform the police about what?" Esther asked.

Ted banged his fist down on the table and his voice boomed, "We're not even sure it's true. That kid who said it, Chinda, she was a liar long before she arrived at the orphanage. They lied to survive; it becomes second nature to them." He appealed to Grace, adjusting his tone to make it more mellow, "You know that dear, you remember the farmer who brought her to us. He caught her stealing fruit, but she denied doing it."

He pointed a finger at Mark. "And now you're going to drag the name of the church through the mud. Tear down all the good work Grace and I have done. Taint the reputation of the orphanage because one kid—a kid that we know to be a liar—has said someone touched her and has talked a few others into going along with her deception. They haven't even given a name. Doesn't that tell you, that their story can't be trusted?" He paused for a few moments, and when he resumed his voice was quiet and reflective. "I reckon someone's put them up to it. I see the Devil at work here. If you wanted to interfere with God's work, wouldn't this be the perfect way to do it? I never fully trusted Dao. I wonder if it's she who's trying to thwart God's work in Thailand."

Grace suddenly seemed more hopeful. "Ted's right, we couldn't believe what some of the children told us. Their stories often turned out to be fiction. Chinda told us she had a rich aunt who was coming to get her. That was a fantasy, she didn't have any relatives. I don't think Dao would be behind this though Ted. She's a good woman who has only ever had the children's best interests at heart."

Annette's gut was churning, she didn't even know this kid, but she felt for her. Why would a child lie about something like that? What if it were true, and the person who did it got away with it? Worse still, what if they continued what they were doing because the child wasn't believed? Maybe Ted was right though. What if it wasn't true and God's work at the orphanage was compromised?

"I hear what you're saying Ted, but I'm sorry, it's my duty to inform the board. The church sponsors the orphanage, so they have a right to know about this. You can tell them what you've told me, and they can read the letter themselves. Then they will make a prayerful decision." Mark spoke with an air of authority and finality that didn't seem to leave room for further discussion.

Ted, blowing out a slow stream of air, said, "Fair enough, I'm sure they'll do what's right."

Annette was relieved to hear that a group of godly people would be deciding what to do in this situation.

***

Mark left for his youth bible study straight after dinner and Grace and Ted went into the lounge room shutting the door behind them. Esther and Annette stood by the sink doing the dishes.

"By the way, I know I said I'd give you a lift, but do you

mind riding the bike tomorrow?" Esther asked. "Violet and I are filling in for Sunday school this week and we have to go over our plan, so I'm having dinner there."

This was great. There was really no need to cause any more drama by discussing Alex. There was enough upset in the house already with this orphanage business. Annette wouldn't have to explain anything. Grace, Mark and Ted would leave early to have a shared dinner before the board meeting. Nobody would be there to notice she hadn't come home.

"Yes, that's okay," she said.

Esther made a clicking sound with her tongue. "Oh... I forgot, everyone's out tomorrow night. You'll be here by yourself." She hesitated. "Did you want to come to Violet's for dinner too?"

"No, I'll be fine, thanks anyway."

Esther responded with a barely disguised smile, "Okay then, if you're sure."

They were both quiet for a while. Annette was caught up in pleasant thoughts of her reunion with Alex, now that all the obstacles had been removed.

The uneasy atmosphere that was there over dinner returned though, when Esther spoke again, "Do you think a child would lie about something like that?"

"No, I don't." Annette surprised herself with the certainty of her response.

Esther eyes were focused on the pot she was scrubbing. "It's odd, because this same issue came up a few years ago. I shouldn't be talking about it I suppose, but you are going to be the pastor's wife." She continued to scrub the same pot, although it appeared to be clean. Annette waited for her to speak. After a few moments, Esther seemed to come to a decision.

She placed the pot upside down on the draining rack

and turned to face Annette.

"It was two years ago, and I hadn't been working at the school long. The school nurse and I ate lunch together sometimes, and, even though she wasn't a Christian, we got along well. One day, she told me she was really worried about a couple of children. One seven-year-old girl kept coming to her with bladder infections and another eight-year-old girl had abdominal pain and had been bleeding. I didn't know what she was getting at. Then, she finally told me exactly what she thought might be happening. You know it was... like what they're talking about with the orphanage, abuse. It's so awful to think about." Esther shook her head and her lip curled with distaste. "The nurse had spoken to both sets of parents and she said they were at a loss about why this was happening and were actually quite angry with her when she suggested that the girls might have been..."

Esther broke off again, took out the plug and slowly wiped the stainless-steel sink where a fatty ring had formed. Annette was feeling very uncomfortable, but it seemed important that she know what had happened. Esther was silent for a while, running even more hot water and continuing to scrub the sink clean. She was about to ask, when Esther spoke again.

"I kind of agreed with the parents, I told her there had to be another explanation too. That maybe she should get a second opinion from a doctor. I only saw that nurse once more. She hadn't been at school for a few days. Then she called one night and asked if I'd have a coffee with her after school the next day. I hesitated because—although I liked her—I thought she was over-dramatising the situation. I guess that's what I preferred to think, and you know what? At that stage, I really didn't want to talk about it anymore."

Annette felt a conflict within herself as well. As she

listened to the story, she was worried about the two girls. Nevertheless, she realised that she too wanted to hear a different explanation. The horror of the nurse's suspicions being correct was unthinkable, but if the nurse was right, those children had needed protection.

Esther continued, "I decided to meet with her. I kind of wish I hadn't, because it didn't change anything, and I ended up being left with suspicions about the whole thing that were probably completely unfounded."

"So, what did she say?" Annette asked.

"That the school had sacked her. That they'd paid her out until the end of term but had asked her to leave immediately. Both children were from our church. One set of parents had asked for a meeting with the principal and our pastor about the matter. Apparently, then it had gone higher in the church and the principal had said the nurse should have spoken to him before speaking to the parents. He told her that her behaviour was inappropriate. He said he had no choice because the church leadership in Melbourne had directed him to terminate her position with the school. The nurse told me that she took my suggestion and talked to a doctor she used to work with at a hospital in Melbourne. That doctor confirmed what she thought, that those symptoms were consistent with... well, you know. She asked me to watch out for the girls. 'It's a coincidence don't you think that they both attend your church?' I remember that's exactly what she said. It felt like an accusation."

There was a crawling, sick feeling welling up inside Annette. Now, it seemed almost certain that those girls had been molested, and that they were members of this church, her church.

"So, did you watch out for them?" Annette's voice had a sharp edge.

"Well, it was so odd. One of the families moved away,

not long after that. The parents that had asked for the meeting stopped coming to church immediately after it all happened. Later, I heard they'd left town. So, I guess we'll never know about the younger girl. And the other one, well she seemed to be okay to me. I don't know, what would I have been looking for? Sometimes I wonder whether I should have done more, got involved somehow, talked to the pastor myself about it, but that wasn't really the right thing to do. It would seem as though I was questioning the decisions that had been made."

"If both girls were in the church doesn't it follow that it would have been someone in the church who did it? Did you suspect anyone?" Annette asked.

"There are over forty men in our church and I know them all. Did I suspect one of them?" She shook her head. "No, there is no way anyone in our church would be capable of doing something like that. Besides, the girls went to the same school, of course it wouldn't have happened there either, and they lived in the same town. Even if something had happened, which I'm pretty sure it didn't. Why would it have to have happened in the church? People love to look for evil in the church. Don't forget that the nurse was an unbeliever."

"Did you ask the older girl whether something had happened to her?"

"Of course not, how do you ask a child something like that? And look what happened to the nurse, nobody seemed to believe her anyway. I'm sure that her parents would have asked her and were satisfied nothing had happened. Anyway, it's not my place to go meddling."

No need to ask Esther the name of the older girl, she didn't need to, she knew who it was.

***

Annette got very little sleep that night and when she did sleep, her dreams left her feeling disturbed and unsettled. In her dream she saw herself as a little girl again. Trying to run but her legs wouldn't move. No sound would come when she tried to scream. A faceless shadow was chasing her.

Suddenly she woke in a cold sweat, but there was no relief, no sense of, Oh, it was just a dream. She still felt terrified, paralysed. Her breath was rapid. Flicking on the bedside lamp helped. The now familiar, old-fashioned furniture and the painting of the vase filled with soft pastel-coloured roses on the wall comforted her a little and her breath deepened. What helped even more though was remembering that she would see Alex soon.

Chapter 16

At closing time, Annette waited until Jane was in the storeroom to yell, "Bye", so that she wouldn't be seen riding off in the direction of the motel. No good arousing suspicion right at the beginning of this venture.

She had kept communication with Jane and Jack to a minimum all day. Had they been complicit in this cover-up? How could they? No, of course they wouldn't have been. This was their daughter. Judging them like this wasn't fair; she didn't know all the details.

Why was she so convinced that nurse was right anyway? The nurse had spoken to Jack and Jane, and they were sure nothing had happened. They must have asked Daisy the question too. Nevertheless, she couldn't help asking herself why it was, that in that whole chain of events, only the non-Christian nurse, seemed to be interested in protecting those little girls.

Time to put these thoughts away, it was in the past, not really her business. More important things to focus on right now.

Pedalling faster, she picked up enough speed for her

hair to billow out in the wind. A rush of adrenaline coursed through her, as she furtively glanced around at the few people on the street. She didn't see anyone she knew, and no-one seemed particularly interested in her movements. The few people that were around, thinned out and then the road was empty as she left the main part of town. When she reached the motel she paused before turning in. Checking to the right and left that there was still no-one on foot and also that there were no cars driving by just at that moment that might spot her.

Alex opened the door just seconds after she knocked. Again, she looked around before brushing past him to get inside as quickly as possible.

"Hi," he said, "really good to see you."

Moving towards her he lifted his hands towards her shoulders. Annette hesitated until his hands made contact, then she ducked away from under them, to the opposite side of the room. There were a few moments of awkward silence.

"Hi," she said.

His hair was still damp, and his face looked scrubbed fresh from an after work shower. She couldn't help but look him up and down, appreciating how his well-muscled physique filled out his jeans and T-shirt.

He smiled, his pleasure at seeing her obvious, while she did her best to hide hers. With some difficulty, she shifted her eyes away to the large picture window that overlooked the motel pool. Safe from view, beside the heavy curtains, she watched some children splashing about in the water. A woman, with a tall drink and a magazine looked up periodically at the children from her deck chair. A couple of men —still in their work clothes—sat at a plastic outdoor table. A tall, longneck Fosters shared between them.

As if he could read her thoughts, Alex asked, "Would

you like a drink?"

Instead of saying no—like she knew she should—she delayed the decision and asked, "What do you have?"

He moved to the bar fridge and opened the door. "I got a few of these, especially for you." Then pulled out a can of Jim Beam and Cola and held it out to her.

In her imagination, the sweet liquid trickled down her throat. Memories flooded back of warm, intimate conversations with Alex. Of a sense of being relaxed and close—not worried about anything—and feeling like everything she said was smart or funny or interesting. The urge to say *yes* was strong, it would be like saying *yes* to her old life. The life she thought she hated so much. She shook her head.

"No, I don't drink anymore."

He raised his eyebrows a little but didn't comment, as he returned the can to the fridge and took out a beer for himself. A familiar hiss sounded loud in the quiet between them as Alex pulled the ring tab off the can. He took a short swig while Annette watched him intently.

"Maybe just pour me a little Jim Beam—into a glass."

"No worries, there may even be some ice here," he said, as he checked the tiny freezer. He found a plastic ice tray and pushed some cubes out into a glass and then poured her a drink. "So, what's been happening?"

Cradling the cold glass in her hand she wondered where to start. How much should she even tell him? She took a sip. It was so sweet and cold. What a lecture she would get from Mark if he could see her now. She gulped down some more. No point stopping now, she'd already sinned. That oh, so familiar, warm buzz followed soon after she emptied the glass, spreading through her chest.

"Well, a lot has happened, but what about you?"

An unpleasant possibility occurred to her. One that she didn't like the thought of it at all. The possibility that Alex may have met someone else by now.

She turned her face away from him and gazed out the window, then asked casually, "Do you have a girlfriend?"

Alex didn't answer immediately. In fact, it was quite a long pause. Why did she want so badly for the answer to be no? Of course, he might have—probably has—he's a good-looking guy. None of her business really. It shouldn't matter to her either way, but the longer he was silent the more she realised it did matter, it mattered a lot. She lowered her head and raised her eyebrows, still waiting for an answer.

"What difference does it make?" he asked.

Heat flushed her face and her response came fast with a snappy tone as she faced him again. "Makes no difference, of course. Up to you. What you do is your business, nothing to do with me if you have a girlfriend. Sorry I asked—" she broke off.

Suddenly she felt ashamed and turned to the window again, trying to appear completely focused on the scene near the pool. What was wrong with her? She was supposed to be engaged. When she tried to think about Mark, all she could do was to picture Alex kissing someone else. Imagine him sitting on the couch with his arm around someone else. She shrugged her shoulders and shook her head a little. How ridiculous, she'd hardly thought about Alex for months.

When she turned back to him Alex was watching her closely. Could he guess her thoughts? So stupid! She shouldn't have asked the question in the first place.

"No, I don't have a girlfriend." He smiled, clearly a little amused by her reaction. The smile faded though, as he continued, "But as I said, what difference does it make? I hear you're getting married."

Tears pricked at her eyes. Hearing that he knew about her pending marriage made her feel sad and alone. The statement sounded so final. The daydreams she'd had of her life with Mark were at odds with the reality so far. Being a born-again Christian was supposed to be a guarantee of happiness. It wasn't working out that way. She sniffled and tried without success to stifle a whimper.

Alex's expression had gone from one of sad resignation to one of real concern. He stepped in close to her. She didn't resist and leaned into his chest. He stroked her hair gently. With his other arm, he hugged her in tight as the sobs surged through her, unrestrained now, and as though from a small child.

Held in Alex's arms, her head cradled on his chest, she cried for a long time. When she finally stopped, she moved away from him, helped herself to another drink and then sat in the only chair. Alex sat on the edge of the bed facing her. There was only concern on his face, not judgement, so she began to talk. The words started as a trickle, but soon became a flood, tumbling out in a continuous flow. It was such a relief to get it out. The doubts, insecurities, confusion that she'd held inside for so long now had found an outlet.

She told him everything. The shock of realising Mark's stepfather was her own father, of what had happened to Daisy. Even why she and Mark were getting married.

"Nothing even happened between us, not really," she said.

There was a slight smile in Alex's eyes when she said this, even though he didn't comment.

After she had spilled it all out, she wanted to blame the alcohol, but was it really? Why had she had badmouthed the church, told secrets that it probably wasn't her place to tell and even let on about her uncertainty about marrying Mark? On her way to the bathroom she stumbled slightly.

When she returned Alex looked as though he was deep

in thought, lips drawn together, eyebrows knitted.

In a gentle voice he asked, "So what are you going to do?"

"About what?" This came out a little snappier than she had meant it to.

Alex raised his eyebrows and leaned back on the bed, away from her and her sudden change in mood.

"About all of it… about any of it?"

Now he was making demands of her too.

"Well, what can I do? I've made a commitment, to God, to Mark, to the church," she said as she threw her hands up. "It's what I want."

"Okay, okay." He raised one hand a little. "It's okay. Let's forget about Mark for a minute—as bizarre as that situation is—can we talk about the little girl? Somebody has to do something about her. You don't know whether it's still happening or not."

Annette's focus shifted completely, immediately. The possibility that something was still happening to Daisy wasn't something she'd considered, or had she?

"What? Why on earth would you say that?"

Annette felt her chest constrict, panic was rising up, her breathing became more rapid. Of course, she knew, that day in Daisy's room she knew, but somehow she'd managed to forget it again.

"From what you've said about the pictures she draws, wetting her pants in church, it seems as though she's petrified of someone there."

Annette didn't speak, she was at the edge of an old memory again. *You're a bad girl.* Fear was sucking her into some other vortex, some other place that wasn't here and wasn't now, but that felt like it was. She knew those words so well; she'd heard them so many times. The words were weighted, weighted with cold dread.

Alex moved towards her. "Are you okay? You look strange."

The sound of his voice snapped her back to the motel room. Her breathing slowed a little. Her body sagged, exhausted, but she was relieved when she saw Alex's face come back into focus. Now, he was staring at her with real concern.

"What happened just then?"

How could she respond? What had happened? What would she say? That it felt like something bad was happening, something terrible, even though nothing was. And she didn't want to say because, as scary as the experience was, the idea of talking about it was somehow even more terrifying.

"I don't know, just felt a bit weird for a minute, must be the alcohol. I'm not used to it anymore you know."

"You went really pale, and it was like you couldn't hear me. Are you sure you're okay?"

"Yes," she said sharply. "I'm okay. We were talking about Daisy, not me."

Alex still looked concerned but didn't pursue it further. He was right though. Somebody should do something about Daisy, but what?

"What do you think I should do? Maybe I should talk to Mark; he's the pastor."

"Remember what I told you in that letter about my mother and what she did to me."

Annette had kept the letter about Alex's childhood misery. Alex had sent it as a warning, and at the time, Annette had passed it off as his mum being a crazy person. Now, Annette had seen evidence that people's beliefs could make them behave strangely. A wave of sadness for Alex washed over her and she felt the urge to hold him close, just like he had held her a little while ago.

Alex was shaking his head slowly, as he spoke, "Well, the pastor knew what was happening, probably half the church knew. My father went to the church and confronted the pastor, asked him why he didn't do anything. The pastor's response was, 'Sometimes it's about the lesser of two evils.' He said he agreed with my father that my mother should never have done those things, but then he went on to tell my father about how much good the church does. 'If we muddy the name of the church because of the actions of one or two people, then Satan wins.'" Alex shook his head again but laughed this time. It was actually more of a scoff.

"Really, you've got to ask yourself who's the devil in this scenario—the women who tortured a child, the people who let it happen, or some mythical creature with horns who gets blamed for everything that goes wrong in the world."

Although, Annette knew that she should feel affronted by Alex's description of Satan as mythical, the truth was she'd had similar thoughts herself. And, as she listened to Alex, she realised that she didn't feel confident to tell Mark. What if he didn't do anything? What if he just wanted to protect the name of the church as well? Two years ago, nobody had believed the nurse. Nothing was done. Would it be any different now? She wouldn't stand by knowing a little girl might be getting hurt. Scary as it felt, she would do something about it, she just didn't know what yet.

***

When Annette asked to sit in the back of Alex's combi on the drive home—hidden from sight—he didn't question or criticise her. He also didn't complain when she asked to be dropped off a short distance from the driveway. When he slid the door open, she slipped out and moved quickly away from the van, not looking back. After a moment, she heard the van door bang shut, and the engine rev as the van pushed off from the gravel siding on the way back to town.

All was quiet in the house and she went straight to her room, not wanting to tempt fate. She sat on the edge of the bed and made herself think about that day in Daisy's room. The picture of the church monster, the speech bubble... Suddenly, inexplicably she felt scared again, no, it was much more than scared. What she felt was gut wrenching, all-encompassing terror. Her breath came in short, sharp rasps as her chest tightened. This was crazy. What was happening to her? The pastel flower painting in the room always made her feel calm, she lay back and tried to focus on it, tried to fight the panic. The pain came then, jerking her down into the soft mattress. Intense and ripping through her, deep inside. Although she was aware that she was moving, it wasn't under her control. Somehow she was being moved, trapped under the weight pressing on her. The peak of the agony corresponded with her being shoved backward rhythmically into the bed, over and over again. Her body was rigid, as though braced against the invisible onslaught that seemed like it would never end. Her muscles were taut like rubber bands ready to snap.

Then, as inexplicably as it had started, it ended. The pain and movement stopped. She heard her breathing and it was loud and laboured. As though, through a haze, she slowly became aware of the room again. Everything was the same as before, the painting still on the wall, she was still alone. Her breathing slowed. She realised how tightly she was holding herself and gently let her muscles relax little by little. There was suddenly no threat, nothing to be scared of and relief flooded through her. It was like waking from a nightmare, but she hadn't been asleep.

There was a sense of being on the edge of understanding more about herself, about why she was, as she was. This experience she'd just had, came from the past, she didn't know how she knew that, she just did. As frightening as re-membering was, the re-experiencing all those awful sensa-tions and feelings again, seemed somehow better now than not remembering. Better than having the badness stuck in-side her, like a rotten apple in a fruit bowl, turning everything bad. There was a sense of release, of explanation. Incomplete though it was, she was getting closer to the truth of her life, of her past and of her present.

Chapter 17

Only Annette and Mark were at the breakfast table. It was Saturday, so she didn't have to rush off to work. She looked across at Mark who was reading the local paper. He had barely acknowledged her when she came in freshly showered and dressed in a pretty, floral dress. Just a "Good Morning", then back to his paper before she could respond or even meet his eyes. It was as though he didn't see her now. Like she was part of the furniture. At least that's how she felt.

What would Mark make of her weird experience alone in her room the other night? Would he be sensitive and caring like he was when they first met? Or would he treat her as the object of disgust, rather than the experience? No point confiding in him it was just too risky. A sudden and intense longing for Alex struck her. Even though she was only four feet away from Mark, she felt completely alone. There was a vast chasm between them and she didn't know how to cross it. All she wanted right now was to be back in Alex's comforting arms.

He had returned to Melbourne for the weekend. The

company only paid for the motel during the week. The thought of a whole weekend here holding her secrets and doubts to herself, began to feel like a gruelling task. Alex had given her his phone number and address. She could make some excuse and be on the 9.30am bus to Melbourne today. Alex would pick her up from the city if she called him. Maybe she would go and visit her mum too. For some reason, connecting with her mum seemed more important to her, after her experience last night. Not only that, she would then have a legitimate reason for going to Melbourne.

The Bible verse in the old-fashioned carved frame that hung above the wood stove mocked her with it's bright gold lettering—*Love never fails.* Well, love seemed to be failing her well and truly. Today, Mark seemed like a stranger. They all felt like strangers, Ted, Grace, Esther. She felt more isolated than ever.

"Annette." Mark's voice broke through her ruminations. "You seem deep in thought."

She smiled a nervous little smile. "I was thinking about my mum, I really should go and see her. Tell her in person about the wedding."

Mark looked genuinely surprised.

"I thought you weren't in touch with her anymore."

Annette hesitated, how could she explain that spending time around Ted, now that she was an adult, gave her more empathy for her mum? That his drinking and violence might help explain why Rose wasn't the world's greatest mother. That maybe Annette should have cut her some slack instead of cutting her off.

"'If you hold anything against anyone forgive them...'" she began.

"'...so that your Father in heaven may forgive your sins.' Matthew 11:25. Very good. Some would say that Rose stopping Ted from seeing you after she threw him out, was un-forgivable. However, a true Christian sees that no-one is beyond forgiveness. I think it's great that you want to wit-ness to your mother."

He smiled at her like he used to when they first met. That smile that made her feel like she was the only person in the world of interest to him. Strangely, that smile wasn't having the same effect that it had before. Her heart wasn't beating any faster.

"I have to go to Melbourne today..." He shook his head as he lowered his voice. "...for a meeting about that orphan-age business." Then, more brightly, "You could come if you like. I could drop you off at your mother's and then pick you up after the meeting."

Now, her heart was thumping. This was unexpected.

"Ah, I'm not sure if I want to go today."

"No time like the present. Why don't you give her a ring and make sure she's home? I would like to leave in half an hour."

Annette made a very short, very strained call to her mother asking if she could visit, and soon they were on their way.

As nervous as she was about seeing her mother and Bill, she was also curious about Mark's meeting.

As they drove past the last few farms of Pleasant Valley, Annette said, "So, I thought the issue at the orphanage was being handled by the local church board."

Mark looked directly ahead at the road in front, but she could see he was troubled. "It was."

When it was clear from the silence that followed that he wasn't going to volunteer anything further, she asked, "Then why today's meeting?"

He turned to her with a serious face. "You do realise that church business, particularly business of this nature is highly confidential."

She nodded.

After a long pause he seemed to come to a decision. "Well, the board voted to let it go as there really wasn't a name given, or even any proof that any of the allegations were true."

Mark was focused on the road and so couldn't have noticed her eyebrows shoot up. He continued on, "I mean even if we informed the Thai police, what would we say? We can't give them any information, not really." He sighed heavily. "Anyway, I thought that would be the end of it. But no, I got a call from the Wellspring church pastor yesterday and it turns out the board at Wellspring voted differently when they were informed. They decided to consult with a local counsellor who apparently..." he elongated this last word, "...is experienced with these sorts of issues. I have no idea why they would consult with a therapist. The pastor is supposed to be the spiritual leader of the church. The pastor is the one people should come to for counselling. And of course, only God can heal pain... Anyway, this counsellor met with the new volunteer house parents before they left for Thailand this week. He *counselled* them about how to ask Dao and the children about what happened. So that's all I know at this stage. The church leaders in Melbourne want to meet with me face to face today to discuss the matter."

Annette was relieved. At least not everyone was ignoring this report. The Wellspring people had stood up for these children. And what had she done for Daisy? She'd done nothing! What though? What could she have done?

"They reiterated the sensitive nature of the issue." He paused and again gave her that grave look. "So please don't discuss it with anyone. You're going to have to learn to keep a lot of things to yourself as a pastor's wife, so you might as well start now."

That wasn't usually a problem. Annette kept most things to herself. But then she'd blurted everything out to Alex. She felt a pang of guilt. Mark was trusting her with information, and she had so recently betrayed him by blabbing to a non-believer about her confusion about the church. Mark would hate that if he knew.

What about this counsellor? Mark didn't sound keen on him, but it sounded as though the Wellspring church board trusted this person. Mark had also said this counsellor was *experienced in these sorts of issues*. Wouldn't that be a better person to talk to about her problems? To help her understand that awful experience she had had alone in her bed the other night. And, the counsellor might have advice about Daisy too. Just then, a tiny flame of hope ignited and began to smoulder inside her. A hope for answers—not just for Daisy—but maybe for herself as well.

***

Annette could see her mother had made some effort to look her best for the visit. Makeup on, hair pulled back into a neat bun, but she looked older. Annette was surprised at how much older she looked. Deep wrinkles at the corners of her eyes and her lipstick bleeding into the vertical lines above her top lip. A wave of emotion took Annette by surprise. Tears pricked at her eyes. Fortunately, at that moment, Rose's focus was elsewhere.

"Is he coming in?" Rose gestured towards the car that sat out in the street.

Mark waved from the driver's seat; Rose waved back.

"No, he's running late for an appointment. You can meet him later when he picks me up."

By then, the unguarded moment had passed for Annette. So when Rose moved towards her, arms outstretched,

Annette allowed the hug, but held herself stiff and separate.

Rose backed off. "Come in," she said, then turned and walked inside.

The house hadn't changed much, except the walls had been painted in a bright canary yellow and there was a new forest-green, suede lounge suite.

"You've changed the colour... it looks nice and bright."

Annette didn't really like it but wasn't sure what else to say.

Rose was beaming. "Oh, I'm glad you like it. Bob did it himself. We had to get rid of the old TV—it broke down —so we thought we would update a few things."

"Oh, is that a colour TV?"

"Yes, it is. It's very nice to watch... when we can get a picture." She laughed, a nervous little laugh. "Anyway, sit down love, make yourself comfortable. Would you like a cup of tea?"

"Umm... yes, okay thanks."

Rose busied herself in the kitchen.

Annette called out, "Where's Bob?"

"He's gone to the footy with the next-door neighbour. That's okay isn't it? He did say he'd stay home to see you, but I thought it would be nice, you know, just the two of us."

Annette looked at the framed photos on the walls. Apart from Rose and Bob's wedding photo, they were mostly of her. She looked like a normal, happy kid in these photos. Not a care in the world. But then, photos were like that. Nobody displayed pictures on their walls of miserable, crying children.

Rose appeared with the teapot, cups and saucers, milk jug, sugar and a plate of Iced VoVo biscuits on a tray. Rose poured the tea.

"How many sugars do you have now?"

"Just one please."

"You always loved these when you were a kid," Rose said, offering the biscuits to Annette.

Annette took one; they tasted great. She relaxed a little. This was nice—having tea with her mother, eating biscuits, making small talk.

"So... who was that man?" Rose asked.

Annette stiffened, that cosy feeling that had begun to settle over her a few seconds ago evaporated. It was a fair question and Annette knew it was coming. She should have answered without reservation. Nevertheless, she hesitated. Religion had never been part of life in this house. She knew her mother had grown up attending a Catholic church, but she really didn't know how Rose felt about God now. It just wasn't ever talked about.

"Boyfriend?" Rose asked, when Annette didn't answer.

"Mum, do you believe in God?"

Her mother's eyebrows shot up. "Gee, that's a big change of subject. Why on earth would you ask me that?"

"Well, you've never said..."

"It's not something you really talk about, you know... religion and politics. They are private matters. You have your beliefs, but there's no need to tell the whole world about them."

Annette was getting irritated now. "I'm not asking you to tell the whole world—though I'm not sure why it's such a big secret—I'm just asking you to tell me."

Rose studied the bottom of her teacup. When she looked up her lips were pursed and there was a hard edge to her voice.

"If you must know, God and I fell out a long time ago. For years, I prayed for things to change and had faith that they would. Or—if they didn't—that it was all part of God's plan. That's what I had learned. Don't question when bad things happen, God is in control. But then when things happen, things that are so evil..." Her voice cracked a little as she broke off. Her eyes were fixed on Annette. "Well, how can anyone believe in loving God after that. You know what I'm talking about don't you, love?"

Annette remembered the bruises and cuts she saw on her mother. How scared they both were of Ted. In a rush of affection, Annette reached out her hand and covered Rose's hand with her own.

Rose was teary now. "I'm so sorry you had to go through that, love. I should have got that bastard out of our lives a long time before I did."

Now, it was Annette's voice that was fractured with emotion. "Did he ever try to contact us after that day he left?"

"No, that miserable bastard wouldn't have dared."

She recalled what Mark had said about Ted being denied access to her. Ted had lied; she had suspected as much when Mark said it. Now, sitting here, she was sure Rose was telling the truth.

"Didn't even write?"

"No, nothing. Would you have wanted to hear from him?"

This was a hard question. At the time, she didn't want to be scared anymore, or for her mum to be hurt anymore, but he was her father. Yes, she would have wanted to know he still cared about her, thought about her. Would rather not have daydreamed at school about him taking her out for an ice-cream or a pizza. On the other hand, she didn't want Rose to feel guilty about kicking him out. And also, her logical self understood that Ted would never have been the father she had daydreamed about, that was obvious now. As a Christian, he should be his best self and even that self was not very loving. Wasn't even very nice.

"I guess not," she said quietly.

"Let's not talk about him anyway." Rose brightened. "Are you going to tell me who that man is?"

Clearly, she couldn't tell Rose the whole story, not at the moment anyway. That also meant that the possibility of inviting Rose and Bob to the wedding wasn't really an option. It hadn't really occurred to Annette that she would feel bad about hurting her mother, but she did. If she had the choice, she would have preferred to have her mother there, at her wedding, instead of Ted.

She sighed and said simply, "He's my boyfriend."

"Well, I thought so, tell me about a bit about him. What does he do?"

"Mark is a church pastor. That's why I was asking you about your beliefs."

"Oh, I see..." She nodded, but her brows were knitted. "But you have no interest in all of that, do you?"

Annette didn't answer. Here was the perfect opportunity to witness to her mother. To tell her mother how joyous it felt to be born again. But if she said that she would be lying. She was joyous when it happened, now she was just confused. Although she still believed in God, there were, oh so many, unanswered questions. The happiness she sought still eluded her, and it didn't seem like the Christians around her were that happy either. Now that she could see the real Mark, behind the façade that the church members saw, she could see that he wasn't happy.

Neither was Esther; she rarely smiled. There was a sadness—a melancholy air about her—that probably had something to do with her relationship with Violet. Ted seemed tense nearly all the time and was outraged about something or other on a regular basis.

Maybe Grace was happy though. She seemed happy, particularly when she was in the garden. Grace seemed able to let the harshness of Ted roll off her. Her cheerful outlook seemed genuine. Annette had seen her at home, and at church, and she was the same. It wasn't a pretence for her. The business at the orphanage had taken its toll on her, but, in general, she seemed to be at peace.

How selfish would she be though, if she put her mother off Christianity by talking about her unfulfilled expectations? Rose's salvation was at stake here.

"Annette, penny for your thoughts?"

Annette looked earnestly at her mother. "Yes, I am into all that. Oh Mum... God has changed my life." Well, that definitely wasn't a lie. "Perhaps it's time to rethink your relationship with God."

Rose smiled at Annette as though she was still a small child, "Well I look forward to meeting Mark, but there is no way my relationship with God is ever going to change."

And with that she picked up the tea things and went out to the kitchen.

There was an awkwardness between them then, that continued until Mark arrived. After a brief introduction, Annette suggested they had a long drive ahead of them and should head off. Mark looked weary and seemed keen to comply. Annette was so caught up in her own thoughts, that it took her a while to realise that Mark was in a very different state of mind than he was on the way to Melbourne. He politely asked her about the visit with Rose, to which Annette replied, "It went okay." And then he didn't speak at all.

***

After they had been on the road for about an hour, she asked how the meeting had gone. His face darkened more.

"I told you, it's confidential."

"Yes, but you also said that as a pastor's wife, I need to learn to keep things to myself and I will. So, don't worry, I won't say anything."

"I shouldn't have told you as much as I did," he snapped. "Please don't ask me again!"

The shred of intimacy that she'd felt when he had taken her into his confidence earlier was shattered. It felt like he had slammed the door on their relationship yet again, shutting her out completely. There was probably no point continuing to question him. How could he be so cold? The truth that she had been denying to herself, rose up like a tidal wave and threatened to swamp her. She gulped and put her hand to her mouth to stifle a sob. Mark didn't love her. It was obvious. He was marrying her because he had to, because it was expedient, practical, and because it was expected after what had happened. She turned her head towards the window as tears silently rolled down her cheeks. Maybe she should just ask him if he did. What if he said *yes?* She wouldn't believe him. Deep down she knew that a yes would be a lie. And what if he admitted that he didn't love her? Would she walk away from this new life she was building? Would she walk away from Mark? She couldn't do that, not now. She had nothing to go back to.

And then, immediately, her thoughts turned to Alex. Of how close she had felt to him. How he'd listened to her, comforted her. There was no point though was there? Alex was a non-believer; she couldn't be with him. They would be *unequally yoked* as the Bible said. Where was God right now when she needed his guidance? But then, how could she expect to hear God's voice when she was thinking about being with another man? She wiped her tears away, then gave herself a mental slap on the face for her wrong thoughts.

Annette spent the rest of the trip hoping and praying for a sign that all was well. That God would show her that the path she was on was the right one. Didn't the Bible say the high road was steep and rocky? Even though Mark continued the drive in complete silence, Annette felt better and stronger.

When they arrived home, Mark went straight to his room and shut the door. When Grace called him at dinner time, he didn't emerge at all.

Chapter 18

Mark still seemed upset on Sunday. When he preached the sermon, Annette could tell there was something wrong. So far, he hadn't cracked his usual opening jokes, in fact, he hadn't even cracked a smile. Mark usually came across as fairly calm and reasoned while he was preaching. This morning, he sounded downright angry. He cautioned the members against having a critical spirit towards the brethren in the church and that the church must stay united at all costs.

In a booming voice, he said, "In Revelation 12:10 the Bible calls Satan, 'the accuser of our brethren'. It's Satan's job to condemn the members of God's family, and any time we do the same, we're doing the Devil's work for him. Who here is without sin and can cast the first stone?"

He thumped his hand down hard on the pulpit. Annette noticed people glancing around at each other—looking surprised and a little uncomfortable.

After returning from the shared lunch at the church, Mark went straight to his room. In the evening he emerged for dinner, but said and ate very little. Grace asked him if he was okay, and he muttered something about not feeling great. Again, he disappeared to his room straight after his plate was empty.

Although Annette was used to Mark shutting her out; she started to worry that something very serious was happening. When she knocked on his door, he asked her to please leave him alone. His voice was soft and she could have sworn she heard it crack a little with emotion. What could have happened at that meeting to upset him so much? He was probably sequestered in his room so that he could pray. No doubt God would help him resolve whatever was wrong. Nevertheless, it took willpower to walk away and not knock again.

She should follow Mark's lead and talk to God about her problems. Going to a counsellor seemed like a stupid idea now. That experience the other night was awful. Why would she even want to think about it, let alone discuss it with a complete stranger? Much better just to forget all about it. But then what about Daisy? She didn't know what else she could do for Daisy.

If there was a therapist the church trusted, then why hadn't Jane taken Daisy to see him already? Wasn't it the job of Daisy's parents to make sure she was okay? But Jack and Jane were mad at the nurse for her assumptions. They didn't believe anything had happened. Maybe, she should talk to them about it, somehow make them believe. If they didn't believe the nurse though, why would they believe her? She wasn't even around at the time. No, better to see the counsellor herself if it was possible, not to talk about her own problems but to talk about Daisy.

***

Annette had asked Alex not to come into the bakery again and he hadn't so far this week. Although she missed him, she was relieved. Her future was clearer before he had arrived. Her plans didn't have to change at all. When she recommitted to God, she also recommitted to His plan for her life. No point mooning over someone that she'd already broken up with once.

On her morning break, she went to the post office and looked through the local yellow pages. There couldn't be that many counsellors in Wellspring. She searched but couldn't find anything at all under C. Damn it! She would just have to ask someone his name. How could she do that without making it obvious why? She was still considering this question as she walked along the river to the spot where she usually ate her lunch. It was a comforting, peaceful place to sit, knowing the church was just up the hill. This spot made her feel closer to God.

Today it wasn't quiet though. As she approached, she could hear muffled voices coming from the church. Nobody was down on the river to see her, so she made her way up the hill, keeping to the cover of the huge redgums. Who would be in the church on a Monday? The ladies had a roster for the weekly cleaning, but these were male voices. She felt a little foolish, sneaking around like this, but she didn't want whoever it was to know she was eavesdropping.

As she came closer, she recognised the voices. It was Ted and Mark and they sounded angry. Like they were arguing. Was it about the orphanage? She knew that Ted didn't believe anything had happened. Maybe at that meeting, Mark had been given confirmation that something had actually happened.

What were they saying? She realised she was straining to hear the words. This was wrong, Mark would tell her what was going on when he was ready. She turned and went back down the hill, to find a quiet place to eat her lunch.

As she walked, an awful possibility began to uncoil inside her, like a snake waking from a long hibernation. Revulsion rose up from the pit of her stomach making her feel queasy. Sucking in deep long breaths helped a little, but she threw her lunch into a bin as she passed by. She no longer had any appetite at all.

The rest of the day at work was a struggle. Her mind went to and fro trying to convince herself that there could be any number of reasons for Mark and Ted's argument. Why think the worst?

***

When she arrived home and walked down the hallway, the sickening feeling came back. Ted was in his bedroom packing a suitcase.

"Where are you off to?" It was a struggle to keep her voice light.

"I'm going on a sabbatical... for a few weeks."

"What do you mean? What's a sabbatical?"

"It means..." he began, enunciating his words carefully as though explaining to a small child, "...I'm going away on my own, to spend time with God, to understand more fully what He wants for me."

"Oh... seems a bit sudden."

Ted's face clouded over. As she watched him slowly coil a leather belt in his hands, Annette immediately regretted her words. There was another belt just like that one when she was young. She took a step backward. Ted sighed, and his face relaxed into a smile.

"We can't always predict when God will call us, and, when he calls, we answer the call and we go." He laid the belt in the suitcase and lifted empty, upturned hands towards her. "Simple as that."

"Okay, hope it goes well then."

"Now, if you don't mind, I've got a lot to do."

She continued down the hall and found Grace in the kitchen making sandwiches.

Annette went past and said a quick, "Hi."

Grace looked up briefly from her work and said, "Hello, love." Then went back to the task at hand.

In front of Mark's door Annette paused and took in a deep breath. Why was she hesitating? She had a right to know what was going on. She was going to be his wife. Ted was her father. This time she knocked, then entered without waiting for a response and closed the door behind her.

Mark's desk was even messier than usual. Open books and notes were spread out over the bed as well. Mark was sitting at the desk staring out the window. When he turned towards her, she noticed dark circles under his eyes and that his hair was ruffled. And... the cause of his messy hair, as he ran his hand through and pulled at it, his face set in a taut mask.

"Yes, what is it?" he said.

"I want to know what's going on," she said, her voice hushed, but firm. "What happened at that meeting about the orphanage?"

"I already told you, it's confidential. Don't keep asking me."

Deciding to try a softer approach, she walked across to his chair and put a gentle hand on his shoulder. "Mark, we're going to be married, we're going to share the good and the bad. Can't you trust me with this?"

He rolled the chair away from her as if something disgusting had just landed on him. Immediately regretting touching him. she pulled her hand away. He faced her now

and looked at her with what appeared to be pure contempt.

"Why don't you ask your father what happened?"

Although his tone was low and measured, the anger
was almost palpable, "And... about the marriage, maybe we
need to rethink that whole idea. A relationship begun and
based on human lust is abhorrent to God."

Annette felt the tears prick at her eyes, but she fought
them back. No don't give him the satisfaction of seeing her
cry. It didn't matter how it started did it, if they loved each
other?

With a shaky voice, she asked, "What are you saying
Mark? Are you saying you don't love me?"

With a loud sigh he slumped into the chair. There was
a long pause before he spoke again, much more calmly this
time.

"I'm sorry, Annette, it's just that it's not a good time for
me right now. Ted's decided to go on this sabbatical, and
I've got a lot of work on that I'm going to have get done
without his help. So please, just leave me alone for now and
we'll sort everything out later." He took her hand, and his
tone softened even more, "Please don't worry. Okay? We've
got to remember that God is in control."

From the exhausted look on Mark's face, it was clear
that there was no point in continuing. Just leave him alone
for now as he'd asked, even though her wedding was now
hanging in jeopardy and all her questions remained unanswered. Maybe she should ask Ted directly as Mark had
suggested, but as she turned to leave Mark's room, she
heard Ted's Valiant start up and drive out of the driveway.

That evening as they ate together, Mark was visibly
more relaxed. Rather than creating a vacuum, Ted's absence
seemed to allow a warmth and intimacy between Grace and
her children that Annette hadn't really seen before. The at-

mosphere was light and almost cheerful. Esther relayed a funny story about what had happened in class that day, Grace talked about what she might cook for Sunday's potluck lunch and Mark suggested they all watch a video together that a church member had recommended. Annette was confused, something very serious was happening. Was she the only one who was concerned now? Shouldn't they be talking about what was going on, rather than acting out this charade that everything was fine? Mark's distress of the last few days seemed to have magically disappeared. He was his old self, but she knew she couldn't afford to let her guard down, not even for a minute, not with so much uncertainty about him and about Ted.

Halfway through the movie Annette excused herself, saying she was tired. The acting was bad, and the message was as subtle as a sledgehammer. She really wasn't in the mood to be pummelled with Christian platitudes. If her suspicions about Ted were true, the hypocrisy of what had occurred was just plain shocking. Had Mark confronted him about it? Had they decided that the answer was for him to go away for a while? Annette was jumping to conclusions. Wouldn't Mark have reported it to the police? Surely he would have. Although her father wasn't a nice man, was he really capable of something so heinous? She couldn't lay her suspicions aside though. Two years ago, the church hadn't handled the situation very well. As much as Annette wanted to be wrong about Ted, she just couldn't convince herself that she was.

***

At work the next day, Annette hoped that Alex would ignore her request not to come in and see her. As well as needing a distraction, she really wanted to talk to him. It felt like there was no one else to trust. By two in the afternoon, he hadn't come in and Annette was disappointed. She knew where to find him though. Once the idea had popped into her head, she couldn't shake it off. Instead of praying for the strength to resist, she plotted how she could see him and still get home at the usual time so as not to arouse suspicion. She asked Jane if she could leave half an hour early to catch the greengrocer before it closed. Alex would most likely have finished work by then.

"I just need to pick up some vegetables for dinner."

Jane looked a little surprised, Annette had never asked to leave early before.

"Yes, that's fine love. As long as you've caught up with the dishes before you go."

Annette worked quickly and was out the door by four thirty. She felt reckless as she cycled to the Tea Tree Motel as fast as she could. The feel of the wind blowing her hair out behind her, gave her a sense of bravado. They couldn't control her, she was eighteen years old, she could do what she bloody well liked. As she turned into the driveway, she was happy to see that his van was outside his room. Excitement coursed through her.

Alex looked surprised, yet pleased, when he opened the door. That was a relief. Mark's frequent and obvious displeasure with her had made her wary—but with Alex there was no need to feel that way. She could relax with him.

"It's nice to see you. I'm really glad you dropped in."

He didn't move towards her to give her a hug, like last time. This time though, she wished he would. He was still in his work clothes, plaster dust clung to his hair and coated the tops of his shoulders. It didn't matter at all to her.

"It's great to see you too," she said.

"Would you like a drink?"

There was no hesitation. "Yes, please."

"Help yourself, if that's okay? I was just about to have a shower."

Before she could tell him she didn't have much time, he took off his T-shirt off and walked into the bathroom. Annette helped herself to a bourbon and coke on ice. The coke bottle was only half full and had gone a bit flat, but she didn't care.

Alex had left the bathroom door open and she could hear the sound of the water hitting his body. As she took a long steady swig of her drink, she imagined him swishing the soap over his skin.

"I can't stay long," she called out.

"Can't hear you, come in and talk to me."

For just a moment, she lingered while she finished her drink. Then, an overwhelming need to feel wanted and close, combined with the delicious tingling of arousal, sent her into the bathroom.

The opaque shower curtain wasn't completely drawn so she could catch glimpses of him through the open edges. He looked good, he looked very good. Really, she should be censoring her thoughts and desires, but she didn't want to. His eyes were closed as the soapy rivulets drained from his hair. He faced towards her and the parts of his torso that she could see, were even more well defined than they used to be. Suddenly he pulled the curtain aside and caught her staring. She didn't look away. Her desire must have been as obvious to him, as his was to her, because she watched as his penis grew hard. The water spat out onto the floor, as they gazed at each other, neither moving.

"Why don't you join me?" he eventually said, his voice a little husky.

Without another word, she undressed. A pool of water was gathering on the floor in front of the shower, but Alex made no move to close the curtain. Annette was enjoying the way he was totally focused on her. It made her so excited. When she was completely naked, he held out his hand to her. She took it and stepped into the shower. Only then did he draw the curtain across.

***

A short time later, they lay on the bed, naked and still damp from the shower. Annette looked at the clock radio next to the bed. It was just after 5pm. She could still go home without arousing any suspicion. But did she want to leave? It felt wonderful to be lying here in his arms. Here she felt far away from all the complications of her new Christian life with Mark.

Why *had* she broken up with Alex? It was that stupid fight in the restaurant. Now that she looked back, it seemed so petty. He was only trying to please her, but it just was never enough. Alex had never been cruel with his words, like Mark had and she couldn't remember a time when Alex had shut her down or sat in judgement of her.

On the other hand, Mark was a Christian and a pastor. He was under a lot of pressure. She had learned that if Satan already has you, like he had her in the past, and like he still had Alex now, he didn't have to try. Mark was under attack by Satan, so was the church. He couldn't be expected to be as easy-going as Alex was. Mark was fighting a war against sin. Alex was just coasting along.

Abruptly she rose from the bed and went into the bathroom. Then, scooped her clothes up off the floor. How she could have been so shameless?

When she came out fully dressed Alex asked, "Hey, what's happening? Can't you stay?"

"No, I can't," she said.

"Why not?"

"I need to get home."

"I thought this..." He waved his hand across the bed. "... meant that you'd changed your mind."

Suddenly, she saw the pain she was causing him. It was written all over his face. His brows were knit together in confusion. It occurred to her that what she doing to him was no better than how Mark was treating her.

Oh God, what have I done?

A feeling of tenderness towards him welled up inside her. She did want to crawl back into bed with him and stay there forever, but it was wrong, and she would not do it.

She walked over to the bed and kissed him softly on the lips. "I'm sorry. I shouldn't have done that."

He turned away from her and she left the room quickly before she gave into her selfish desires again.

***

As she cycled home, the slight soreness from the pressure of the bicycle seat, became a bittersweet reminder both of her sin and of her pleasure. She couldn't help but relive the delicious sensations of an hour before. Again she felt his hungry kisses on her mouth as the water tumbled down on their bodies. The sensation of being pinned against the shower wall and the hardness of his chest against her nipples as he rubbed against her. Then the moment when she moaned with pleasure, after which, he turned off the shower, carried her out of the bathroom and gently lay her on the bed. The anticipation of his tongue on her and the intensity of it, flicking her into ecstasy. Then, pulling him up by his shoulders, before it was too late, and directing him inside her. Her climax—which came simultaneously with his—was exquisite.

Had it ever been so good with Alex before? Probably,

but she couldn't remember ever wanting it that badly, nor feeling so close to him. Nothing else mattered, it was as though nothing even existed outside that room. Sex was like food in that way, you could eat the same thing over and over. Then when you were really hungry again, the same food still tasted fantastic and new. And she had been hungry, ravenous, for physical touch, for affection, for intimacy, for love. Alex had given her all that she lacked.

It was different this time, though. This time, she felt as though she was fully there, whereas she had been slightly removed before. Not fully present, sometimes in the past it had even felt as though her mind and her body were acting separately. Why was it different now? It didn't matter. All she wanted to think about at this moment was their bodies entwined, the intimacy between them and how good it all felt. She refused to think about what had happened afterwards. How she had treated him. And, the knowledge that she had sinned, and sinned grievously, also hung there at the edge of her consciousness. A knowledge that threatened to taint this experience black. She would worry about that later. Just for now she would keep their encounter cocooned and safe from judgement. Just for a little longer.

Chapter 19

Annette remained lost in thought all through dinner. Not until later that evening did she realise Esther was angry with her.

Both Grace and Mark had gone out to Bible studies straight after dinner. Annette and Esther were left alone in the kitchen. Annette was drying a casserole dish and looking out the window. She smiled to herself.

Esther banged down a pile of dishes on the bench, startling Annette out of her daydream. When she looked towards the noise, Esther was staring at her.

"What's going on, Annette?"

What was she talking about? She couldn't possibly know what had happened. Annette drew her eyebrows together, attempting to appear completely puzzled by the question.

"I don't know what you mean?"

"Don't pretend you don't know what I'm talking about."

Annette was worried. Her sense of bravado evaporated. She didn't speak.

"I was driving past, and I saw you, I saw you ride into the Tea Tree Motel."

Esther spat out the last few words as though removing something poisonous from her mouth.

Shit! What an idiot! She hadn't checked if anyone was around before she'd turned into the entrance of the motel. Risked everything for what? A few moments of pleasure?

"So, I pulled up on the side of the road and watched you." Esther was shaking her head, her tone dropped lower.

The anger and disgust dissipated and her expression shifted to one of sadness. "I saw a man open the door to you Annette, I saw you go inside with him. There would only be one reason you would go into a man's motel room wouldn't there?"

Annette scrambled to come up with a feasible explanation for what Esther had seen. Then, she sighed. Even if she could come up with something believable—which was unlikely—she really didn't want to lie.

"He's an old boyfriend," Annette said softly. "It's only happened once, believe it or not."

"It really doesn't matter does it? If it was one time or fifty times. Sin is sin."

"I know." Annette lowered her eyes in shame. She felt dirty now. What she had done was disgusting to God. It was also a betrayal of this family.

"I'm sorry. I won't see him again. I hope you can forgive me."

Even as she said it, she wondered whether it was possible for her not to see Alex again. She remembered the look on his face when she left the room.

"Obviously you haven't changed at all. And, it's not just me you need forgiveness from is it? You need to ask God for forgiveness... and Mark, of course. How could you do that to us?"

Maybe Esther was right, maybe she hadn't changed. How would Mark react? Would he be jealous? He would be outraged, she was pretty sure about that, but jealous? Maybe not. He really wasn't showing much interest in her, not in that way. That was no excuse of course, she should have been stronger, had more willpower. She really did not want to face Mark about this.

"I don't know what happened... I guess when he turned up, I realised how lonely I was feeling."

Esther's expression softened. A little spark of hope returned, that Esther at least, could understand how hard this new way of life was for her.

"I get that it's not easy to be a Christian. Sometimes you can feel very alone..." Esther sighed heavily. "...and there are sacrifices to be made."

Esther paused, and when she spoke again, she had a faraway look. "We can't just do whatever we feel like though, even if we think no-one else will find out," her voice faltered, as a tear dribbled down her cheek. She wiped it away and turned sharply towards Annette She shook her head for emphasis. "You can't be doing things like that."

Maybe this one aberration of hers wasn't going to ruin everything after all. Obviously, Esther could empathise with her because of her own relationship with Violet. How far had those two had taken their feelings for each other?

"So, you won't tell Mark?" Annette asked.

Esther's eyebrows shot up in surprise. "Of course, I will. I have to tell Mark."

"But I thought you understood, you know, because of you and Violet."

The sting of the slap across her face was so unexpected, that Annette just stood there stunned, staring at Esther. Esther looked shocked as well.

"I'm sorry... I can't believe I did that."

Annette rubbed her face, which was still stinging. Her astonishment was quickly replaced by indignation. This wasn't fair. In the eyes of the church, Esther was just as much a sinner as she was. Esther looked as though she might cry again. She turned away from Annette and twisted a strand of hair in her hand. She stood doing that for quite a while.

Then she said in a deadpan voice, "I don't understand why you would say that. What do you mean because of me and Violet?"

Esther wasn't denying the relationship, but neither was she admitting to anything. Before now Annette had only a strong suspicion, but Esther's current behaviour was removing any doubt that something was going on. Although she knew that using this knowledge against Esther was a shitty thing to do, she felt cornered.

"What I mean is..." She paused for effect. "...how can you sit in judgement of my sin when you and Violet are lovers?"

Esther rested her elbows on the bench, took her head in her hands and began to sob. Annette felt instantly remorseful.

What a bitch I am!

This was not something she ever would have done before she became a Christian. She was a much more, live and let live, sort of person then. Now, she was just as judgemental as the rest of them.

"I'm sorry, I didn't mean to upset you."

Esther lifted her head and looked at Annette. Her voice quivered between sobs as she spoke.

"I never meant for it to happen. God knows, I've prayed over and over for those feelings and urges to leave me. Violet doesn't see it the same way I do. She believes a loving God will accept us as we are. I wish that were true, but I don't agree. I know it's wrong, but eventually, I guess I gave into it. You're right, I am no better. Like you, I'm just not strong enough to overcome the temptations of the flesh."

"How long have you been together... that way?"

Esther gave out what sounded like a choked laugh, but she wasn't smiling.

"It's been going on for five years. Since the last year of high school. No one has ever suspected, not until now. Nobody would believe a pious, piano-playing, churchgoing, Christian primary school teacher could be a... a lesbian." She whimpered, again on the verge of tears, then sniffed and continued, "Oh don't worry, I've tried to stop. After I went away to uni, I refused to see her when I visited here, except at church of course. It was really hard on her during those years. I dated Christian boys, but I just didn't feel what I felt with Violet," Her voice shifted, now there was a pleading quality to it. With her head lowered she said, "Annette, you have to believe me, I don't want to be like this. I'm trying to change. I started seeing a counsellor in Wellspring a few weeks before you came to live here, I know I need help to change, I've tried to do it alone, but I can't. I'm so sick of living a lie."

"Is it helping, seeing a counsellor?"

"I'm not sure, I thought she would tell me how to stop, that's what I wanted, but it isn't turning out that way. The sessions are more focused on how I really feel about the relationship, which is not what I expected. I find I'm questioning a lot of things I've always just accepted... and I don't know if that's a good thing or not."

Annette was relieved to hear out loud that she wasn't the only one with doubts and questions.

"I shouldn't be talking this way when you are such a new Christian."

"No, it's okay," Annette reassured her, "and you don't have to worry Esther, I won't say anything about this."

Esther let out a sigh. "Really? Thank you, I appreciate that... How did you know about us? I mean, I know we spend a lot of time together, but how did you know we were lovers and not just good friends?"

Annette smiled and said, "It's the way Violet looks at you that gives it away. It's not that easy to find someone who loves you that much."

Annette thought of Alex then. No, it wasn't easy to find someone like that. Would God really want Esther to throw away her relationship with Violet? Annette wasn't sure, and if she wasn't sure about Esther, how could she be so certain that she shouldn't be with Alex.

Annette needed to figure things out, and fast. And she knew that somehow, that old, deep, unresolved turmoil was keeping her confused about what she wanted. She decided to take a risk and confide in Esther, even though she wasn't sure whether she could trust her.

"Remember you told me about those girls that were abused. I know it sounds crazy, but I think something like that happened to me too. I don't know who or when, I can't remember any details except the awful feelings and the pain. If I could understand what happened, maybe I would make better choices. I think I need a little help to work through things as well."

Esther raised her eyebrows then nodded. "Yes, it does sound crazy. If something that bad happened why wouldn't you remember it, all of it?" Although, Esther didn't seem to believe Annette, her tone was gentle. "Sounds like you do need help though. I'll give you the number of the place where I go. It's the only place in Wellspring. There's another counsellor at the practice. I've heard that he understands about that sort of thing."

Of course, it must be the same counsellor that the Wellspring church board had brought in to advise them, the one she had tried to find. It seemed that it was God's plan for her to go there after all.

"A teacher who's on the board of Wellspring church told me that just last week. It seems that they got that counsellor involved in this orphanage business. I think the teacher told me because he wanted to make the point that our church hadn't taken any action. Apparently, the counsellor was to give the new house parents advice on questioning the children about what had happened to them."

Now that the conversation had shifted, Annette realised she was holding her breath.

"And do you know if they found out what happened, who it was?"

"I don't know actually," Esther said, then paused. "It's odd. When I asked the teacher about it yesterday at morning tea, he said I shouldn't be asking about it, that it was confidential. He was quite snappy with me. Not really fair when he brought it up in the first place..."

Esther's expression suddenly darkened, a look of realisation spreading across her face. "You're not thinking..."

Annette was about to respond when Esther laughed a little, shook her head, and said, "No, of course you're not, sorry, that was just a ridiculous thought. Let's ask Mark what happened, he'll know."

"Hmm, yes, I believe he does know," Annette said.

***

A few days later Annette was on the bus to Wellspring to see the counsellor. No wonder she couldn't find him in the phone book. He was a psychologist. Of course, he would be listed under "P" not "C". Esther had explained that the counsellors were husband and wife, working from their home.

Tap, tap, tap—her fingers drummed on the armrest. The woman sitting next to her looked at Annette's hand, then smiled at Annette. Annette smiled back at her, then rested her hands on her thighs. She took a deep breath. Maybe it wouldn't be so bad. Talking things over seemed to have been good for her relationship with Esther. At least someone else in the house knew about her struggles now. And she and Esther had become closer in the days that followed their confrontation. Esther seemed more relaxed around her. Maybe she was relieved to have shared her secret too. Although, Esther hadn't said that she would keep what she knew about Alex to herself, Annette felt confident that she would. It seemed to be an unspoken agreement that they would keep each other's secrets.

Annette's heart started hammering as she walked through the gate leading to the counsellor's front door. It was an older-style weatherboard home, with white, wrought iron lacework under the curved corrugated roof of the verandah. Not the sterile, modern environment that she had pictured. She didn't know why but the leadlight image of a kookaburra set into the front door comforted her. Strangely, the neglected front garden did too. There were two silver cat bowls below an old church pew that sat on a faded rug on the wide verandah. Was she even at the right house? She walked back and checked the number on the letterbox again. No, this was it. She rang the front doorbell.

"Hi, Annette is it?" asked a friendly voice. The man opened the screen door for her to enter. "I'm Murray, come on in."

Too late to run away now. She followed Murray through the doorway as he padded along the hallway in his old slippers and lead her into an oddly furnished room.

Mismatched recliners with the leather worn down in places sat almost opposite each other. There was an old-fashioned chaise covered in faded floral tapestry in front of a bay window. Annette was surprised when he gestured towards the one of the recliners, rather than the chaise.

Murray must have noticed her expression and he chuckled. "Don't worry there's no lying down anymore, but you can put your feet up if you like." He tapped the bar on the side of the recliner.

Annette sat stiffly upright on her armchair, feet firmly on the ground. Murray on the other hand sank back into his, looking very much at ease.

"Well Annette, do you want to start by telling me a bit about what's brought you here today?"

Now that she was here, Annette did not want to talk. Although, the words were boiling up inside her—threatening to overflow into a raging torrent she couldn't control —she had to keep herself in check. She didn't know this man. How could she trust him? Murray sat silently with a gentle smile on his face, looking at her. Why didn't he speak? The silence continued, she could hear the clock on the mantelpiece—tick tock, tick tock. She stared out of the bay window, trying to compose herself. Through the lace curtains, she could see a willow tree, swaying gently in the breeze. Thoughts tumbled in, one on top of the other, one minute it was about Mark and how sweet he'd been when they met, then the next minute it was the betrayal. Bringing her to his home to face Ted and then Ted's subsequent disdain of her. And then Mark's disdain of her. One face, then another face, looking down on her, both disapproving, both unloving. Pictures came then of childhood, her mother bruised and bloody. Ted—with Johnny Walker bottle in hand—yelling abuse at them both, then slamming the door and roaring out the driveway. Esther's story about

Ted hitting her mother. Then she pictured herself again in Daisy's bedroom, Daisy's white terrified face and the sickening drawing. This was quickly followed by the memory of her own experience alone in her bed. She felt nauseous, she felt hot. Her chest was tight, she was struggling to breathe.

From what seemed like a long distance away, she heard a gentle, but firm voice. "Annette, look at me."

As though she was seeing through a thick fog, her eyes moved slowly from the window towards Murray's voice.

"Annette, you're safe in this room, nothing can hurt you here."

As she looked into Murray's kind eyes and then down at his grey, sheepskin scuffs, she believed him. She was safe here.

Then, she dissolved into tears. "I don't understand what's wrong with me."

"That's okay, we'll figure out what's going on."

She began to feel a little better. Murray passed her a white handkerchief which she took and blew her nose.

"You have so much sadness for one so young," he said, looking sad himself. "If the sadness was a well, how deep would it be?" he asked.

Annette pictured herself looking into a well, she couldn't see anything but blackness.

"There's no bottom in the well," she decided.

"Trust me," Murray reassured her, "there is a bottom and we will find it together."

Like a child, she let herself be held by his words and then she told him her story. At times he asked questions to clarify some detail or other, but mostly he just listened.

She hesitated before telling him about what had happened with Alex. Was Murray a Christian? Would he sit in judgement? Would he remind her that she'd sinned?

"Do you believe in God?" she asked.

"Is it important for you to know that?"

Everyone else she knew seemed to be on one side or another —for or against Christianity—for or against God. Maybe Murray wouldn't take a side. Maybe, he would even... take her side.

When she didn't answer, he said, "You know, you may want to think of me as a pimple on the bum of the church. And, as you can imagine it becomes hard for people to squeeze out their stuff... so to speak, if they think I have strong opinions one way or another."

Annette laughed and it was okay because Murray laughed with her. She shook her head and said, "No, well I guess it's not important."

So, she told him about that afternoon with Alex at the motel—not the details of course.

"We... well, you know. We did it."

She searched his face and could tell he understood what she meant. Nevertheless his gentle smile didn't waver. Even when she explained how she'd become engaged, his face held no judgement. It sounded ridiculous when she said it out loud. Even more ridiculous that she was going along with it—that it was what she wanted. But Murray didn't say it was ridiculous, he did ask though if she still wanted to marry Mark—given how she felt about Alex.

The dream she'd had that day, back in Tracy's flat, came back to her. She didn't know why, but it seemed important so she recounted it to Murray.

"There was so much water. The plant was drowning. And the woman, she just watched on oblivious, and he kept pouring the water on, until there was no chance of the pansy surviving. I don't understand the dream, or why it was so disturbing."

"You are the architect of your dreams; you know that don't you? You created the dream and you know what it means. Perhaps not consciously, but somewhere deep inside, you know."

Towards the end of the session, he said that he agreed with her, bad things had happened. Those bad things that she remembered and those that maybe, she didn't, he called them "traumatic memories". He said these memories aren't like normal memories, that they get stuck inside us when we're children and then cause us problems as adults. He said it was okay that she didn't remember everything, that she may, or she may not and that was okay too. She could still feel better, and that he could help her with that.

When it was time to leave, she dangled the crumpled, moist handkerchief in the space between them.

"Where do I put this this?" she asked.

"Keep it, maybe give it a wash and bring it next time." He smiled his gentle smile, and said, "Just in case."

"Oh, I can't afford to come every week."

"Don't worry. There's some government funding that will cover the cost."

***

On the way home, she relived the session, the things she'd said, the things Murray had said. She felt lighter, more hopeful. That was, until it dawned on her that the whole session had been about her. She hadn't talked about Daisy, or the orphanage at all. Why hadn't she talked about those things? Murray knew about the orphanage. Perhaps he could have either confirmed or denied her suspicions. What was wrong with her? She should have asked.

Ted was due back the day after her next appointment with Murray. She shook her head from side to side a little. No, she wouldn't think about him coming back right now. She would talk about it all in her next session. For now, she would focus on sorting herself out.

Chapter 20

The next day was Friday and it was busy at work which made it easier not to think about things. In the late afternoon, when the after-school rush was over —not long before closing—Annette was doing the daily clean of the display fridges. Daisy was at her usual table near the kitchen door doing homework. Apart from Daisy, the café was empty.

Jane looked up from her food prep for the following day and asked, "Where's your father? I heard he's gone away for a while."

Annette turned and looked at Jane. It was hard to identify Jane's mood right now. Was she angry?

"He's away on a Sabbatical," Annette said.

Jane's mouth curled slightly into what appeared to be a sneer.

Annette continued uncertainly, "Umm, I'm not sure where he went."

Annette noticed Jane glancing over at Daisy. Daisy seemed focused on her homework. Annette didn't think Daisy was listening to their conversation. Jane lowered her voice though when she spoke again. This time there was no mistaking the contempt.

"You and I need to talk."

Annette was shocked, Jane had never had a cross word with her. She waited for Jane to continue, tense now. Jane pursed her lips and turned to Daisy.

"Daisy you can go upstairs and watch TV now."

Daisy looked up from her work. "I'm supposed to finish this for tomorrow." Her eyebrows rose. "Don't you want to check it? You always want to check it."

"Well then, go upstairs and finish it. I'll come and check it later."

Daisy packed up her things. "Can I have a coke?"

Jane usually said no to soft drink, but this time she went to the fridge, got a bottle of coke and opened it. Then she walked over to Daisy saying, "Now, go when I ask you to."

When they were alone again, Jane went over and locked the front door, turning the open sign over to closed. She sat down heavily at the table that Daisy had just vacated and indicated to Annette to join her. Annette slowly took off her apron, hung it on its hook and sat down opposite Jane.

Jane sighed. "Annette, you've been a really good worker and I'm sorry to have to do this..." All the anger seemed to have disappeared, now Jane simply looked deflated.

Annette could guess what was coming, but still, she couldn't quite believe it.

"...I have to let you go."

It was so unexpected, out of the blue. Annette knew she hadn't done anything different from usual.

"But... why? I don't understand."

"Oh, please don't ask me that. It's been a difficult week, what with the rumours that are flying around and... I just can't have you working here anymore. That's it, that's the end of it!"

"What rumours are you talking about? Are they about me?"

"No, not about you." Jane paused. Her expression softened, just a little. "Well of course there's been talk about you ever since you arrived, but that's not what I mean."

"Well, who then, and what does it have to do with me?"

Jane sat for a moment; her head cocked to the side. She shook her head and whatever she was about to say was left unspoken. Then she rose and walked over to the till, opened it and counted out a bundle of notes.

"This more than covers your pay for the next two weeks."

Annette was stunned. "What? You want me to finish right now, this afternoon?"

"Yes, that's what I want." Jane was holding out the money. "Please take this and go."

Annette stood up walked stiffly over to Jane, took the money then turned quickly and left before Jane could see the tears spilling down her cheeks.

The rain that pelted down as she cycled away from the bakery camouflaged her tear-streaked face. It was so unfair. This was about Ted, she knew it. She could guess the content of the rumours. It would be, what she herself had suspected. She forced the words into her head. Ted probably had molested those children in Thailand. Her stomach lurched. It was sickening. Her own father. That was why he had tried to discredit the girl that had spoken out. And, Mark had sent him away for two weeks. What would that achieve? Not only that, but Ted was supposed to be a Christian. How could he possibly turn up at church every week and pretend he was if he had done those unspeakable acts? He couldn't, could he? So, maybe she was wrong. Maybe she should be sure before she condemned him. A

Christian couldn't do a thing like that. Yeah sure, she had seen some behaviours from the Christians she had met in Pleasant Valley that didn't seem particularly Christ like, but they were only human after all. But this, this was on a different level. A Christian couldn't possibly commit a heinous crime like this.

As she neared the Tea Tree Motel, she didn't hesitate as she turned into the driveway. Not caring if anyone saw her. She needed to see Alex. She needed to be with someone she could trust. Was it fair, after what she had said to him last time? No, she didn't care if it was fair or not, right now she just had to see him. As she got closer, she saw a different car in front of his motel room.

A man in overalls raked leaves on the lawn opposite Alex's room.

She stepped off her bike and called out to him, "Umm, excuse me."

The man looked up.

"There's usually someone staying here, his name is Alex, but... that's not his car."

"Oh, Alex." The man scratched his head. "Yep, I know who you mean. He's one of the workers at the new hospital."

She nodded.

"They all leave on Fridays, love. We rent the rooms out to other people over the weekend." He drew his eyebrows together in an expression that said he was surprised that wasn't obvious to her.

Oh fuck!

How could she have forgotten that? She felt ashamed, just expecting him to be there waiting for her. Of course, he had his own life in Melbourne. A life she hadn't really asked about. So focused on her own problems, even when she was with him.

The let-down she felt at not seeing him came out as a little whimper. The man's expression changed to one of concern. He propped his rake against a nearby wall and walked towards her.

"Oh love... tsk, tsk," he said, clicking his tongue. "Please don't cry. If you want to leave him a note, I can give it to him. They're usually back by Sunday night."

Annette nodded, not trusting herself to speak. She followed him to the reception office. The man handed her some notepaper, a pen and an envelope. She was thankful for the privacy of the envelope.

"Just pop his name on it and leave it on the counter when you go." he said, and then gestured towards a chair by the door. "You're welcome to sit in here until the rain stops if you like. I need to get back to it." He left her hurriedly, as if relieved to escape before there were any more emotional displays.

She took a brochure from a stand to rest the paper on, and then sat down heavily. What now? She sighed. Jane had said people were talking about her as well. What were they saying? Were they questioning her worthiness to be a pastor's wife? Well, why wouldn't they? She was kidding herself. If the rumours about Ted were true, then she was from rotten stock. No wonder she felt so bad on the inside. She wasn't good enough and that's why Mark didn't want her, not really, especially not now. This life was not for her.

On the scrap of paper she wrote.

Please come and get me.
A

She stared at the note in her hand and pictured Alex sweeping her into his arms. Was that what she wanted? And what about Daisy, the promise she had made to herself about Daisy. Daisy... the possibility struck her like a bolt of lightning, quickly followed by a wave of nausea. Was Ted the church monster? Had Ted been the one molesting Daisy, before he went to Thailand? Maybe even since he'd returned. How though? When would he have the opportunity?

The time for hiding from the truth was over. She had to know for certain about Ted one way or the other. With a new sense of purpose and determination she took the note from her lap, crumpled it, then walked over and threw it in the wastepaper bin next to the reception desk. Leaving the envelope and pen on the counter she walked outside and saw that the same man was still raking leaves from the garden beds around the office.

"Sorry, I changed my mind. I'll catch up with Alex during the week," she said, as she took her bike from its stand and mounted it.

The man nodded and gave her a wave as she cycled away.

***

As difficult as it was to keep silent about her suspicions that night, she decided that she would wait until after she had spoken to Daisy. If Mark was covering this up, then he was no more likely to tell her now than he was before. Annette wasn't the only one who was quiet during dinner. Esther looked troubled, as though she had something on her mind. Maybe she should seek Esther out and ask what was wrong after dinner. There was no opportunity though. Esther excused herself before everyone had finished, leaving half her food uneaten. They all heard her car drive out soon after.

Grace looked surprised. "I didn't know she was going out tonight."

Mark shrugged. "Probably had a music practice, she said they were doing a new song on Sunday."

"Oh." Grace seemed to relax a little. "Odd that she didn't say so, though."

Mark sighed, then said, "Don't worry about it, Mum."

And with that, he stood up and left the table himself and went to his room leaving Grace looking confused.

She turned to Annette, "Is there something going on that I should know about?"

Annette didn't trust herself to answer. She shrugged and gave her head a slight shake.

"I'll clear up if you like," she offered.

Grace gave her an appreciative smile. "Thanks love, I am feeling a little tired."

Grace cleared a few dishes from the table while the kettle boiled. Then she made herself a cup of tea and went into the lounge room. Shortly after, Annette heard Grace chuckling along with the canned laughter of a comedy show on the TV.

For the first time, Annette considered the impact this whole thing might have on Grace. This was her husband, an elder of the church, a lay pastor and a Christian. Someone who had made a commitment to be faithful to her alone. Grace seemed to only see the best in people. How would she cope? Maybe that was one of the reasons Mark was keeping it quiet. She was his mother after all. Maybe he was protecting her? Imagine if the whole congregation found out. Grace would be humiliated. Ted would bring disgrace down on the whole family.

***

The next day Annette carried out her plan to speak to Daisy. Clearly, she wasn't welcome at the bakery, so she would have to be careful not to run into Jane. She hoped to catch Daisy playing in their backyard that backed onto the river.

Annette approached the yard by making her way uphill from the path by the river. Her heart was beating fast. She wasn't sure whether she was more nervous because she might get caught sneaking around, or whether it was for fear of what Daisy might say.

She was in luck. From her position to the side of the backyard, partially hidden by a huge redgum, Annette could see Daisy playing hopscotch on the concrete path that led out to the clothesline. Daisy had drawn the squares and numbered them in chalk and while Annette watched she threw a stone into the second square. She jumped into the first square and then into the third square, but instead of continuing to the fourth square, she suddenly sat down heavily in the third square. She turned and picked up the stone from the second square, then with her back to her house, twisted the sharp end of the stone into the palm of her hand.

Annette was too shocked to act for a moment; she couldn't believe what she saw. Why would Daisy hurt herself like that? Well, she could think of one reason why.

She stepped out from behind the tree and called to Daisy in a hushed, but firm, voice, "Daisy!"

Daisy dropped the stone and looked around to see where the voice was coming from. Her face went red, but she came over to the fence with a smile on her face.

"Mum said you weren't coming back; she wouldn't tell me why. Are you coming back to work here?"

There was a pleading quality to Daisy's voice. Annette was not prepared for questions so she changed the subject.

"Why were you hurting yourself, Daisy?"

Daisy looked at the ground. The smile that appeared

when Daisy had first seen Annette vanished. She kicked the dust at her feet and after a long pause, she said, "I do it when the bad things come into my head. It helps me not to think of them anymore."

Annette steeled herself and asked, "What bad things do you think of, Daisy?"

Daisy shook her head. "I'm not allowed to talk about it," she said.

Now Annette could see a tear dribbling down Daisy's cheek.

"It's okay Daisy, don't cry. I'm not going to get you into trouble, but can you tell me who told you you're not allowed to talk about it?" Annette asked.

"Well... he said not to tell anyone, that's why I lied to Mum when she asked me the first time. Then, when I told her the truth last week, she said not to talk about it. She said I've done a sinful thing and then lied about it. She told me to ask God for forgiveness and then forget it ever happened. She said not to think about it ever again." Daisy stopped for a few seconds, then said quietly, "But I can't stop thinking about it, I've tried, and I've tried, but I can't."

This was not what Annette had expected to hear. When she had played this conversation over in her head, she had imagined herself asking Daisy to tell her parents. But Daisy had already told—her mother at least—and nothing had happened.

"Have you told your dad?" she asked.

"No, Mum said he doesn't need to know."

How could Jane let Daisy believe she was the one who had done wrong? She knew she probably shouldn't be asking Daisy to go against her mother's wishes but she had to persevere. She had to know the truth.

"Daisy, it was the church monster who hurt you, wasn't it? I need you to tell me who the church monster is."

Daisy's face went pale, her eyes opened wide.

"No, he said I wanted him to do it, and everybody would think I was a bad girl. I told Mum, and she thinks I'm bad. You'll think I'm bad too. And it's not even true." Daisy was starting to sound hysterical now, the pitch of her voice raised higher. "I didn't want him to do it, I didn't."

"Of course, you didn't Daisy. It's not your fault, you didn't do anything wrong." Annette said as gently as she could. Daisy looked up at Annette and sniffed.

"You don't think I'm bad?"

"No, Daisy, whoever did it is the bad one, not you."

Daisy looked less distraught now, more hopeful. Her mouth turned up into an ever so slight smile.

"Daisy! Come inside now!"

Daisy jumped when she heard Jane's voice from the direction of the flyscreen door. Her time was up, so at the risk of upsetting Daisy again, she asked in a gentle voice, "Daisy, it's really important that you tell me who it was? Was it one of the elders?"

Annette didn't need to hear a response, Daisy's face as screwed up again in confirmation as she fought back a new wave of tears.

Jane opened the door but didn't step outside. "Daisy come away from the fence and come inside now!"

Daisy looked up at the house towards her mother and then turned slowly back to Annette. She mouthed the words almost soundlessly, but there was no mistaking what she said.

"It was Elder Ted... It was your dad."

Then Daisy sniffed once more, wiped her eyes, turned and walked towards the house.

Chapter 21

As Annette cycled home, she realised she wasn't surprised by Daisy's response. It was only confirmation of what she already knew was true. It was Ted who had molested those children at the orphanage, as well as Daisy and the other girl who had moved away. Maybe there were others. He worked with children after he left her and Rose...

What was confusing now was the way people had responded. If the church leaders, the school principal and both sets of parents knew about the two girls, why had none of those people done anything? Why weren't the police involved then? Why weren't they involved now that they all suspected that Ted had molested the children at the orphanage? Why had no one stopped him? Annette felt a growing sense of outrage surging up from the pit of her stomach. Why was no one protecting these kids? Did no one care about their suffering?

And Ted, how could he? It made her sick to think about it. How could he stand up in church and pretend to be a Christian? He was the same as he'd always been. She hated him, the bastard!

And then, out of nowhere, a memory came to her. Her family at the beach on a summer evening. Ted, in a rare good mood, had suggested it. Annette must have been about seven years old. Rose sat on the beach watching, while Ted raced Annette into the warm water. Then the two of them body-surfed into shore on the waves. Later, Rose came in too, and stood in the shallows. The three of them threw the brightly, coloured beach ball to each other. Annette and Ted—further out—splashed about, diving forward or throwing themselves back to catch the ball before it hit the water. Afterwards, Ted went and bought dinner from the kiosk on the beach. They ate hot fish and chips and drank icy cold coke from glass bottles as they sat on their towels. Rose and Ted —not fighting—but chatting and laughing like the other normal, happy couples having fun on the beach.

Annette's anger died down as she reflected on that perfect memory. What remained was sadness. Who was she sad for—for herself, for her mother, for those children Ted had damaged? Maybe even for him, for her father. Why did he have to be like that when, sometimes, he could be so wonderful?

Other memories came back then of her mother, bruised, bleeding, crying. Annette cowering in her room too scared to come out; so paralysed with fear, she couldn't do anything to help Rose. Couldn't try to stop him. Annette suddenly felt very young and alone. She was still scared of Ted. Although it felt better to acknowledge it, she would not let the fear get the better of her again, like it did when she was young.

Suddenly it seemed important that she talk to her mother. Rose knew the real Ted. Rose knew the father Annette had grown up with, the good and the bad, not this fake, charming church-goer who had fooled everyone here.

And Rose had finally stood up to Ted, just as Annette may have to do soon. Although Rose might be shocked to hear this new information about Ted, Annette would tell her anyway.

She headed towards the service station on the outskirts of town. There was a phone booth there. She fished in her bag for coins and her small address book. Her hand was shaking as she dialled the number.

"Hello, Bob speaking."

"Hi, Bob, it's me."

"Annette, it's good to hear from you. How are you?"

"I'm okay," she lied. "Can I speak to Mum?"

"Sorry love, she's not home. Can I help?"

"No," her voice cracked with disappointment. "It doesn't matter."

"You don't sound okay. Where are you, anyway? Your mum is so worried about you. You know we can come and get you if you want?"

For the briefest moment Annette was tempted to say yes. It would be so good to get away from this awfulness. The thought of leaving Mark now didn't distress her at all, but if she left now, what would happen to Daisy? Her resoluteness returned. She wouldn't abandon Daisy, she just wouldn't. Ted's behaviour had to stop. She didn't really know what to do, but she would figure it out.

"Annette, I mean it. You can come and stay with us for as long as you want."

"Thanks Bob, maybe I will, but not now. Please tell Mum I called."

"Can you give me a phone number, so she can call you back?"

"Umm... no it's okay. I'll call again soon. Bye."

Before he could say more she hung up. She had one ten cent piece left. Alex. Alex would know what to do. He had said, *call anytime.* She dialled his number, it rang a few times and then went to an answering machine. Disappointed, she hung up without leaving a message. Tomorrow night he would be back in town. She would see him then.

Standing there in the phone booth she considered going to the police. What would happen? Would they talk to Daisy? Daisy was so terrified maybe she wouldn't talk to them especially since Jane had told her not to talk about it. Then what? Annette didn't know the name of the other girl it had happened to. She couldn't even tell them where Ted was, even if they wanted to talk to him. And what about the orphanage? The Australian police may not get involved with a crime that was committed overseas. No, she didn't think she had anything concrete enough yet. So far it was only what she had heard. If nobody in the church confirmed what she was saying perhaps the police wouldn't investigate at all and Ted would continue to hurt other children. And why would those who knew in the church talk to the police now? They had kept it a secret so far. Maybe she could convince Mark to talk to the police. Maybe he didn't know about Daisy and the other girl. Yes, he was protecting his mother, but if he knew that children were still at risk, right here in this town, then surely, as a pastor, he would make sure they were protected from Ted. The police would believe the story if it came from Mark. She cycled home feeling at least as though she had a semblance of a plan.

Annette walked towards the house after putting her bike away in the shed. There were raised voices coming from the kitchen. She stepped lightly on the path so as not to make any noise. It sounded like Esther and Mark were arguing.

"You have to tell her," Esther was saying.

"Why, what purpose would that serve?"

Annette hesitated outside before opening the kitchen door. They must not have heard her arrive. Here she was eavesdropping again, without intending to, but this time she felt justified. Mark had kept secrets from her once too often.

Mark continued, "She would be devastated, she loves those kids, and he's her husband. An elder of the church."

"Yes, but how can you possibly think it's okay for her to continue living with him? Sleeping in the same bed as him? It's disgusting!" Esther spat out the last few words.

Annette opened the door and stepped into the kitchen. They were sitting at the table. They looked up at her briefly, both clearly embarrassed, then they looked away. Esther picked up her cup, drank from it, then cradled it in her hands. Mark took a sip from his glass of water and then set it back down on the table slowly. Nobody spoke for a few seconds.

Eventually, Mark said, "Hi." Then he rose from his chair, walked across and placed his glass on the sink. "Sorry, got to go, I've got a sermon to finish."

Annette's heart was beating fast again and when she spoke, she struggled to keep her voice under control.

"No," she said firmly.

She moved towards the kitchen table and pulled out a chair but remained standing with her hands on the back of the chair.

"Stay right there."

Annette kept a stony glare on Mark as he stood there for a few moments. Then he refilled his glass and took his seat again at the table.

Annette looked across at Esther who was shifting in her seat and said, "You stay too."

Esther gave a slight nod.

Thank God!

Esther seemed to be onside. This couldn't remain hidden any longer. Annette sat down.

"I'm not quite sure what it is you think you heard..." Mark began slowly.

"Don't worry, I know what you were talking about. I know about Ted; I know what he did to those children at the orphanage."

She let that sink in for a moment. Then, she turned her attention to Esther, raising her eyebrows. "Obviously you knew as well."

"No," Esther said, shaking her head, "I wasn't sure of anything up until a few moments ago. After you and I talked the other night, I called my colleague who's on the board and asked him again what the outcome was, of speaking with Dao and the Thai children. All he would say is, that 'it's being handled' and that I should 'ask my brother about it.'" She smiled, but it wasn't a happy smile. "Knowing that things in the church are often *handled* by sending people away on *Sabbatical...*" She looked pointedly at Mark. "It added up. I haven't been able to ask Mark about it until now because Mum's been around. He's just confirmed that it was Ted who abused those children."

They both looked at Mark. He looked heavenward and sighed before speaking.

"It is being handled," he said, shaking his head at Esther. "These things have to be managed delicately. There's a lot at stake. I've already told you, Annette, that this is confidential information, which I didn't have permission to share with you, but since he's your father, I guess it's important that you know what's been put in place."

Annette felt herself relax slightly. Something was being done after all.

"Ted agreed to undergo specialised psychiatric care in a private church hospital in Sydney. He's receiving the most up to date treatment from one of our most prominent and skilled psychiatrists for his... sinful tendencies."

"What if the treatment doesn't work?" Esther asked. "And how will we know either way?"

"I'm assured that at the end of the two weeks he will be either cured, or, at worst, he may need a further two weeks of treatment." He paused again, looking closely at his glass of water. "I'm told they run tests to check, they measure his response to images." He looked up and then at each of them in turn. "That's how they assess whether he's still a risk or not."

Annette was confused. She looked across at Esther, who didn't look as though she understood either.

"How do they measure it? How can they be sure?" she asked.

Mark huffed in frustration. "Do I have to spell it out for you? Isn't it obvious? They measure the blood flow to... you know, his penis, while he's looking at stimulating pictures." He shook his head.

"Oh," said Annette, regretting that she'd asked.

They were all quiet for a while.

"He did it to Daisy as well," Annette said softly, breaking into the silence.

"Oh no," Esther said. "How do you know?"

"I asked her."

"That all makes sense then," Esther said, with a heavy sigh. "He offered to help the Sunday school teacher. He actually asked to do it. I remember thinking how unusual that was because most men think Sunday school teaching is beneath them. He suggested separating the kids into age groups for their benefit. 'More specialised teaching', he said, 'We should take some of the load off the Sunday school teacher.'" She shook her head. "Daisy and the other girl —the girl that left town—they were the only ones in their age group. He was their only teacher for about six months until he went to Thailand." Her mouth curled into an expression of contempt. "We made it easy for him didn't we? That nurse knew something was wrong, but nobody listened to her. I didn't listen to her. All this wouldn't have happened, if we'd stopped him back then." She turned to Mark. "I'm sorry, Mark, I should have told you about all this at the time."

Annette was watching Mark while Esther was speaking. Now he was shifting in his seat; he looked uncomfortable and didn't meet Esther's gaze. Realisation slowly dawned on her.

"You knew about the girls here in the church, didn't you?"

Mark didn't speak straight away, then he looked at Annette.

Stony faced, he said, "The pastor told me because he thought I should know, because of Mum. This was before the other family had left, at the time when the leaders were trying to decide what to do. That family wanted us to report it to the police, but that wasn't considered an option. This is a small town, something like that can bring down a church in the eyes of the community. What about our witness to unbelievers? Satan would win because who would want to join a church like that? And what if he hadn't done it? Our church would be dragged through the mud for nothing." He sighed slowly and then began again. "It was decided that I would sit down with him and confront him. I was nearly finished at the seminary, and they felt, because of my personal involvement and because Ted may have sinned against my mother, that it should be me. Well, Ted denied everything. He was very angry that he had been accused when all he was trying to do was to further God's work."

Mark paused, he seemed less sure of himself now. There was a hint of pleading in his voice. "Look, I'm not sure I believed him, but I had no proof. Jane had asked Daisy about it and Daisy had denied that anything had happened. The other girl had recounted details to her parents, but it was still only her word against his. What was I supposed to do?" He threw up his hands. "It wasn't my decision anyway. When I reported back to the church leaders, well, all were agreed that, even if it was true, he would be too frightened to ever do it again. For everyone's sake, it was decided that it would be best though, that he go away for a while, at least until everything had settled down. It seemed as though God provided the perfect solution with the work in Thailand..."

Annette shook her head slowly, as she tried to take it all in.

Esther asked, "And the other family?"

"You recall we have a church member in the police force?" Mark addressed this to Annette.

"Hmm, the one you had track me down... You didn't say he was in the police force," Annette said.

"Yes, the same one. We brought him down, and he, the pastor and I had a chat with the family. The police member explained to them that, because Daisy had denied that anything had happened, it would be their daughter's word against Ted's. That it was unlikely there would be enough evidence to get it to court. And even if it did go to court, what a gruelling process that would be for their daughter. The pastor talked to them about the damage it would do to the church. He explained that the plan was to send Ted away. The couple realised there was no point proceeding. Sadly, the parents stopped attending our church and made the decision to leave town anyway, but it was probably for the best. New start and all that."

As the impact of what the church had done finally sank in, Annette's eyes opened wide and she said in amazement, "You sent him to an orphanage?"

"You've got to understand, we weren't sure he'd done it. Even so, he had been warned that if he were ever accused again, he would be expelled from the church, Mum would be informed, and the police would be called. We felt sure the threat of all that would be enough. The leaders would never have agreed to send him if we felt there were any risk to those kids."

Annette looked at Mark shaking her head. "But now he's done it again, and none of those things have happened."

"I know." Mark sounded frustrated. "It was different this time though. Yes, he denied it again at first when I confronted him, but when he understood that there was no doubt this time, he became contrite. He begged for help to have this affliction removed from him. He said it was like a devil possessed him, and he couldn't control it. It was clear to me that all he wants is to stop. He wants to be the man God called him to be." Mark paused, looking at Annette. "Annette, can you not find it in your heart to have some compassion for your own father? Forgiveness, it's a cornerstone of Christianity. Have you both forgotten that?"

It seemed to be a rhetorical question. He asked it as though he were delivering a sermon. Then, without waiting for an answer, he stood and continued in his preacher's voice.

"A thing like this, it may seem black and white to those who don't have the burden of leadership, but a lot of factors have to be considered." He slapped his hand down on the table. "We're talking about people's lives here."

With that he turned and left the room. The sound of his bedroom door slamming shut reinforced that the discussion was well and truly over.

Mark had been persuasive and Annette felt a pang of guilt. She hadn't thought of Ted's behaviour as an *affliction*. The way Mark described it was as though it were an illness. And yes, it was true, she couldn't feel any compassion for Ted, not about this. Did it make her heartless that she was angry with him, that she wanted him to be punished for what he had done? Was she not a good Christian because she didn't want to forgive him? Something fundamental was missing in Mark's speech though. What about the children? Where was the compassion for them? Who was protecting them? How would they be healed from the damage Ted had done? They seemed to be the forgotten ones in this whole hideous business. And, yes, Ted must be sick in some way to do this, but he had the power of choice. He could have chosen not to act on his desires.

Esther's voice interrupted her thoughts, "I don't care what he says, I'm going to tell Mum. Ted can't live here anymore."

"And the police, will you come with me to the police?"

Annette was hopeful, maybe if Esther went with her...

"No, I'm sorry, but I agree with Mark on that. What's the point? Daisy denied it when it happened, the other girl's gone. You heard Mark, a policeman was involved and even he said not to bother. Mum would be even more upset. No, Ted can just go away again, leave quietly, make some excuse and move on."

"And if he does it again, somewhere else, to some other child?"

"You heard Mark; he's having treatment. He'll be cured."

"What if he's not cured, Esther, what then?" Annette asked quietly.

There was no response, and the question was left hanging

as Esther left the house.

As she sat there in the kitchen, a certainty settled in upon her. It was with a sense of pure relief she made the decision that she wouldn't marry Mark. Like taking off a jumper on a stifling, hot day. She really didn't feel anything towards him now, except, perhaps, disappointment.

A few weeks ago, this realisation would have been crushing for her; she would have felt as though she had no future. Now she felt free, unshackled from this gloomy, lifeless relationship. Mark who had once seemed so attractive to her, who had seemed to be the key to everything she wanted and needed, now seemed cold, harsh and unfeeling.

She should go to Mark right now and tell him she was not going to marry him. She didn't think he would care too much, but he might care about how it appeared to the church members. Would he throw her out? He might decide it was safer for her to be out of the way in case she talked to anyone about Ted. And then what? What could she do to protect Daisy if she were back in Melbourne? No, she wouldn't tell him yet, as much as she wanted to be free of him, she had to see this through.

And what about the church? She could choose to be unshackled from that too, with its hypocrisy and its endless rules and regulations. How would God feel though, about her reneging on her commitments to Mark and to the church? Was she ready to give up on God too? She knew from listening to sermons that she couldn't measure God by the way his followers behaved. Yet, God's people were behaving so badly, it did make Annette question God's very existence. Even if He did exist, how could He let those children be hurt that way? Was that God's will? Was that part of God's plan? No, of course it wasn't. Ted had acted out of his own selfish desires. But why didn't God stop him? He's supposed to be all seeing, all powerful. There was a Bible

verse from Romans, that was often quoted to explain suffering: *For those who love God, all things work together for
good...* When Annette thought of Daisy, of the other girl, of
the children at the orphanage, this didn't make sense.

As she struggled with these complex issues, she thought
of Murray, who wouldn't tell her whether he was a Christian or not. He seemed kind, like he really cared. She wished
she could talk to him again now. Time was running out.
Even though it was the weekend, maybe she should just try
to call Murray. He probably wouldn't answer, but she was
at a loss as to her next move. At least she could leave him a
message, asking for an earlier appointment.

Grace still wasn't home, so she went into Grace's bedroom and closed the door. There was a phone extension by
the bed and Annette was confident that Mark couldn't hear
her.

To her surprise, Murray answered shortly after she dialled.

"Ahh, I'm not sure how this works..." she began tentat-
ively, "...but I'm really not sure what else to do."

"Is there something specific on your mind that you
want to talk about?" he asked.

Annette could hear voices and laughter in the background.

"Yes, yes there is."

"Okay, then give me a minute, and I'll go and pick up
the other extension." Then she heard him say, "Will you
hang this up for me, love?"

The sounds of laughter continued until she heard his
voice again, and then a click as the other line disconnected.

"Okay, I'm here," he said.

"It's about my father..."

She told Murray about Daisy and the other girl, including what the policeman had said at the time. Also, that Ted

had then been sent to an orphanage and what had happened there. She relayed what Mark had told her this evening about Ted's treatment, and about the church's decision not to report Ted after all that had happened. She wasn't sure what she'd been hoping for, but Murray's response was almost as disappointing as that of everyone else.

"Leave it with me," he said.

When she asked what he planned to do, he told her he couldn't say more than that. He asked her if she'd thought about moving back to Melbourne and said that he could make a referral to a good psychologist for her. She told him she wanted to stop Ted, but it sounded like Murray was telling her to leave it alone.

Quite convinced that nobody cared at all, except her, she hung up the phone. Now she felt absolutely and completely alone.

It was a cool evening, so she put a cardigan over her shoulders, took a small blanket and went out into the garden. She sat down on an old wooden bench seat and looked up at the night sky, to the vast expanse of stars. So much clearer than in the city. The sound of a night owl came to her through the trees. She sat there for a long time. And the longer she sat there, the less alone she felt. Was it God's presence near her in the garden? Or, simply, the presence of the natural world calming her spirit? She could accept that she really didn't know what to do now. She had asked those who she thought could help and they wouldn't. But still, a certainty had settled in on her. And that was, that she would not leave this town. Not until she knew for sure that no child would ever again be at risk from Ted.

Annette felt a sense of purpose now that she'd never really felt before. Did it come from God? Maybe... She trusted that she would be strong enough to manage whatever eventuated. Grace's car came down the driveway and pulled into the garage, but Annette stayed right there in the garden, pulling the blanket more tightly around her. Grace and Mark's muffled voices carried softly across the yard from the kitchen, and then it was quiet again. Shortly after that, she heard Esther's Datsun drive in, and then the back door close quietly. Still, Annette stayed there. She had a goal, a goal that was beyond her own desires. And that felt good. Eventually she crept quietly inside and went to bed feeling more at peace than she had for a long time.

Chapter 22

In the early hours of the morning, the phone rang, rousing Annette from a deep sleep. The ringing stopped abruptly, and she heard Mark answer, he spoke in a hushed voice.

Then she heard Grace and Esther's concerned voices asking, "What's wrong? What is it?"

"Go back to bed, it's a church issue," Mark said. "I'll explain in the morning."

When Annette woke, both Mark and Esther had left. Esther usually left before them for music practise, but where was Mark?

Grace explained that he'd been called to Melbourne for an urgent meeting.

"On the Sabbath too, tsk, tsk. You'd think it could wait until Monday," Grace said, clicking her tongue and shaking her head while she tossed scrambled eggs in a pan. "And why are you still in your nightie? You'll make us late for church."

Church was the last place Annette wanted to be, but what else was she going to do? At least she might see Jane and get a chance to convince her to go to the police.

Grace continued prattling, "Though I'm not sure what sort of sermon we'll get with Elder Jacobs only having a few hours this morning to prepare."

Annette returned to her room to get dressed. Clearly, Grace still didn't know what was going on.

Later that morning, when Annette and Grace arrived at the church, Annette saw Esther standing outside talking with Violet.

"I just need to pop over to the toilet block before the service," Annette said to Grace.

After Grace had entered the church, Annette approached Esther and Violet and asked if she could speak to Esther alone for a moment.

"Don't worry, she knows the whole story." Esther gestured towards Violet.

Did Violet know everything? All about Ted? And about her and Alex? She probably did. Yet, she could see the compassion in Violet's eyes.

"I can't imagine how hard this must all be for you," Violet said gently.

Annette felt tears prick at her eyes. Violet sounded like she actually cared. But then, Annette had trusted church people before and look what had happened. A flash of anger dried her tears.

"I suppose you agree with them—that the church's reputation is more important than protecting children."

"On the contrary—" Violet began.

Esther cut her off and said impatiently, "No actually, when I told her she said that it should be reported to the police and... I'm starting to agree. Now, what did you want to talk to me about? I have to get inside; we're about to start the pre-service music."

Annette was both surprised and pleased at Esther's change

of heart.

"Well, I was going to ask when you are going to tell Grace?"

Esther sighed and rubbed her eyes. They had dark circles beneath them, as though she hadn't slept much.

"I plan to tell her as soon as we get home from church. No choice now anyway."

"What do you mean?" Annette asked.

"There was a phone call this morning, early. Mark told me before he left, that Ted snuck out of the treatment facility during the night. That's why Mark left this morning; the leadership called him to Melbourne to discuss the situation."

She paused, as though considering whether to continue, "Looks like the treatment wasn't working and he refused to take the medication they prescribed. He's still denying it happened. He's calling it a vendetta against him."

"A vendetta?"

The singer was at the door calling Esther in. Esther glanced at Violet, and with a slight shake of her head, she walked into the church.

Violet patted Annette on the shoulder softly and said, "Go in and find a seat."

Everyone was standing for the music when she went in. She couldn't see Daisy, Jane or Jack anywhere. Coincidence? She didn't think so. She went and stood next to Grace.

Up on the rostrum, Elder Jacobs was shuffling through his notes, looking nervous. Annette didn't hold high hopes for this sermon either, she'd heard Elder Jacobs preach before. Soon, the last strains of music quieted down, and the singer asked people to be seated. When everyone was seated, Elder Jacobs rose to his feet. Before he had reached the lectern, he stopped suddenly. Annette looked in the direction the elder was facing.

Her heart began to race, and her chest tightened. Her vision blurred slightly as the fear took hold.

Ted was striding in through the open side door with his hand raised towards the other elder. He moved to the lectern and took the microphone in his hand.

"Sorry, Elder Jacobs, if you would just give me a few moments?"

Annette breathed as deeply as she could.

No, I refuse to be intimidated by you!

She called on her new sense of purpose to help calm this terror that was threatening to overwhelm her. Although her heart was still beating fast, she kept breathing deeply. She would not let her emotions control her. Her mission here was too important.

As her surroundings came back into focus, she could see Esther's face from her seat at the piano. Esther looked as shocked as Annette felt. Then she glanced sideways at Grace. Grace looked extremely confused—obviously this was unexpected for her as well.

Elder Jacobs was still standing halfway between his seat and the lectern, looking more uncertain than ever. Finally, he inclined his head slightly towards Ted and then returned to his seat.

"As some of you know, I've recently been away on a Sabbatical," Ted said.

Annette heard a loud scoff from the back of the church. She looked around as others did, to see where it came from, but she couldn't tell.

Ted shook his head and said slowly, "Hmm, I can see why God told me that I had to come here today and speak out." He smiled, then picked up a Bible from the lectern and held it up. "Friends let's read from the word of God. Turn with me to Matthew 5:11."

The sound of people shuffling through their Bible to

find the text seemed to release some of the tension in the air.

Ted lifted the Bible higher and—without opening it—recited, "'Blessed are you when people insult you, persecute you and falsely say all kinds of evil against you because of me.'"

He lay the Bible down and paused before speaking again. "Friends, evil has been spoken about me."

The sound of people catching their breath in shock or surprise rippled through the congregation.

"But I don't care about that because—as we just read in Matthew—I am blessed when I am persecuted. And I don't blame anyone, either. You are not acting alone; you are in league with our enemy. Who is our enemy?" Ted's voice grew louder as he gestured to towards the congregation.

The church members responded in chorus, "The Devil!"

"I ask again church, who is our enemy?"

Louder this time, they yelled, "The Devil," and, "The Devil is our enemy!"

"Yes, the Devil!" Ted banged his fist on the pulpit. "Does the Bible not say in 1st Peter that he '...prowls around like a lion looking for those he can devour?'"

"Yes! Yes!" the congregation replied in chorus.

Ted paused and looked around the congregation. In a low voice he said, "God is my witness, he knows my heart. That I would not speak against anyone, let alone a leader of the church if He did not clearly direct me to do it."

Again, hushed gasps and whispers swept through the audience.

Ted waited until it was quiet and looked directly at Grace, "I'm sorry I have to do this Grace, but we should have spoken out against sin when we first witnessed it."

Annette looked at Grace who was shaking her head

slowly, a tear dribbling down her cheek. She took Annette's hand and held it tightly. The church was deathly silent.

Ted continued, his voice rising again, "I apologise to the family of God that we didn't call out this grievous sin when it happened. As leaders, we are even more account-able to the church. We need to be of perfect repute, upright, holy and disciplined. Unfortunately, your leader, Mark, has not shown himself to be a true leader. Have you not wondered church, how he came to be engaged to my daughter so quickly? I'm ashamed to say it of my own flesh and blood, but she..." He pointed to Annette. "...was sent here as an agent of the Devil, she is a temptress!"

Annette realised she was holding her breath. She felt glued to her seat, helpless to do anything. She felt the pres-sure of Grace's hand on hers, as one by one, the church members turned and craned their necks to stare at her. She sunk down lower in her seat.

"Mark—although he was ensnared—is not blameless either. He showed no self-control. And then, rather than admit his sin to you all and ask forgiveness, he chose to cast aspersions at me instead, to cover his own sin." Ted was nodding as he spoke.

The whispering was growing louder now, no longer hushed.

Suddenly a loud, strident voice cut through all the oth-ers. "Stop it!" It was Esther. She was standing. "How dare you?"

The whispering stopped. Annette felt relieved as eyes turned away from her and towards Esther. Before Esther could say more though, Ted gestured towards her with an upturned palm.

"And Esther—I'm sad to say—has also been hiding her sin from you all."

Grace dropped Annette's hand and stood up.

"Ted, what are you doing?" She shook her head slowly. There was a dazed look on her face.

"Grace, I don't know why God has allowed your children to have been as much of a blight on you, as my daughter has been on me, but it's not our place to question. And I'm sorry to have kept this from you, I guess I was trying to protect you, but it's time for you to know that your daughter has been—and still is—in an unnatural relationship with that one."

Ted pointed his finger at Violet. Again, whispers ran through the congregation. Stares moving back and forth between Violet and Esther. Esther was crying. She stood and slowly picked up her sheets of music and her handbag. Looking straight ahead she crossed the front of the church, towards the door. Violet stood as well and began to make her way along her pew.

"Yes, best you both leave; your deviant acts are abhorrent to God, and not only that..." Ted thundered towards their receding backs, "...you have deceived God's church!"

Esther rushed out the door. The whispering stopped when Violet halted abruptly. She turned slowly and lifted a forefinger at Ted, as though about to speak. Ted stood his ground at the pulpit, a defiant look on his face, while the silence continued. Annette—hopeful now— waited like everyone else to hear what she would say. But eventually, Violet bit her lip, turned away and followed Esther out.

Grace was shaking her head, looking at the floor, tears streaming down her cheeks.

Annette wanted so badly to speak out against him, to accuse him in front of everyone, as he had done to her, but what would be the point? Who would believe her now? She looked around frantically, trying to think of what to do.

Now that Esther and Violet had left, people were talking more loudly. The service was quickly degenerating into chaos. Some were getting up out of their pews to go and talk to others. Those that were seated either side of Grace and Annette had left and gone elsewhere.

Finally, Elder Jacobs stood up from his seat and walked over to the pulpit. With an uncharacteristic authority, he said, "I think it might be best to leave it at that, Ted."

The congregation quieted down. People that were standing or moving around, found a seat. Ted hesitated for the first time that morning; his confidence seemed to waver as he surrendered the microphone to Elder Jacobs. He stepped away from the pulpit and took Elder Jacobs's seat on the stage.

"Umm, we might forgo our closing songs today," Elder Jacobs said, inclining his head towards the empty piano stool. "But I think, right now, we need to come together in prayer."

The elder prayed for the unity of the church, but Annette didn't want to hang around any longer. She couldn't face the accusing stares again.

"I'll wait in the car," she whispered to Grace.

Grace kept her head bowed but opened her eyes and fidgeted around in her bag and handed Annette the keys. Annette slipped out while most of the congregation still had their heads bowed and eyes closed.

As she waited in the car, she soon heard the chatter as the doors opened and people began to leave the church. The sound wasn't as lighthearted and cheerful as it usually was. Even from the carpark, she could hear that people were agitated and upset. She kept her head down, she didn't want to look at anyone. Ted had won. Now, she was helpless to do anything about him. One car after another pulled out, and even though her window was down, no one came near or spoke to her.

She looked up when she heard Ted's voice. Grace was

walking towards the car and Ted was following close behind her. All the other cars around them had left.

"As I said, God told me I had to bring the truth to light." He threw his hands up in the air. "I didn't want to do it."

Grace didn't speak until she was seated in the car. She wound her window down and said in a low, steady voice, "They are my children, Ted. It's too much." She shook her head. "Don't come home, not yet anyway. I need time to think and to pray and to mend this with my children."

With that, she turned the key and began to reverse out.

Ted walked alongside the car saying, "You can't do that, you need to submit to me, you don't have authority over me. I'm your husband."

Grace didn't respond and drove away while Ted continued to shout at her in the distance.

The drive continued in silence for a few minutes, then Grace spoke, almost as though she were talking to herself. "They must all think I'm so stupid. Even Ted thinks I didn't know, but I did know about Esther, I've known for a long time. I guess what I didn't know was how to deal with it, so I just didn't. Pretended it wasn't happening. Pretended that I believed they were just friends. Now they've both been shamed in front of the whole church, and it's my fault too. Maybe if I'd talked to her about it; helped her to see it was wrong."

She shook her head again. Annette wasn't sure how to respond, she struggled to think of something to say to make Grace feel better.

Then again, maybe she should tell Grace the whole truth about Ted, since Esther hadn't had the opportunity. The timing seemed off though, Grace was suffering enough.

Suddenly Grace turned to her, as though she had just

remembered Annette was there.

"Well, I don't suppose there will be a wedding now... I never did think it was a good enough reason to marry. Nobody should be yoked together for the rest of their lives because of a momentary lapse." Her look was soft, empathetic. "You don't love him anyway, do you?"

Annette was taken aback. Was it that obvious now?

"I thought I did, I really did..." she said. Trying to muster up an enthusiasm she no longer felt. "...but no... I don't love him."

"Well in that case—and my dear, I'm so sorry to say this —probably the best thing for you to do is to go back to Melbourne."

Annette nodded her head. Of course, no-one would want her around now after Ted's speech.

As they turned into the driveway Annette said, "I'll go and pack my things."

Grace stayed in the car. "Yes dear, and I'll take you to the train in the morning. Right now, I need to go and talk to Esther."

She turned the car around, and it soon disappeared out of the driveway again and Annette was left alone.

Chapter 23

What now? She went into her bedroom and hauled her suitcase off the top of the wardrobe. As it came down, the hard metal edge hit her in the shins. She threw the case across the room with as much force as she could muster. It hit the oval, wardrobe mirror which cracked in the middle. Some small shards fell out onto the floor and onto the suitcase which had landed in the middle of the room. Most of the pieces stayed tenuously attached around the edges of the oval, their sharp edges creating pointy triangles that threatened to fall.

Annette sat down heavily on the bed and began to cry in frustration. She felt completely powerless. Of course, she couldn't change anything, achieve anything. Why did she ever think she could make Ted accountable? She couldn't even be a decent Christian— she'd committed such a serious sin with Mark. The gravity of what they had done hadn't really hit her until today. Mark was a leader in the church and that made it so much worse. The shock and disgust on the church members faces when they had turned to her was undeniable. A wave of shame swept over her again as she recalled the moment of her disgrace. Ted's words repeated over and over in her head. "Temptress", "Agent of the Devil".

She was sinking into a miry swamp of shame, that threatened to engulf her. Looking up she saw her cracked and broken reflection in the fractured remains of the mirror. She stared at her image with an ironic smile.

Yep that's how I feel on the inside too. I'm damaged goods, bad, broken.

Then, she shook herself trying to shake off the shame. No, no time for that now, she had to think, she couldn't stay here. Grace wanted her gone, but where would she go? She didn't want to stay with Bill and Rose. Tracy thought she was crazy. She had burned her bridges with Alex. Or had she? Was it too late?

The sound of a car in the driveway didn't fully register with Annette, until the car door slammed shut. She snapped to attention as the back door opened and footsteps moved around inside the house. Too late to clean up the mess she'd made of the mirror. She didn't move, hoping no one would come looking for her.

A few seconds later, Ted appeared in the doorway, his tall frame filling the space.

"Where's Grace?" he asked. His tone was demanding.

Annette was suddenly on guard, her breath quickened.

"She's not here, she went to see Esther." Despite her fear of him, she couldn't keep the accusation out of her voice.

Ted seemed to notice the state of the room for the first time. "What happened here?"

She wouldn't give him the satisfaction of knowing how much his words had affected her.

"Umm, it broke when I got my suitcase down," she lied.

He walked into the room and his shoes crunched on the broken glass. He moved around to the foot of the bed until he towered over her.

"So, you're leaving. That's good." He leaned forward, punctuating his words by poking her in the middle of the chest. "You should never have come in the first place. Someone like *you* has no place in the church."

He stepped back and smiled an unpleasant smile. Was he looking forward to seeing the effect of his hurtful words? Maybe he was expecting her to cry.

She didn't. Something in her snapped. Although he had poked her chest hard, she couldn't really feel it now, she was so furious. Maybe it was the blatant hypocrisy in his statement. Or, perhaps it was the look of pure disgust on his face. All fear left her, she stood up and before Ted realised what was happening, she drew her arm back and slapped him hard across the face with all the force of her rage.

Shocked, he rubbed his face where a red mark was starting to appear, his eyes were wide.

"Why you little bitch!"

Now Annette saw again the man who had beaten her and her mother so many times. When she saw that expression on his face, there was no doubt in her mind what would happen next. She almost gave in to the terror... almost. But no, she wouldn't try to run; she would stand her ground come what may. She wasn't finished with him yet.

"It was *you* who hurt those children at the orphanage and *you* who hurt the little girls here in the church." She spat the words out at him. "It wouldn't surprise me one bit, if you hurt the kids at the children's home where you worked as well."

He smiled. Annette sucked in a breath. Why was he smiling?

"And what are you going to do about it? Who do think would believe the little slut who seduced a church pastor?'

She hit him a second time on the same cheek.

His smile disappeared and his face went red. Holding her by one shoulder, he grabbed at the V in her dress where the buttons began. Then he ripped the dress apart until her bra and undies were exposed. Then pushed her down on the bed and pinned her flailing arms at the wrists with his hands.

Annette stopped struggling; her body went limp. Now she was unable to move or to think.

Ted spread her legs apart, until he was standing between them looking down at her.

"This is all you're good for. All you were ever good for."

He placed her arms above her head and held them with one hand, with the other grabbed the top of her undies.

In her stupor, and as though through a thick fog, memories came to her. This had happened before—not exactly like this—but still... like this. Awful memories came back. One after the other, at different ages, five, six, seven years old. It was like watching a movie in her mind, of film clips of her life. Somehow, she knew these memories were real, not imagined, this had really happened. Her body stayed limp. She couldn't fight it before, and she couldn't fight it now.

Through the fog she heard a voice. A muffled voice, as though from a long way off. She struggled to come back to the surface, as though she were under muddy water. Not hearing clearly, not seeing clearly.

"Annette!"

The voice was louder now. She could make out her name. It wasn't Ted's voice, but it was familiar... Who was it?

"Annette, are you there?"

Suddenly, she became aware of the room again. Ted let go of her hands and stood up straight, looking around uncertainly. She could still feel his legs against hers and couldn't bear him near her.

"Get away from me!" she screamed.

The voice called her name again, more frantic this time. It sounded like it was coming from the back door. It was Alex. What was Alex doing here?

She couldn't think about that now. The sensation of Ted being so close was all encompassing. Getting away from him was the only thing that mattered.

"I said, get away from me!"

Ted took a step away and as he did, she drew her knees towards her and kicked him as hard as she could with both feet. He stumbled over the suitcase and then cried out as he fell backwards. At the same time, Annette heard footsteps coming towards her from the kitchen.

Ted slowly pushed the suitcase out of the way, his arm scraping across shards of glass. Then he rose to his feet. She recoiled, wriggling quickly back towards the bedhead. He seemed unsteady, as though he might topple over at any moment. With his left hand, he reached behind his back as if trying to touch something there. His expression was confused. Then, he stopped short, crying out in pain. As he cried out, he fell again, forward this time, landing face down on the shattered glass.

A few moments later, Alex appeared at her bedroom doorway. Annette sat up and pulled her dress around her as best she could. She couldn't quite take in what she saw. Nothing seemed real. She wanted to wake up from this nightmare, but she couldn't.

"Are you okay?" Alex asked, taking a step into the room.

She watched him as he stopped in his tracks and took in

the whole scene. A look of horror spread across his face.

A large shard of glass from the mirror was protruding from Ted's upper back. Blood was slowly soaking through his white shirt, and then down onto the floral carpet. He was trying to push himself up with his right arm, without succeeding. Blood was dripping down his forearm. Then, he slumped down on the floor and lay still.

"What happened? Who is he?" Alex indicated towards her ripped dress. "Did he try to..."

Annette couldn't speak yet; she put her hand over her mouth and nodded. This was all real. What she had re-membered was real. What Ted had attempted a few minutes ago was real, and, Ted lying there in a pool of his own blood was also real.

"Help me," Ted said in a weak voice. And tried to lift himself up again.

Neither Annette nor Alex moved. Alex looked at An-nette. Ted slumped forward again. Head to the side, eyes closed, face pale.

"Is... is he dead?" she whispered, hand still covering her mouth.

A long moment went by as Alex moved closer to Ted and knelt by his side.

Alex looked at her. "No, he's unconscious, but he's still breathing."

"When he heard you coming, he stood up and I kicked him, he fell back. You have to believe me; I didn't mean for that to happen."

"Of course, I believe you; you were defending your-self."

The fear and anger were gone. There was no threat now, just her father lying helpless in front of her, his life seeping away from him.

"He's my father," her voice was flat. "He tried to rape

me. Just then he did, and then I remembered all the times it happened before, when I was a kid."

Alex nodded slowly. He didn't seem surprised.

"And not only me; he's done it to other kids. He did it to Daisy."

Her voice sounded cold as she accused and condemned Ted. She was his judge and jury right now. She had tried and convicted him. He deserved to die. He might anyway, even if they called an ambulance. If they did nothing, he would surely die, there was so much blood.

The cankerworm spoileth, then fleeth away.

No, he wouldn't, not anymore...

"I know he's done horrible things. What do you think though? Right now, shouldn't we call for help?" Alex asked.

Was this really what she wanted for her own father? If he lived, there would probably be no justice, but did she really want to be responsible for his death? The enormity of what she was contemplating suddenly hit her and she sprang into action.

"I'll call for help, you stay with him."

Alex nodded; he looked relieved.

In the hall, Grace had all the emergency numbers listed on the wall above the phone on the hall table. Annette's hand shook as she dialled the number for the ambulance.

Chapter 24

Later that evening, Annette and Alex sat on a cold, hard, metal bench at the police station. A uniformed police officer stood opposite them on the other side of the corridor.

Mostly, the last few hours were a bit of a blur. But not everything. She closed her eyes, saw again the bloodstained shirt with the mirror fragment protruding through. Then felt his hands on her, tearing at her clothes. She blinked hard and opened her eyes, forcing the images away. Alex was watching her; he took her hand and squeezed it gently. Grateful, she leaned against him.

"Why did you come?" she asked.

He reached into his pocket and pulled out a screwed-up piece of paper.

"The motel manager gave this to me when I arrived this afternoon. He said you were upset. So, I went straight to the house to find you."

"Hmm, I threw that in the bin." She pointed at the paper. "I didn't think it was fair to you and besides, I thought I could handle things. Obviously, I can't handle anything."

A tear slid down her cheek. "I'm so glad you came."

One of the uniformed police that had questioned them at the house, walked towards them down the corridor.

"Come this way," he said and indicated towards the corridor.

Alex and Annette got up.

"No, not you," he said to Annette.

Alex smiled weakly at her, patting her hand with his other hand as he let go. He seemed quite nervous now. She watched them pad along the lino floor until they went through a glass door and disappeared out of sight.

Annette sat down again and tried to make sense of the last few hours. The person on the phone had said not to move Ted and not to remove the glass from his back, but to tourniquet the cut to his arm. She'd grabbed a clean tea towel from the kitchen and run back to the room.

When she got there, the chest of drawers was open, and clothes were spilling out of the top drawer. She could see that while she had been gone, Alex had found some T-shirts and wrapped one around Ted's forearm. This seemed to have slowed the bleeding. The other he had wrapped loosely around the glass fragment. A green T-shirt, turned rusty brown with blood.

Annette found herself rooted to the spot, not able to approach the body on the floor.

"They said not to pull the glass out," she said.

Again, she tried to move forward but couldn't.

"It's okay," Alex said gently. "I'll stay with him, you go and put some other clothes on." He indicated towards the chest of drawers.

Annette looked down; she had forgotten about her torn dress. She grabbed jeans and a T-shirt from the open drawer. After she had put the fresh clothes on in the bathroom, she stared at the dress on the floor. It had been a favourite dress, but now she hated it. It was a disgusting reminder of what had happened. Without a second thought, she went out into the kitchen and opened the door to the firebox of the wood stove. Using a poker, she pushed the dress in a little at a time so as not to smother the few smouldering coals that were left from the morning. After she saw the material lick the coals into bright flames, she closed the firebox door.

The ambulance arrived a few moments later, sirens wailing. Two ambulance officers ran in carrying a stretcher. She directed them to her room but didn't go in herself, but stood against the wall outside the room. The sounds inside the room were loud and urgent.

"Lost a lot of blood" and "BP low." And directions to Alex: "Yes, lift gently with us on three. One, Two, Three lift!"

Then they were walking past her with the stretcher.

"You're his daughter? Will you come in the ambulance with him?"

She shook her head. They looked surprised.

"Okay, but make sure you notify any other family members."

She nodded numbly. After the ambulance left all was quiet.

Alex said, "You'd better call his wife."

Annette dialled Violet's number. "I need to speak to Grace."

"You sound awful," Violet said. "Are you okay?"

"Tell Grace there's been an accident. It's Ted."

"What happened?" Violet asked.

Annette hesitated as she began to relive it all again.

"Just tell her please. Tell her the ambulance has taken him to Wellspring hospital."

Annette slammed the phone down and stared at it for a

few moments.

The two uniformed police arrived at the house shortly after the ambulance had left. The police questioned them both. Annette delivered her version of events in a flat voice. She tried to relay the facts. All the while fighting to avoid the horrible emotions that threatened to overwhelm her if she gave into them even for a second.

Alex also told them what he knew of what had happened. One of the officers asked Alex whether he had "actually seen" Ted attack Annette.

Alex hesitated, then shook his head. "No, I didn't, but it was obvious what had happened. Her dress was ripped open."

"Hmm," was all the officer said, as he wrote on his little notepad.

"But there is no dress now, is there?" He looked pointedly at Annette.

"Clearly there has been some sort of scuffle that has left the victim seriously injured. You two need to realise that it's very important we hear a completely accurate account of the sequence of events that occurred in that room."

He looked at Annette, and then at Alex, as though waiting to hear something other than what they had already recounted. The other officer walked outside as a message came through on his radio. After a short time he returned and informed them the point of the shard had passed between two ribs and pierced Ted's spleen. And that the cut on his arm was not serious.

"They are taking him into surgery now."

Tears sprang to Annette's eyes, still not sure what she felt. What if he did die?

"Maybe I'd better go to the hospital?"

"No, you both need to come to the station with us. We need to take statements."

When they were outside—walking towards the police car—one of the policemen told them their rights.

Time was really dragging now. Alex had been gone for ages. And the seriousness of Annette's situation was really starting to sink in. The police didn't believe them. So stupid, burning that dress! At least it would have been some sort of evidence of what had actually happened. Why were they told their rights? Did that mean one, or even both of them, might be charged? With what? Manslaughter... maybe even murder... if Ted died. And what if they blamed Alex? This was nothing to do with him. He wouldn't have even been there if she hadn't written that note. If he hadn't shown up when he had though, the unthinkable would have happened again.

One of the officers had told her that she could make a phone call, but who would she call? For a fleeting moment she thought of calling Mark. He knew the truth about Ted. He could explain what he knew to the police, but would he? No, she couldn't trust him to tell the truth, if the truth made the church look bad. He had ignored Ted's behaviour before, it was too risky. Besides, the fact that Alex had been at the house would be hard to explain. She wasn't ready to deal with that. Maybe Grace... but no, Grace had washed her hands of Annette. Probably blamed her for Ted's revelations in church earlier today, for her son's disgrace. And Esther—it was hard to predict what Esther would do. Yes, she was extremely upset with Ted, but that didn't mean she would tell what she knew. Even with all that had happened, she still may want to protect the church from a scandal. No, she decided, she wouldn't call any of them.

"Excuse me," she said to the officer who was keeping an eye on her. "Can I make my phone call now?"

Soon she was in a tiny room with nothing else in it but a desk, the chair she sat on and a phone. The officer was standing outside, visible through the glass door. She held her breath as the phone rang over and over for, what seemed to be, an endless amount of time. When she finally heard Rose's voice at the other end, she couldn't speak for a moment. Her mother—the one that she had shunned for so long—now felt like her only lifeline. She hadn't told Rose anything of her life since going to live in that bungalow. Now, she wanted to tell her everything. Not yet though. She needed an answer first. The answer to a question —the question that had started to circle around her like a shark, ever since the memories had returned. Before she could ask Rose for help she had to know. There was no time for small talk. She launched straight in, telling Rose what she'd remembered. Those awful memories that had come to her when Ted was attacking her.

"Did you know? Did you know he did that to me?"

"Yes, I knew."

Annette's heart sank. Suddenly she felt ill, her mother knew. How could she let that happen?

Rose continued, "I had no idea you didn't remember. I assumed you wouldn't want to talk about it, so I never brought it up. I caught him at it; he didn't see me at the time and I was too stunned to do anything at that moment. But that's why I threw him out, love. The very next day. I threatened to go to the police if he didn't leave. He said he'd kill me if I did. I told him I didn't care. It was one thing to do those things to me, but not to my little girl. No, I wouldn't have it." Rose's voice broke a little. "Anyway, he asked if anyone else knew and I didn't answer him. Not answering that question saved me, I think. I do believe he would have killed me, if he wasn't so scared of Mum and Dad going to the police; he didn't know if I'd told them or not. He left that day and never came back." Rose sighed heavily. "I'm so sorry love. I really hadn't considered the possibility that you hadn't remembered. And I'm so sorry it went on for so long. I didn't know how long he'd been at it. Until now, I could only guess."

Annette began to sob into the phone.

"What's happened, love? Why has this come up now? Have you seen him again?"

The officer had told her to be quick, and now he was pointing his finger at her through the window. As briefly as she could, she explained the day's events to Rose, saying she would tell her the whole story later.

Rose assured her that she and Bob would be there as soon as possible. Then said, "That bastard won't be getting away with it again. Not if I can help it! He just had me so shit scared of him that I couldn't talk to to the police. I should have talked to them years before when the neighbours dobbed him in for hitting me and I definitely should have dobbed him in for what he did to you. I know that now. Maybe none of this would have happened."

Annette hung up the phone, feeling slightly more hopeful. But would the police even believe Rose? Since she didn't report it at the time.

When she looked up, a man in a suit was talking to the police officer. He opened the door and she rose from the chair.

"Come this way Annette."

They walked down the corridor in the direction Alex had gone earlier. The man told her that he was Detective Smythe from the Russell Street Criminal Investigation Bureau. Annette was even more frightened. She and Alex weren't criminals.

"We told the other officers the truth, I swear we did."

Detective Smythe just smiled and nodded. He directed her into a room a little further on than the one Alex had entered. This room was also sparsely furnished with a desk that had two chairs on one side of it and one on the other. A woman in a grey pencil skirt and a white shirt stood up when Annette entered.

As the woman shook Annette's hand, she said, "Detective Anderson, Russell Street CIB. Nice to meet you."

She smiled at Annette as well.

"Take a seat. Would you like a cup of tea or coffee?" the female detective asked.

Annette sighed. And it occurred to her that she hadn't had anything to eat or drink for a really long time.

"Yes, tea please."

"Milk and sugar?"

She nodded, a little confused by the apparent kindness. Detective Anderson left the room.

Although Annette was almost too scared to hear the answer, she had to know.

"Do you know how Ted's surgery went?" she asked Detective Smythe.

"They had to remove his spleen, but apparently the spleen is something you can live without. Who knew?" His smile was grim. "They said he's lucky to have survived such a deep cut to the organ though."

The detective didn't really look as though he was delivering good news. His expression made it seem like he might have preferred the alternative. Annette was confused, maybe Ted's life was still in danger.

"So, he'll be okay?" she asked.

"Yes, he's stable now and we've been told he'll make a full recovery."

Despite everything, Annette felt relieved. She didn't want him dead and she certainly didn't want to be the cause of his death. Detective Anderson returned with the tea and a couple of shortbread biscuits on a plate. Annette sipped at the tea, preferring to stare into the cup, rather than into the faces of the two detectives who sat opposite her.

They didn't speak while she drank. After a few moments of silence, she decided to try to explain what had happened again. Maybe these detectives would believe her.

"It really was an accident; I didn't mean for him to get cut like that. I just wanted to get him away from me. Alex wasn't even there when Ted fell, you can't blame him."

When she looked up. Detective Anderson was shaking her head.

"We would like to take a full statement from you. Please just go through what happened step by step. Also, we would appreciate you telling us anything else that you think would be relevant to our investigation."

Annette went through the series of events again. It was difficult to discuss the specifics of when Ted put his hands on her, but Detective Anderson empathised with her, saying how difficult this must be to talk about. Annette felt safer recounting it this time. They didn't sound as though they doubted her—like the local police had—when they asked questions. They just seemed to be clarifying the details of what happened.

The tears flowed freely as she told of him ripping her dress, pushing her down. She hadn't planned to, but she also told them about what she had remembered in those moments. What he'd done to her when she was so young. Also, what she'd seen and heard him do to Rose. The words spilled out of her, as though she were describing a movie she was watching. The memories were still vivid, but they had a different quality to them now. They were memories of the past. Situated in the past. They weren't part of her present anymore.

When the retelling came to an end, it became clear to Annette that those memories had been holding her captive, making her needy, keeping her stuck. She couldn't see it before, but now it was as though a veil over the past had been lifted.

She was the woman in her dream. Ted was the one with the bucket, pouring out the water. On her. She had been oblivious her whole life. Never realising, until now, that she was allowing what he had done to her; to drown her hopes, her dreams and her relationships; to keep her isolated from others; to make her feel like she was different from everyone else. She was the one watching on as Ted's actions continued to destroy her life, even after he'd left. Everything would be different now; deep down she knew that.

Chapter 25

Finally, Annette was done. Detective Anderson snapped off the cassette recorder.

"Thank you for that. What he has done to you in the past and attempted to do again today is particularly heinous because you are his daughter. I'm so sorry you had to go through all of that. We really appreciate you being brave enough to tell your story. I'm not sure how much you know about your father, love, so some of this may be a little hard to hear, but he has been on our radar before now. As you have confirmed, he has a history of violence—sexual and otherwise—and not just towards you and your mother.

Recently, we had a report from Murray Thomas, a psychologist in Wellspring, regarding what had occurred at the orphanage in Thailand. Later, he called us regarding the girls in the church here, after you disclosed to him what you knew."

Annette was relieved. Murray did take action, after all.

"Counselling is usually confidential, but you should know that he was legally obligated to tell us because one of those girls was still at risk from Ted. I'm just telling you that because we may need to take further statements from you about those matters as well."

Annette nodded her agreement.

Detective Anderson continued, "When we looked into our records, we saw a report had been made about him before. In 1971, he met and then married a woman who was a cottage mother in a family group home in a suburb of Melbourne."

"A family group home, what's that?" Annette asked.

"It's a home where a woman, or a couple, are paid to live with and care for children who are wards of the state. That is, children whose parents are dead or otherwise incapable of looking after them. The idea was that the children would feel like they were part of a family, more so than when they were in an institution."

Detective Anderson began again, "So after their marriage, your father became a cottage parent working alongside his new wife. Did you know about that?"

"Yes, I knew he worked with children, but I didn't understand why he wanted to... until now."

"I know this must be shocking for you."

Annette didn't speak; it was shocking, knowing what she now knew about Ted.

"I'm sorry, but it does get worse. The local police station, near the home, received an anonymous typewritten letter that Ted was sexually abusing two young girls in the home and that it had been going on for some time. The police investigated, but the children denied that anything had happened. They were probably too scared to say. And, also, the person who made the report hadn't come forward. Nothing can be done if there are no witnesses," she added, as if by way of excuse. "A few weeks after the children were interviewed, your father's second wife died due to a fall down the stairs."

Annette closed her eyes and tried to breathe deeply, but she couldn't keep her chest from hammering. Rose had said, *He would have killed me.*

"After Murray's report to us about the orphanage, we looked up those two girls. They were aged ten and eleven at the time, so they're young women now. After much reassurance from us that they would be kept safe from Ted, they were prepared to make statements about the abuse."

The detective paused; she seemed well practised at delivering bad news, but this story appeared to be disturbing even to her.

"The younger one asked to see us again yesterday. She came to down to headquarters and told us that she witnessed Ted push his wife down the stairs. The poor woman wasn't dead when she reached the bottom. Allegedly, Ted..." The detective paused, watching Annette's face carefully.

Annette felt numb, she waited for what she had already guessed was coming.

"Well... he broke her neck... The police attended, but there was no evidence to suspect that it was anything other than an accident. The girl hadn't told anyone—he had threatened to kill her and her friend as well if she said anything. So, she kept that secret for six years." Detective Anderson let out a heavy sigh. "We only found out about the murder yesterday."

Murder! It was too much. Was he all bad? *This murderer! This child molester!* Could this be the same man who had played with her and Rose on the beach that day so long ago?

Detective Smythe was still talking. "We knew he wasn't in the area because Daisy's mother had told us he was away on Sabbatical."

Annette let out a deep breath. "So, you've spoken to Jane?"

"Yes, she's bringing Daisy in today to make a statement."

"We have been keeping this investigation highly confidential internally—"

The female detective looked across at her colleague when he interjected.

"Listen we generally trust our members. However, in this case, we are aware that you made allegations to Murray that a member of the force, who is also a member of the church, obtained information about you, in order that Ted's current family could determine your whereabouts. You also alleged that the same police member advised church leaders not to report the sexual abuse of children. So, the officers who attended the scene today weren't aware of the full investigation. They were just trying to do their job and piece together what appeared to have happened," Detective Smythe explained. "Because your allegations against that police member haven't been investigated yet, we couldn't take any risks that our investigation of your father would be compromised in any way. Even more so now that it has become a murder investigation."

Detective Anderson continued quickly, "Not that we would ever minimise the seriousness of the sexual molestation. You can survive that, though. You can't survive murder." She smiled apologetically.

Yes, Annette had survived. Daisy had survived. The other children had survived. But at what cost? She couldn't help wondering how different her life might have been if Ted had been different. She really should be focused on what the police were saying right now. She could think about all this later. Maybe talk to Murray, or the psychologist he had recommended. The realisations kept tumbling in though. Was this why she had a problem with alcohol? It wasn't until she was deprived of drinking, when she came to Pleasant Valley, that she realised how much she had depended on it to numb her feelings. Was this why she couldn't say no to sex, because she wasn't allowed to say no as a child? She forced herself to pay attention to Detective Smythe.

"Fortunately, you had described to Murray where Ted was. Turns out that Murray was well informed about the facility in Sydney and its purpose. He was also aware of the church's habit of sending problem members there to be cured. We asked the police in Sydney to pick him up and escort him back to Melbourne. They were to pick him up today. We thought you, Daisy and his family here were all safe with him away interstate. Nobody realised until this morning that he had left the facility last night and driven back here. We were heading down here anyway to take a formal statement from Daisy. Anyway, don't worry, we have him under police guard at the hospital and he's been charged with first degree murder as well as a bevy of sex offences. After the anaesthetic had worn off, we questioned him about his how his injuries occurred. He said it was an accident, that he came in to say goodbye to you and he tripped over the suitcase. We also returned to the house and checked the firebox of the wood stove and recovered fragments of what well may be, the dress you were wearing when the incident occurred. That also serves to corroborate your story. Anyway, it's unlikely there will be any assault charges laid against you, given Ted's account of events."

Annette's tea was long finished, but she still cradled the cup to her chest.

"What do I do now?" she asked.

Detective Smythe said, "You're free to go, but at this stage, you do need to stay in town and keep us informed of your whereabouts. Your friend was going to get his car and then come back for you. Best you wait for him; you'll probably need some support for the next little while. Go and get some rest and we'll contact you tomorrow. Here are our cards if you need to talk to us in the meantime." They both handed her a printed card. "We have Alex's address here in town. Is that where you will be? Or, will you stay at your current address?

She didn't hesitate with her response; she couldn't even contemplate the thought of returning to that house.

"I'll be with Alex. My mother is coming to town as well. Would you give her the address when she arrives please, so she can find me at the motel?"

"Oh, that's excellent, yes, we want to take a statement from her as well. We've seen that there were historical reports from neighbours who made calls about violence at your home. When the police attended though, your mother would not disclose what had occurred."

"Hmm, I think she'll tell you all about it now," Annette said.

After being escorted out of the room, she saw Daisy, Jack and Jane sitting on the same bench that she and Alex had been sitting on. Daisy looked scared; Jack was talking to her and holding her hand. Jane stood as Annette approached, and then motioned Annette to join her at the other side of the corridor, out of earshot of the other two. Both Daisy and Jack smiled a worried smile when they saw Annette.

"They said that he attacked you. That's awful, I'm so sorry. Are you okay?"

Annette nodded; she was starting to feel okay now.

"I'm so very sorry for my behaviour. When Daisy told me last week, I didn't know what to do. I thought it would be best for her, for everyone, if she forgot it ever happened. And I knew Jack would be furious. I felt like I had to let you go; you would have been a constant reminder to her and to me. After the police called, I told Jack, and he convinced me that it was wrong to let it go unpunished. He said it was important for Daisy to know she didn't do anything wrong. I didn't understand that at first; I thought why would someone just do that to her without provocation? She must have done something to invite it."

Annette felt a flash of shame. Ted had delivered the message to her over and over again that she was a *bad girl*. The shame was quickly replaced by anger, because she knew now that she wasn't bad, she was just unlucky. None of this was her fault.

When she responded, she spoke for herself as much as for Daisy. "No, it wasn't her fault, and it's high time the wrong was handed back to the wrongdoer. He told her that she was responsible; he told her she was bad. He made her take on the shame and the guilt that he should have carried. And no child should ever have to carry that."

The words sprang from somewhere deep inside and a burden lifted from her. She refused to carry his shame, his badness anymore.

"Yes, I'm starting to understand that now. I just wish she'd told us when it happened."

"She was too scared and too ashamed. Her suffering has to stop now though, and she'll need help with that."

"We'll get her all the help she needs, don't worry. And thank you, I'm not sure she would have ever said anything if it hadn't been for you. You know she adores you."

"She's a lovely little girl, and that should never have happened to her."

Annette walked towards Daisy. As she did, she began to formulate a plan. Why couldn't she do what Murray did and help people too? Help children like Daisy, and adults as well. Although completing high school would have seemed like a ridiculous idea such a short time ago, now, she felt as though anything was possible. She would finish her schooling then go on to study to psychology. Not only would she heal; she would help others to heal.

Daisy jumped up and hugged Annette tightly. When they withdrew, they both had tears flowing freely down their cheeks.

Jack shook her hand and thanked her.

"Look, I understand that you may not want to, after the way I've behaved, but you're welcome to come back to work if you like," Jane said.

Annette looked up towards the glass doors at the far end of the corridor that led out to the carpark. She could see Alex outside in the sun, leaning against his van. She let out a deep sigh, as a certainty settled in on her.

She smiled at the three of them. "Thanks anyway, but I think it's time for me to move on. I'll come and visit though. If you want?" she asked, looking at Daisy.

"Yes, please," Daisy responded, smiling, as she wiped away her tears.

Jane looked puzzled. "I'm confused, you and Mark are engaged, aren't you?"

Jane obviously hadn't heard about what had happened at church that morning.

"No, I don't think we are. Not anymore."

As Jane followed Annette's gaze, the confusion left her face. She said with a grin, "Ah, I think I understand. That's the young fellow that came into the bakery that day, isn't it? I thought there was something between you two."

Annette smiled, said her goodbyes and continued down the hall towards Alex. Before she reached the door, a familiar figure came through it, walking quickly towards her.

"Annette, I'm glad I caught you," Violet said, a little breathless. "I can't imagine how shocking this has been for you. How are you doing, after everything?"

"Have you heard about Ted? About everything he's done?"

She nodded slowly. "Yes, I took Grace to the hospital to see him. They wouldn't let her in. They told her about the charges, including the murder. She and Esther are waiting here now, in interview rooms, to make statements." She hesitated, weighing her words. "We wondered, Annette, when we heard about the children here and in Melbourne and at the orphanage. Did he... touch you, Annette?"

"Yes, he did."

Violet shook her head sadly, "I don't know what to say. I want to say he's the Devil incarnate, that he's evil, a monster, but he's... also your father."

Annette knew it was going to take a while to sort all that out because it was true. He had behaved like a monster —and—he was her father.

"Have you heard of the cankerworm, in the Bible?" she asked Violet.

Violet nodded. "Is that how you see him?"

"Hmm, yes... I don't want him to destroy any more lives."

"The police sound pretty confident that he will be in prison for a very long time, because of the murder" Violet said, shaking her head. "It's a shame it took a murder for everyone to take notice."

Annette sighed heavily. It was a shame.

"And you and Esther, what will you do now after what happened in church today?"

"We will stay here to be near Grace until after the trial. Then we will move to Melbourne. Find a little church that accepts us just as we are. Ted did us a favour really, telling the whole church. Otherwise, we may have gone on for years keeping us a secret. Sneaking around. We haven't told

Grace that we're moving yet, but we think she'll understand."

"I'm glad for you. How is Grace doing... and Mark, what about him?"

"I think Grace is still in shock at the moment, but she's strong; her faith will get her through. And Mark, well..." She sighed. "Mark is a pastor, so of course he's gone straight into damage control. You shouldn't worry about him. The church will forgive him. They've known him since he was little."

Annette looked towards the door; Alex was standing in the doorway, watching them talk. Violet followed the direction of Annette's gaze.

"Hey, it looks like someone's waiting for you. Go on get out of here, leave this town and be happy. And, remember Annette..." Violet took her hand and squeezed it gently. "...'the Lord will restore the years that the cankerworm has devoured.'"

Annette gave Violet a hug and then walked down the corridor.

Although she didn't know where she stood with God —that was something she would work out later—Violet's parting words stayed with her. She was confident that her life would be restored to her, whether God was part of it or not. She would heal. She was strong. She was a survivor.

Annette walked to the door, took Alex's hand, and went out into the bright sunshine.